GW01110651

Frank Danby

Twilight

outlook

Frank Danby

Twilight

1st Edition | ISBN: 978-3-75240-625-2

Place of Publication: Frankfurt am Main, Germany

Year of Publication: 2020

Outlook Verlag GmbH, Germany.

Reproduction of the original.

TWILIGHT

BY

FRANK DANBY

CHAPTER I

A couple of years ago, on the very verge of the illness that subsequently overwhelmed me, I took a small furnished house in Pineland. I made no inspection of the place, but signed the agreement at the instance of the local house-agent, who proved little less inventive than the majority of his *confrères*.

Three months of neuritis, only kept within bounds by drugs, had made me comparatively indifferent to my surroundings. It was necessary for me to move because I had become intolerant of the friends who exclaimed at my ill looks, and the acquaintances who failed to notice any alteration in me. One sister whom I really loved, and who really loved me, exasperated me by constant visits and ill-concealed anxiety. Another irritated me little less by making light of my ailment and speaking of neuritis in an easy familiar manner as one might of toothache or a corn. I had no natural sleep, and if I were not on the borderland of insanity, I was at least within sight of the home park of inconsequence. Reasoned behaviour was no longer possible, and I knew it was necessary for me to be alone.

I do not wish to recall this bad time nor the worse that ante-dated my departure, when I was at the mercy of venal doctors and indifferent nurses, dependent on grudged bad service and overpaid inattention, taking a so-called rest cure. But I do wish to relate a most curious circumstance, or set of circumstances, that made my stay in Pineland memorable, and left me, after my sojourn there, obsessed with the story of which I found the beginning on the first night of my arrival, and the end in the long fevered nights that followed. I myself hardly know how much is true and how much is fiction in this story; for what the *cache* of letters is responsible, and for what the morphia.

The house at Pineland was called Carbies, and it was haunted for me from the first by Margaret Capel and Gabriel Stanton. Quite early in my stay I must have contemplated writing about them, knowing that there was no better way of ridding myself of their phantoms, than by trying to make them substantial in pen and ink. I had their letters and some scraps of an unfinished diary to help me, a notebook with many blank pages, the garrulous reticence of the village apothecary, and the evidence of the sun-washed God's Acre by the old church.

To begin at the beginning.

It was a long drive from Pineland station to Carbies. I had sent my maid in advance, but there was no sign of her when my ricketty one-horse fly pulled up at the garden gate of a suburban villa of a house "standing high" it is true, and with "creeper climbing about its white-painted walls." But otherwise with no more resemblance to the exquisite and secluded cottage *ornée* I had in my mind, and that the house-agent had portrayed in his letters, than a landscape by Matise to one by Ruysdael.

I was too tired then to be greatly disappointed. Two servants had been sent in by my instructions, and the one who opened the door to me proved to be a cheerful-looking young person of the gollywog type, with a corresponding cap, who relieved me of my hand luggage and preceded me to the drawing-room, where wide windows and a bright fire made me oblivious for the moment of the shabby furniture, worn carpet, and mildewed wallpaper. Tea was brought to me in a cracked pot on a veneered tray. The literary supplement of *The Times* and an American magazine were all I had with which to occupy myself. And they proved insufficient. I began to look about me; and became curiously and almost immediately conscious that my new abode must have been inhabited by a sister or brother of the pen. The feeling was not psychic. The immense writing-table stood sideways in the bow-window as only "we" know how to place it. The writing-chair looked sufficiently luxurious to tempt me to an immediate trial; there were a footstool and a big waste-paper basket; all incongruous with the cheap and shabby drawing-room furniture. Had only my MS. paper been to hand, ink in the substantial glass pot, and my twin enamel pens available, I think I should then and there have abjured all my vows of rest and called upon inspiration to guide me to a fresh start.

"*Work whilst ye have the light*" had been my text for months; driving me on continually. It seemed possible, even then, that the time before me was short. I left the fire and my unfinished tea. Instinctively I found the words rising to my lips, "I could write here." That was the way a place always struck me. Whether I could or could not write there? Seated in that convenient easy-chair I felt at once that my shabby new surroundings were sympathetic to me, that I fitted in and was at home in them.

I had come straight from a narrow London house where my bedroom overlooked a mews, and my sitting-room other narrow houses with a roadway between. Here, early in March, from the wide low window I saw yellow gorse overgrowing a rough and unkempt garden. Beyond the garden more flaming gorse on undulating common land, then hills, and between them, unmistakable, the sombre darkness of the sea. Up here the air was very still, but the smell of the gorse was strong with the wind from that distant sea. I wished for pens and paper at first; then drifted beyond wishes, dreaming I knew not of what, but happier and more content than I had been for some time past. The air was healing, so were the solitude and silence. My silence and solitude were interrupted, my content came abruptly to an end.

"Dr. Kennedy!"

I did not rise. In those bad neuritis days rising was not easy. I stared at the intruder, and he at me. But I guessed in a minute to what his unwelcome presence was due. My anxious, dearly beloved, and fidgetty sister had found out the name of the most noted Æsculapius of the neighbourhood and had notified him of my arrival, probably had given him a misleading and completely erroneous account of my illness, certainly asked him to call. I found out afterwards I was right in all my guesses save one. This was not the most noted Æsculapius of the neighbourhood, but his more youthful partner. Dr. Lansdowne was on his holiday. Dr. Kennedy had read my sister's letter and was now bent upon carrying out her instructions. As I said, we stared at each other in the advancing dusk.

"You have only just come?" he ventured then.

"I've been here about an hour," I replied—"a quiet hour."

"I had your sister's letter," he said apologetically, if a little awkwardly, as he advanced into the room.

"She wrote you, then?"

"Oh yes! I've got the letter somewhere." He felt in his pocket and failed to find it.

"Won't you sit down?"

There was no chair near the writing-table save the one upon which I sat. A further reason why I knew my predecessor here had been a writer! Dr. Kennedy had to fetch one, and I took shallow stock of him meanwhile. A tall and not ill-looking man in the late thirties or early forties, he had on the worst suit of country tweeds I had ever seen and incongruously well-made boots. Now he sprawled silently in the selected chair, and I waited for his opening. Already I was nauseated with doctors and their methods. In town I had seen everybody's favourite nostrum-dispenser, and none of them had relieved me of anything but my hardly earned cash. I mean to present a study of them one day, to get something back from what I have given. Dr. Kennedy did not accord with the black-coated London brigade, and his opening was certainly different.

"How long have you been feeling unwell?" That was what I expected, this was the common gambit. Dr. Kennedy sat a few minutes without speaking at all. Then he asked me abruptly:

"Did you know Mrs. Capel?"

"Who?"

"Margaret Capel. You knew she lived here, didn't you? That it was here it all happened?"

"What happened?"

"Then you don't know?" He got up from his chair in a fidgetty sort of way and went over to the other window. "I hoped you knew her, that she had been a friend of yours. I hoped so ever since I had your sister's letter. Carbies! It seemed so strange to be coming here again. I can't believe it is ten years ago; it is all so vivid!" He came back and sat down again. "I ought not to talk about her, but the whole room and house are so full of memories. She used to sit, just as you are sitting now, for hours at a time, dreaming. Sometimes she would not speak to me at all. I had to go away; I could see I was intruding."

The cynical words on my lips remained unuttered. He was tall, and if his clothes had fitted him he might have presented a better figure. I hate a morning coat in tweed material. The adjective "uncouth" stuck. I saw it was a clever head under the thick mane of black hair, and wondered at his tactlessness and provincial garrulity. I nevertheless found myself not entirely uninterested in him.

"Do you mind my talking about her? Incandescent! I think that word describes her best. She burned from the inside, was strung on wires, and they were all alight. She was always sitting just where you are now, or upstairs at the piano. She was a wonderful pianist. Have you been upstairs, into the room she turned into a music room?"

"As I told you, I have only been here an hour. This is the only room I have seen."

My tone must have struck him as wanting in cordiality, or interest.

"You didn't want me to come up tonight?" He looked through his pocketbook for Ella's letter, found it, and began to read, half aloud. How well I knew what Ella would have said to him.

"She has taken 'Carbies'; call upon her at once ... let me know what you think ... don't be misled by her high spirits...." He read it half aloud and half to himself. He seemed to expect my sympathy. "I used to come here so often, two or three times a day sometimes."

"Was she ill?" The question was involuntary. Margaret Capel was nothing to me.

"Part of the time. Most of the time."

"Did you do her any good?"

Apparently he had no great sense or sensitiveness of professional dignity. There was a strange light in his eyes, brilliant yet fitful, conjured up by the question. It was the first time he seemed to recognize my existence as a separate entity. He looked directly at me, instead of gazing about him reminiscently.

"I don't know. I did my best. When she was in pain I stopped it ... sometimes. She did not always like the medicines I prescribed. And you? You are suffering from neuritis, your sister says. That may mean anything. Where is it?"

"In my legs."

I did not mean him to attend me; I had come away to rid myself of doctors. And anyway I liked an older man in a professional capacity. But his eccentricity of manner or deportment, his want of interest in me and absorption in his former patient, his ill-cut clothes and unlikeness to his brother professionals, were a little variety, and I found myself answering his questions.

"Have you tried Kasemol? It is a Japanese cure very efficacious; or any other paint?"

"I am no artist."

He smiled. He had a good set of teeth, and his smile was pleasant.

"You've got a nurse, or a maid?"

"A maid. I'm not ill enough for nurses."

"Good. Did you know this was once a nursing-home? After she found that out she could never bear the place...."

He was talking again about the former occupant of the house. My ailment had not held his attention long.

"She said she smelt ether and heard groaning in the night. I suppose it seems strange to you I should talk so much about her? But Carbies without Margaret Capel.... You *do* mind?"

"No, I don't. I daresay I shall be glad to hear all about her one day, and the story. I see you have a story to tell. Of course I remember her now. She wrote a play or two, and some novels that had quite a little vogue at one time. But I'm tired tonight."

"So short a journey ought not to tire you." He was observing me more closely. "You look overdriven, too fine-drawn. We must find out all about it. Not tonight of course. You must not look upon this as a professional visit at all, but I could not resist coming. You would understand, if you had known her. And then to see you sitting at her table, and in the same attitude...." He left off abruptly. So the regard I had flattered myself to be personal was merely reminiscent. "You don't write too, by any chance, do you? That would be an extraordinary coincidence."

He might as well have asked Melba if she sang. Blundering fool! I was better known than Margaret Capel had ever been. Not proud of my position because I have always known my limitations, but irritated nevertheless by his ignorance, and wishful now to get rid of him.

"Oh, yes! I write a little sometimes. Sorry my position at the table annoys you. But I don't play the piano." He seemed a little surprised or hurt at my tone, as he well might, and rose to go. I rose, too, and held out my hand. After all I did not write under my own name, so how could he have known unless Ella had told him? When he shook hands with me he made no pretence of feeling my pulse, a trick of the trade which I particularly dislike. So I smiled at him. "I am a little irritable."

"Irritability is characteristic of the complaint. And I have bored you horribly, I fear. But it was such an excitement coming up here again. May I come in the morning and overhaul you? My partner, Dr. Lansdowne, for whom your sister's letter was really intended, is away. Does that matter?"

"I shouldn't think so."

"He is a very able man," he said seriously.

"And are you not?" By this time my legs were aching badly and I wanted to get rid of him.

"In the morning, then."

He seemed as if he would have spoken again, but thought better of it. He had certainly a personality, but one that I was not sure I liked. He took an inconceivable time winding up or starting his machine, the buzz of it was in my ears long after he went off, blowing an unnecessary whistle, making my pain unbearable.

I dined in bed and treated myself to an extra dose of nepenthe on the excuse of the fatigue of my journey. The prescription had been given to me by one of those eminent London physicians of whom I hope one day to make a pen-and-ink drawing. It is an insidious drug with varying effects. That night I remember the pain was soon under weigh and the strange half-wakeful dreams began early. It was good to be out of pain even if one knew it to be only a temporary deliverance. The happiness of a recovered amiability soon became mine, after which conscience began to worry me because I had been ungrateful to my sister and had run away from her, and been rude to her doctor, that strange doctor. I smiled in my drowsiness when I thought of him and his beloved Margaret Capel, a strange devotee at a forgotten shrine, in his cutaway checked coat and the baggy trousers. But the boots might have come from Lobb. His hands were smooth, of the right texture. Evidently the romance of his life had been this Margaret Capel.

So this place had been a nursing-home, and when she knew it she heard groans and smelt ether. Her books were like that: fanciful, frothy. She had never a straightforward story to tell. It was years since I had heard her name, and I had forgotten what little I knew, except that I had once been resentful of the fuss the critics had made over her. I believed she was dead, but could not be sure. Then I thought of Death, and was glad it had no terrors for me. No one could go on living as I had been doing, never out of pain, without seeing Death as a release.

A burning point of pain struck me again, and because I was drugged I found it unbearable. Before it was too late and I became drowsier I roused myself for another dose. To pour out the medicine and put the glass down without spilling it was difficult, the table seemed uneven. Later my brain became confused, and my body comfortable.

It was then I saw Margaret Capel for the first time, not knowing who she was, but glad of her appearance, because it heralded sleep. Always before the drug assumed its fullest powers, I saw kaleidoscopic changes, unsubstantial shapes, things and people that were not there. Wonderful things sometimes. This was only a young woman in a grey silk dress, of old-fashioned cut, with puffed sleeves and wide skirts. She had a mass of fair hair, *blonde cendré*, and with a blue ribbon snooded through it. At first her face was nebulous, afterwards it appeared with a little more colour in it, and she had thin and tremulous pink lips. She looked plaintive, and when our eyes met she seemed a little startled at seeing me in her bed. The last thing I saw of her was a wavering smile, rather wonderful and alluring. I knew at once that she was Margaret Capel. But she was quickly replaced by two Chinese vases and a conventional design in black and gold. I had been too liberal with that last dose of nepenthe, and the result was the deep sleep or unconsciousness I liked the least of its effects, a blank passing of time.

The next morning, as usual after such a debauch, I was heavy and depressed, still drowsy but without any happiness or content. I had often wondered I could keep a maid, for latterly I was always either irritable or silent. Not mean, however. That has never been one of my faults, and may have been the explanation. Suzanne asked how I had slept and hoped I was better, perfunctorily, without waiting for an answer. She was a great fat heavy Frenchwoman, totally without sympathetic quality. I told her not to pull up the blinds nor bring coffee until I rang.

"I am quite well, but I don't want to be bothered. The servants must do the housekeeping. If Dr. Kennedy calls say I am too ill to see him."

I often wish one could have dumb servants. But Suzanne was happily lethargic and not argumentative. I heard afterwards that she gave my message verbatim to the doctor: "Madame was not well enough to see him," but softened it by a suggestion that I would perhaps be better tomorrow and perhaps he would come again. His noisy machine and unnecessary horn spoiled the morning and angered me against Ella for having brought him over me.

I felt better after lunch and got up, making a desultory exploration of the house and finding my last night's impression confirmed. The position was lonely without being secluded. All round the house was the rough garden, newly made, unfinished, planted with trees not yet grown and kitchen stuff. Everywhere was the stiff and prickly gorse. On the front there were many bedrooms; some, like my own, had broad balconies whereon a bed could be wheeled. The place had probably at one time been used as an open-air cure. Then Margaret Capel must have taken it, altered this that and the other, but failed to make a home out of what had been designed for a hospital. By removing a partition two of these bedrooms had been turned into one. This one was large, oak-floored, and a Steinway grand upon a platform dominated one corner. There was a big music stand. I opened it and found no clearance of music had been made. It was full and deplorably untidy. The rest of the furniture consisted of tapestry-covered small and easy-chairs, a round table, a great sofa drawn under one of the windows, and some amateur water colours.

On the ground floor the dining-room looked unused and the library smelt musty. It was lined with open cupboards or bookcases, the top shelves fitted with depressing-looking tomes and the lower one bulging with yellow-backed novels, old-fashioned three-volume novels, magazines dated ten years back, and an "olla podrida" of broken-backed missing-leaved works by Hawley Smart, Mrs. Lovett Cameron, and Charles Lever. Nothing in either of these rooms was reminiscent of Margaret Capel. I was glad to get back to the drawing-room, on the same floor, but well-proportioned and agreeable. Today, with the sun out and my fatigue partly gone, its shabbiness looked homely and even attractive. The position of the writing-table again made its appeal. Suzanne had unpacked my writing-things and they stood ready for arrangement, heaped up together on the green leather top. I saw with satisfaction that there were many drawers and that the table was both roomy and convenient. The view from the window was altered by the sunlight. The yellow gorse was still the most prominent feature, but beyond it today one saw the sea more plainly, a little dim and hazy in the distance but unmistakable; melting into the horizon. Today the sky was of a summer blue although it was barely spring. I felt my courage revive. Again I said to myself that I could write here, and silently rescinded my intention of resting. "*Work whilst ye have the light.*" I had not a great light, but another than myself to work for, and perhaps not much time.

The gollywog put a smiling face and a clean cap halfway into the room and said:

"Please, ma'am, cook wishes to know if she can speak to you, and if you please there is no...."

There tumbled out a list of household necessities, which vexed me absurdly. But the writing-chair was comfortable and helped me through the narrative. The table was alluring, and I wanted to be alone. Cook arrived before Mary had finished, and then the monologue became a duet.

"There's not more than half a dozen glasses altogether, and I'm sure I don't know what to do about the teapot. There's only one tray...."

"And as for the cooking utensils, well, I never see such a lot. And that dirty! The kitchen dresser has never been cleaned out since the flood, I should think. Stuffed up with dirty cloths and broken crockery. As for the kitchen table, there's knives without handles and forks without prongs; not a shape that isn't dented; the big fish kettle's got a hole in it as big as your 'and, and the others ain't fit to use. The pastry board's broke...."

I wanted to stop my ears and tell them to get out. I had asked for competent servants, and understood that competent servants bought or hired whatever was necessary for their work. That was the way things were managed at home. But then my cook had been with me for eight years and my housemaid for eleven. They knew my ways, and that I was never to be bothered with household details, only the bills were my affair. And those my secretary paid.

"It was one of them there writing women as had the place last, with no more idea of order than the kitchen cat," cook said indignantly, or perhaps suspiciously, eyeing the writing-table. I had come here for rest and change, to lead the simple life, with two servants instead of five and everything in proportion. Now I found myself giving reckless orders.

"Buy everything you want; there is sure to be a shop in the village. If not, make out a list, and one of you go up to the Stores or Harrod's. If the place is dirty get in a charwoman. Some one will recommend you a charwoman, the house-agent or the doctor." I reminded cook that she was a cook-housekeeper, but failed to subdue her.

"You can't be cook-housekeeper in a desert island. I call it no better than a desert island. I'd get hold of that there house-agent that engaged us if I was you. He said the 'ouse was well-found. Him with his well-found 'ouse! They're bound to give you what you need, but if you don't mind expense...."

Of course I minded expense, never more so than now when I saw the possibility before me of a long period of inaction.... But I minded other things more. Household detail for instance, and uneducated voices. I compromised and sanctioned the appeal to the house-agent, confirming that the irreducible minimum was to be purchased, explaining I was ill, not to be troubled about this sort of thing. I brushed aside a few "buts" and finally rid myself of them. I caught myself yearning for Ella, who would have saved me this and every trouble. Then scorned my desire to send for her and determined to be glad of my solitude, to rejoice in my freedom. I could look as ill as I liked without comment. I could sit where I was without attempting to tidy my belongings, and no one would ask me if I felt seedy, if the pain was coming on, if they could do anything for me. And then, fool that I was, I remember tears coming to my eyes because I was lonely, and sure that I had tired out even Ella's patience. I wondered how any one could face a long illness, least of all any one like me who loved work, and above all independence, freedom. I knew, I knew even then that the time was coming when I could neither work nor be independent; the shadow was upon me that very first afternoon at Carbies. When I could see to write I dashed off a postcard to Ella telling her I was quite well and she was not to bother about me.

"I like the place, I'm sure I shall be able to write here. Don't think of coming down, and keep the rest of the family off me if you can...."

I spent the remainder of the evening weakly longing for her, and feeling that she need not have taken me at my word, that she might have come with me although I urged her not, that she should have understood me better.

That night I took less nepenthe, yet saw Margaret Capel more vividly. She stayed a long time too. This time she wore a blue peignoir, her hair down, and she looked very young and girlish. There were gnomes and fairies when she went, and after that the sea, swish and awash as if I had been upon a yacht.

Unconsciousness only came to me when the yacht was submerged in a great wave ... semi-consciousness.

But I am not telling the story of my illness. I should like to, but I fear it would have no interest for the general public, or for the young people amongst whom one looks for readers. I have sometimes thought nevertheless, both then and afterwards, that there must be a public who would like to hear what one does and thinks and suffers when illness catches one unawares; and all life's interests alter and narrow down to temperatures and medicine-time, to fighting or submitting to nurses and weakness, to hatred and contempt of doctors, and a dumb blind rage against fate; to pain and the soporifics behind which its hold tightens.

Pineland did not cure me, although I spent hours in the open air and let my pens lie resting in their case. Under continual pains I grew sullen and resentful, always more ill-tempered and desirous of solitude. Dr. Kennedy called frequently. Sometimes I saw him and sometimes not, as the mood took me. He never came without speaking of the former occupant of the house, of Margaret Capel. He seemed to take very little personal interest in me or my condition. And I was too proud (or stupid) to force it on his notice. I asked him once, crudely enough, if he had been in love with Margaret Capel. He answered quite simply, as if he had been a child:

"One had no chance. From the first I knew there was no chance."

"There was some one else?"

"He came up and down. I seldom met him. Then there were the circumstances. She was between the Nisi and the Absolute, the nether and the upper stone...."

"Oh, yes, I remember now. She was divorced."

"No, she was not. She divorced her husband," he answered quite sharply and a little distressed. "Courts of Justice they are called, but Courts of Injustice would be a better name. They put her to the question, on the rack; no inquisition could have been worse. And she was broken by it...."

"But there was some one else, you said yourself there was some one else. Probably these probing questions, this rack, were her deserts. Personally I am a monogamist," I retorted. Not that I was really narrow or a Pharisee, only in contentious mood and cruel under the pressure of my own harrow. "Probably anything she suffered served her right," I added indifferently.

"It all happened afterwards. I thought you knew," he said incoherently.

"I know nothing except that you are always talking of Margaret Capel, and I am a little tired of the subject," I answered pettishly. "Who was the man?"

"The man!"

"Yes, the man who came up and down to see her?"

"Gabriel Stanton."

"Gabriel Stanton!" I sat upright in my chair; that really startled me. "Gabriel Stanton," I repeated, and then, stupidly enough: "Are you sure?"

"Quite sure. But I won't talk about it any more since it bores you. The house is so haunted for me, and you seemed so sympathetic, so interested. You won't let me doctor you."

"You haven't tried very hard, have you?"

"You put me off whenever I try to ask you how you are, or any questions."

"What is the good? I've seen twelve London doctors."

"London has not the monopoly of talent." He took up his hat, and then my hand.

"Offended?" I asked him.

"No. But my partner will be home tomorrow, and I'm relinquishing my place to him. It is really his case."

"I refuse to be anybody's case. I've heard from the best authorities that no one knows anything about neuritis and that it is practically incurable. One has to suffer and suffer. Even Almroth Wright has not found the anti-bacilli. Nepenthe gives me ease; that is all the doctoring I want—ease!"

"It is doing you a lot of harm. And what makes you think you've got neuritis?"

"What ailed your Margaret?" I answered mockingly. "Did you ever find that out?"

"No … yes. Of course I knew."

"Did you ever examine her?" I was curious to know that; suddenly and inconsequently curious.

"Why do you ask?" But his face changed, and I knew the question had been cruel or impertinent. He let go my hand abruptly, he had been holding it all this time. "I did all that any doctor could." He was obviously distressed and I ashamed.

"Don't go yet. Sit down and have a cup of tea with me. I've been here three weeks and every meal has been solitary. Your Margaret"—I smiled at him then, knowing he would not understand—"comes to me sometimes at night with my nepenthe, but all day I am alone."

"By your own desire then, I swear. You are not a woman to be left alone if you wanted company." He dropped into a chair, seemed glad to stay. Presently over tea and crumpets, we were really talking of my illness, and if I had permitted it I have no doubt he would have gone into the matter more closely. As it was he warned me solemnly against the nepenthe and suggested I should try codein as an alternative, a suggestion I ignored completely, unfortunately for myself.

"Tell me about your partner," I said, drinking my tea slowly.

"Oh! you'll like him, all the ladies like him. He is very spruce and rather handsome; dapper, band-boxy. Not tall, turning grey...."

"Did she like him?" I persisted.

"She would not have him near her. After his first visit she denied herself to him all the time. He used to talk to me about her, he could never understand it, he was not used to that sort of treatment, he is a tremendous favourite about here."

"What did she say of him?"

"That he grinned like a Cheshire cat, talked in *clichés*, rubbed his hands and seemed glad when she suffered. He has a very cheerful bedside manner; most people like it."

"I quite understand. I won't have him. Mind that; don't send him to see me, because I won't see him. I'd rather put up with you." I have explained I was beyond convention. He really tried hard to persuade me, urged Dr. Lansdowne's degrees and qualifications, his seniority. I grew angry in the end.

"Surely I need not have either of you if I don't want to. I suppose there are other doctors in the neighbourhood."

He gave me a list of the medical men practising in and about Pineland; it was not at all badly done, he praised everybody yet made me see them clearly. In the end I told him I would choose my own medical attendant when I wanted one.

"Am I dismissed, then?" he asked.

"Have you ever been summoned?" I answered in the same tone.

"Seriously now, I'd like to be of use to you if you'd let me."

"In order to retain the *entrée* to the house where the wonderful Margaret moved and had her being?"

"No! Well, perhaps yes, partly. And you are a very attractive woman yourself."

"Don't be ridiculous."

"It is quite true. I expect you know it."

"I'm over forty and ill. I suppose that is what you find attractive, that I am ill?"

"I don't think so. I hate hysterical women as a rule."

"Hysterical!"

"With any form of nerve disease."

"Do you really think I am suffering from nerve disease? From the vapours?" I asked scornfully, thinking for the thousand and first time what a fool the man was.

"You don't occupy yourself?"

"I'm one of the busiest women on God's earth."

"I've never seen you doing anything, except sitting at her writing-table with two bone-dry pens set out and some blank paper. And you object to be questioned about your illness, or examined."

"I hate scientific doctoring. And then you have not inspired me with confidence, you are obsessed with one idea."

"I can't help that. From the first you've reminded me of Margaret."

"Oh! damn Margaret Capel, and your infatuation for her! I'm sorry, but that's the way I feel just now. I can't escape from her, the whole place is full of her. And yet she hasn't written a thing that will live. I sent to the London Library soon after I came and got all her books. I waded through the lot. Just epigram and paradox, a weak Bernard Shaw in petticoats."

"I never read a word she wrote," he answered indifferently. "It was the woman herself...."

"I am sure. Well, good-bye! I can't talk any more tonight, I'm tired. Don't send Dr. Lansdowne. If I want any one I'll let you know."

Margaret came to me again that night when the house was quite silent and all the lights out except the red one from the fire. She sat in the easy-chair on the hearthrug, and for the first time I heard her speak. She was very young and feeble-looking, and I told her I was sorry I had been impatient and said "damn" about her.

"But you are all over the place, you know. And I can't write unless I am alone. I'm always solitary and never alone here; you haunt and obsess me. Can't you go away? I don't mean now. I am glad you are here now, and talking. Tell me about Dr. Kennedy. Did you care for him at all? Did you know he was in love with you?"

"Peter Kennedy! No, I never thought about him at all, not until the end. Then he was very kind, or cruel. He did what I asked him. You know why I obsess you, don't you? It used to be just the same with me when a subject was evolving. You are going to write my story; you will do it better in a way than I could have done it myself, although worse in another. I have left you all the material."

"Not a word."

"You haven't found it yet. I put it together myself, the day Gabriel sent back my letters. You will have my diary and a few notes…."

"Where?"

"In a drawer in the writing-table. But it is only half there…. You will have to add to it."

"I see you quite well when I keep my eyes shut. If I open them the room sways and you are not there. Why should I write your life? I am no historian, only a novelist."

"I know, but you are on the spot, with all the material and local colour. You know Gabriel too; we used to speak about you."

"He is no admirer of mine."

"No. He is a great stylist, and you have no sense of style."

"Nor you of anything else," I put in rudely, hastily.

"A harsh judgment, characteristic. You are a blunt realist, I should say, hard and a little unwomanly, calling a spade by its ugliest name; but sentimental with pen in hand you really do write abominably sometimes. But you will remind the world of me again. I don't want to be forgotten. I would rather be misrepresented than forgotten. There are so few geniuses! Keats and I…. *Don't go to sleep.*"

I could not help it, however. Several times after that, whenever I remembered something I wished to ask her, and opened dulled eyes, she was not there at all. The chair where she had sat was empty, and the fire had died down to dull ash. I drowsed and dreamed. In my dreams I achieved style, an ambient, exquisite style, and wrote about Margaret Capel and Gabriel Stanton so glowingly and convincingly that all the world wept for them and wondered, and my sales ran into hundreds of thousands.

"We have always expected great things of this author, but she has transcended our highest expectations...." The reviews were all on this scale. For the remainder of that night no writer in England was as famous as I. Publishers and literary agents hung round my doorsteps and I rejected marvellous offers. If I had not been so thirsty and my mouth dry, no one could have been happier, but the dryness and thirst woke me continuously, and I execrated Suzanne for having put the water bottle out of my reach, and forgotten to supply me with acid drops. I remember grumbling about it to Margaret.

CHAPTER II

I began the search for those letters the very next day, knowing how absurd it was, as if one were still a child who expected to find the pot of gold at the end of the rainbow. I made Suzanne telephone to Dr. Kennedy that I was much better and would prefer he did not call. I really wanted to be alone, to make my search complete, not to be interrupted. If it were not true that I was better, at least I was no worse, only heavy and dull in body and mind, every movement an almost unbearable fatigue. Nevertheless I sat down with determination at the writing-table, intent on opening every drawer and cupboard, calling to Suzanne to help me, on the pretence of wanting white paper to line the drawers, and a duster to clean them. In reality, that she should do the stooping instead of me. But everywhere was emptiness or dust. I crawled to the music room after lunch and tried my luck there, amid the heaped disorderly music, but there too the search proved unavailing. It was no use going downstairs again, so I went to bed, before dinner, passing a white night with red pain points, beyond the reach even of nepenthe. I had counted on seeing Margaret Capel again, getting fuller instructions, but was disappointed in that also.

The next day and many others were equally full and equally empty. I looked in unlikely places until I was tired out; dragging about my worn-out body that had been whipped into a pretence of activity by my driving brain. Dr. Kennedy came and went, talking spasmodically of Margaret Capel, watching me, I thought sometimes, with puzzled enquiring eyes. My family in London was duly informed how well I was, and the good that the rest and solitude were doing me. I felt horribly ill, and towards the end of my second week gave up seeking for Margaret Capel's letters or papers. I was still intent upon writing her story, but had made up my mind now to compile it from the facts I could persuade or force from Dr. Kennedy, from old newspaper reports, and other sources. It was borne in upon me that to go on with my work was the only way to save myself from what I now thought was mental as well as physical breakdown. I saw Margaret elusively, was never quite free from the sense that I was not alone. The chills that ran through me meant that she was behind me; the hot flushes that she was about to materialise. In normal times I was the most dogmatic disbeliever in the occult; but now I believed Carbies to be haunted.

When I was able to think soundly and consecutively, I began to piece together what little I knew of these two people by whom I was obsessed. For it was not only Margaret, but Gabriel Stanton whom I felt, or suspected, about the house. Stanton & Co. were my own publishers. I had not known them as Margaret Capel's. Gabriel was not the member of the firm I saw when I made my rare calls in Greyfriars' Square. He was understood to be occupied only with the classical works issued by the well-known house. Somewhere or other I had heard that he had achieved a great reputation at Oxford and knew more about Greek roots than any living authority. On the few occasions we met I had felt him antagonistic or contemptuous. He would come into the room where I was talking to Sir George and back out again quickly, saying he was sorry, or that he did not know his cousin was engaged. Sir George introduced us more than once, but Mr. Gabriel Stanton always seemed to have forgotten the circumstance. I remembered him as a tall thin man, with deep-set eyes and sunken mouth, a gentleman, as all the Stantons were, but as different as possible from his genial partner. I had, I have, a soft spot in my heart for Sir George Stanton, and had met with much kindness from him. Gabriel, too, may have had a charm—they were notoriously a charming family,—but he had not exerted it for my benefit. He and all of them were so respectable, so traditionally and inalienably respectable, that it was difficult to readjust my slowly working mind and think of him as any woman's lover; illegitimate lover, as he seemed to be in this case. I wrote to my secretary in London to look up everything that was known about Margaret Capel. Before her reply came I had another attack of pleurisy—I had had several in London,—and this brought Ella to me, to say nothing of various hungry and impotent London consultants.

As I said before, this is not a history of my illness, nor of my sister's encompassing love that ultimately enabled me to weather it, that forced me again and again from the arms of Death, that friend for whom at times my weakness yearned. The fight was all from the outside. As for me, I laid down my weapons early. I dreaded pain more than death, and do still, the passing through and not the arrival, writhing under the shame of my beaten body, wanting to hide. Yet publicity beat upon me, streamed into the room like midday sun. There were bulletins in the papers and the Press Association rang up and asked for late and early news. Obituary notices were probably being prepared. Everybody knew that at which I was still only guessing. It irked me sometimes to know they would be only paragraphs and not columns, and I knew Ella would be vexed.

When the acuteness of this particular attack subsided I thought again of

Margaret Capel and Gabriel Stanton, yet could not talk of them. For Ella knew nothing of the former occupants of the house, and for some inexplicable reason Dr. Kennedy had left off coming. His partner, or substitute, whose Cheshire-cat grin I easily recognised, made no secret, notwithstanding his cheerfulness, of the desperate view he took of my condition. I hated his futile fruitless examinations, the consultations whereat I was sure he aired his provincial self-importance, his great cool hands on my pulse and smug dogmatic ignorance. "The pain is just here," he would announce, but not even by accident did he ever once hit upon the right spot.

Fortunately Ella was there. She must have arrived many days before I recognised her. The household was moving on oiled wheels, my meals were brought me now on trays with delicate napery and a flower or two. Scent sprays and early strawberries, down pillows and Jaegar sheets, a water bed presently, and all the luxuries, told me undeniably she was in the vicinity. I had always known how it would be. That once I admitted to helplessness she would give up her home life and all the joys of her well-filled days, and would live for me only. Because her tenderness for me met mine for her and was too poignant for my growing weakness, I had denied us both. Her the joy of giving and myself of taking. Now, without acknowledgment or word of gratitude, I accepted all.

"Don't go away," were the first words I said to her. I! who had begged her so hard not to come, repudiated her anxiety so violently.

"Of course not. Why should I? I always like the country in the early spring," she answered coolly. "Do you want anything?" She came nearer to the bed.

"What has become of Dr. Kennedy?" I asked.

"I thought you did not like him. Suzanne told me that often you would not see him when he called. And you were quite right. It was evident he did not know what was the matter with you."

"No one does."

"You have not helped us." Her eyelids were pink, but otherwise she did not reproach me.

"And now I am going to die, I suppose."

"Die! You are not going to die; don't be so absurd. I wouldn't let you, for one thing. And why should you? People don't die of pleurisy, or neuritis. You are better today than you were yesterday, and you will be better still tomorrow. I know."

Outside the room she may have wept, for, as I said, her eyelids were pink.

Inside it she was all quiet confidence and courage.

"I want Dr. Kennedy. Get him back to me." I did not argue with her whether I would live or die, it was too futile.

"This man Lansdowne is F.R.C.S. and M.D. London," she reminded me.

"I don't care if he's all the letters of the alphabet. He grins at me, talks smugly, patronises me, pats my shoulder. He will send his carriage to follow the funeral. I see in his face that he has made up his mind to it."

Nurse interfered and said that Dr. Lansdowne was most able.

"Send her out of the room." I was impatient at her interference.

"All right, nurse, I'll sit with Mrs. Vevaseur until you've had your dinner. You won't talk too much?" she said to me imploringly.

"Perhaps," I answered, and smiled. It was good to have Ella sitting with me again.

"The doctor did not wish her to speak at all, nor to see visitors."

I don't know how Ella managed to get that authoritative white-capped female out of the room, but she did; she had infinite tact and resource.

"Shall I get my needlework? Or would you rather I read to you? You really mustn't talk."

"Neither. You are not going away?"

"I am staying as long as you want me."

Not a word about the times when I had told her brutally to let me alone, when I had almost turned her out of the house in London, finally fled from her here. That was Ella all over, and characteristic of me that I could not even thank her. When she said she would stay it seemed too good to be true. I questioned her about her responsibilities.

"What about Violet and Tommy, the paper?" For Ella, too, was bound on the Ixion wheel of the weekly press.

"It's all right; everything has been arranged, in the best possible way. I am quite free. I shan't go away until you ask me to go."

Then I began to cry, in my great weakness, but hid my eyes, for I knew my tears would hurt her. I gave way only for a moment. It was such a relief to know her there, to feel I was being cared for. Paid service is only for the sound.

Ella pretended not to notice my little breakdown, although she was not far off it herself. She began to talk of indifferent things. Who had telegraphed, or rung up; she told me that the news of my illness had been in the papers. All my good friends whom I had avoided during those dreary months had forgotten they had been snubbed and came forward with genuine sympathy and offers of help. I soon stopped her from telling me about them. It made me feel ashamed and unworthy. I could not recollect ever having done anything for anybody.

"About getting Dr. Kennedy back?"

"He neglected you disgracefully; wrote me lightly. I don't wonder you told him not to call."

"I want him back."

"Then you shall have him back. You shall have everything you want, only go on getting better." She turned her face away from me.

"Have I begun?"

She made no answer, and I knew it was because she could not at the moment command her voice.

So I stayed quiet a little while. Then I began again to beg her to rid me of Lansdowne.

"After all, he is independent of his profession," she said at length thoughtfully, thinking of his feelings and how not to hurt them. "He married a rich woman."

"He would. And I am sure he has no children," I answered.

"Good heavens! How did you know? You are cleverer when you are ill than other people when they are well."

That is like Ella, too, she has an exaggerated and absurd opinion of my talent. Just because I write novels which are paid for beyond their deserts!

I don't know how she did it, I don't know how she accomplished half of the magical wonderful things she did for my comfort all that sad time. But I was not even surprised, a few days later, when I really was better and sitting up in bed; propped up by pillows, I admit, but still actually sitting up; that Dr. Kennedy, tall and unaltered, with the same light in his eye, even the same dreadful country suit, lounged in and sat on the chair by my side. Ella went away when he came in, she always had an idea that patients like to see their doctors alone. She flirts with hers, I think. She is incurably flirtatious in her leisure hours.

"You've had a bad time," he said abruptly.

"You didn't try to make it any better," I answered weakly.

"Oh! I! I was dismissed. Your sister turned me out. She said I hadn't recognised how ill you were. I told her she was quite right. I didn't tell her how often you had refused to see me."

"Did you know how ill I was?"

"I'm not sure." He smiled, and so did I. "Were you so ill?"

"I know now what Margaret Capel felt about Dr. Lansdowne."

"He is a very able fellow. And you've had Felton, Shorter, Lawson."

"Don't remind me."

"Anyway you are getting better now."

"Am I? I am so hideously weak."

"Not beginning to write again yet! You see, I know all about you now. I've taken a course of your novels."

"Thinking all the time how much better Margaret Capel wrote?"

"You haven't forgotten Margaret, then?"

"Have *you*?" He became quite grave and pale.

"I! I shall never forget Margaret Capel."

Up till then he had been light and airy in manner, as if this visit and circumstance and poor me, who had been so near the Gates, were of little consequence.

"Did you think how much worse I wrote than she did, that I was no stylist?"

"Why do you say that?"

I was glad to see him and wished to keep him by my side. I thought what I was going to tell him would secure my object.

"She told me so herself" I shot at him, and watched to see how he would take it. "The last time I saw you, the night the pleurisy started, she sat over there by the fireside. We talked together confidentially, she said she knew I would write her story, and was sorry because I had no style." There was a flush on his forehead, he looked to where I said she sat.

"What else did she say?" He did not seem to doubt me or to be surprised.

"You believe I saw her, that it was not a dream?"

"There is an unexplored borderland between dreams and reality. Fever often bridges it. Your temperature was probably high. And I, and you, were so full of her. Go on. Tell me what she wore."

"She was dressed in grey, a white fichu over her shoulders."

"And a pink rose."

"Her hair...."

"Was snooded with a blue ribbon." He finished my sentences excitedly.

"No. It was hanging in plaits."

"Oh, no! Not when she wore the grey dress." He had risen and was standing by the bed now, he seemed anxious, almost imploring. "Think again. Shut your eyes and think again. Surely she had the blue ribbon."

I shut my eyes as he bade me. Then opened them and stared at him.

"But how did you know?"

"Go on. There was a blue ribbon in her hair?"

"The first time I saw her. The next time her hair was hanging down her back, two great plaits of fair hair, and she had on a blue dressing-gown."

"With a white collar like a fine handkerchief, showing her slender throat."

"How well you knew her clothes."

"There was a sense of fitness about her, an exquisite sense of fitness. She would not have worn her hair down with that grey dress."

"You know I really did see her."

"Of course. Go on. Tell me exactly what she said, word for word."

"About my bad style."

"About your good sense of comradeship with her."

"She said I would write the story. Hers and Gabriel Stanton's."

I told him all she had said, word for word as well as I could remember it, keeping my eyes shut, speaking slowly, remembering well.

"She told me of the letters and diary, the notes, chapter headings, all she had prepared...."

I turned my head away, sank down amongst the pillows, and turned my head away. I didn't want him to see my disappointment, to know that I had found nothing. Now I recognised my weakness, that I was spent with feverish nights and pain.

"I can't talk any more." He put his hand upon my pulse.

"Your pulse is quite strong."

"I am not," I said shortly. I wished Ella would come back.

"You looked for them?" I did not answer.

"I am so sorry. Blundering fool that I am. You looked, and looked ... that is why you kept me at arm's length, would not see me, wanted to be alone. You were searching. Why didn't I think of it before? But how did I know she would come to you, confide in you?"

He was talking to himself now, seemed to forget me and my grave illness. "I might have thought of it though. From the first I pictured you two together. I have them. I took them ... didn't you guess?" I forgot the extreme weakness of which I had complained, and caught hold of his coat sleeve, a little breathless.

"You took them ... stole them?"

"Yes. If you put it that way. Who had a better right? I knew everything. Her father, her people, nothing, or very little. And she had not wished them to know."

"She was going to write the story, whatever it was; to publish it."

"No! not immediately, not until long afterwards, not until it would hurt no one. They were in the writing-table drawer, the letters, in an elastic band. She was not tidy as a rule with papers, but these were tidy. The diary was bound in soft grey leather, and there were a few rough notes; loose, on MS. paper. You know all that happened there; the excitement was intense. How could I bear her papers, his letters, her notes to fall into strange hands. I was doing what she would wish, I knew I was carrying out her wishes. The day she ... she died I gathered them all together, slipped them into my greatcoat pocket; the car was at the door. I hurried away as if I had been a thief, the thief you are thinking me."

"Got home quickly, gloated over them all that evening."

"I swear to you, I swear to you I have never opened the packet. I have never looked at them. I made one parcel of them all, of the letters, diary, notes; wrapped them all together in brown paper, tied it up with string, sealed it.

"You've got it still!" I was in high excitement, all my pulses throbbing, face flushed, hands hot, breathless.

"In the safe at my bank. I took it there the next morning."

"You are going to give me the packet?"

"But of course." He seemed suddenly to recollect that I was an invalid, that he was supposed to be my doctor. "I say, all this excitement is very bad for you. Your sister will turn me out again. Can't you lie down, get quiet,—you've jumped from 90 to 112." His hand was on my pulse again. I knew I was going beyond my tether and cursed my weakness.

"You won't change your mind!" I was lying on my back now, quite still, trying to quiet myself as he had told me. "Promise!"

"I'll get the packet in the morning, as soon as the bank is open, and come straight on here with it. You must find some place to put it. Where you can see it, know it's there all the time. But you mustn't open it, you must get stronger first. You know you can't use it yet."

"Yes, I can."

"It would be very wrong. You wouldn't do it well."

"I'm sick of being ordered about." But I could barely move and breathing was becoming difficult to me, I had a sense of faintness, suffocation, the room grew dark. He opened the door and called nurse. Ella came in with her. I was conscious of that.

"What does she have when she is like this? Smelling salts, brandy?" Nurse began to fan me; my cheeks were very flushed.

Ella opened the windows, wide, quietly; the scent of the gorse came in. I did not want to speak, only to be able to breathe.

Nurse telegraphed him an enquiring glance. Strychnine? her dumb lips asked. He shook his head.

"Oxygen. Have you got a cylinder of oxygen in the house?" He took the pillows from under my head.

I don't know what they tried or left untried. Whenever I opened my eyes I sought for Ella's. I knew she would not let them do anything to me that might bring the pain back. I was only over-tired. I managed to say so presently. When I was really better and Dr. Kennedy gone, Ella said a bitter word or two about him. Nurse too thought she should have been called sooner. A good nurse, but dissatisfied up to now with all my treatment, with my change of doctors, with my resistance to authority, and Ella's interference.

"Ella." She had been sitting by the fire but came over to me at once.

"What is it? I am only going to stop a minute. Then I shall leave you to nurse. That man stopped too long, over-excited you. We mustn't have him again, he doesn't understand you."

"Yes he does; perfectly." My voice may have been faint, but I succeeded in making it urgent. "Ella, I want to see him again in the morning, nothing must prevent it, nothing. Don't talk against him, I want him."

"Then you shall have him," she decided promptly. Notwithstanding my terrible weakness and want of breath I smiled at her.

"I suppose you've fallen in love with him," she said. Love and love-making were half her life, the game she found most fascinating. They were nothing to do with mine.

"See that he comes. That's all. However ill I am, whether I'm ill or not, he is to come."

"You noticed his clothes?"

"Oh, yes!"

Nurse I suppose thought we had both gone mad. But she came over to me and lifted me into a more comfortable position, fanned me again, and when the fanning had done its work brought *eau de Cologne* and water and sponged my face, my hot hands. She told Ella that she ought to go, that I ought to be alone, that I should have a bad night if I were not left to myself. Ella only wanted to do what was best for me.

"I am sure you are right, nurse. I shan't come in again. Sleep well."

"You are sure?"

"Quite sure that Dr. Kennedy shall come in the morning, if I have to drag him here. It's a pity you will have an executioner instead of a doctor; he seems to do you harm every time he comes. You had your worst attack when he was here before. Good-night. I do wish you had better taste."

She kept her light tone up to the last, although I saw she was pale with anxiety and sympathy. Days ago she had asked me if the nurses were good and kind to me, and if I liked them, and had received my assurance that this one at least was the best I had ever had, clever and untiring. If only she had not been so sure of herself and that she knew better than I did what was good for me, I should have thought her perfect. She had a delightful voice, never touched me unnecessarily, nor brushed against the bed. But she was younger than I, and I resented her authority. We were often in antagonism, for I was a bad invalid, in resistance all the time. I had not learnt yet how to be ill! The lesson was taught me slowly, cruelly, but I recognised Benham's quality long before I gave in to her. Now I was glad that Ella should go, that nurse should minister to me alone. I wanted the night to come … and go. But my exhaustion was so complete that I had forgotten why.

CHAPTER III

I seem to be a long time coming to the story, but my own will intervene, my own dreadful tale of dependence and deepening illness. Benham was my day nurse. At ten o'clock that night she left me, considerably better and calm. Then Lakeby came on duty, a very inferior person who always talked to me as if I were a child to be humoured: "Now then be a dear good girl and drink it up" represents her fairly well. Then she would yawn in my face without apology or attempt to hide her fatigue or boredom. Nepenthe and I were no longer friends. It gave me no ease, yet I drank it to save argument. Lakeby took away the glass and then lay down at the foot of the bed. I thought again, as I had thought so many times, that no one ever sleeps so soundly as a night nurse. I could indulge my restlessness without any fear of disturbing her. Tomorrow's promised excitement would not let me sleep. Their letters, the very letters they had written to each other! I did not care so much about the diary. I had once kept a diary myself and knew how one leaves out all the essentials. I suppose I drowsed a little. Nepenthe was no longer my friend, but we were not enemies, only disappointed lovers, without reliance on each other. As I approached the borderland I wished Margaret were in her easy-chair by the fireside. I did not care whether she was in her grey, or with her plaits and peignoir. I watched for her in vain. I knew she would not come whilst nurse snored on the sofa. Ella would have to get rid of the nurse from my room. Surely now that I was better I could sleep alone, a bell could be fixed up. Two nurses were unnecessary, extravagant. I woke to cough and was conscious of a strange sensation. I turned on the light by my side, but then only roused the nurse (she had slept all day) with difficulty. I knew what had happened, although this was the first time it had happened to me, and wanted to reassure her or myself. Also to tell her what to do.

"Get ice. Call Benham; ring up the doctor." This was my first hæmorrhage, very profuse and alarming, and Lakeby although she was inferior was not inefficient. When she was really roused she carried out my instructions to the letter. Once Benham was in the room I knew at least I was in good hands. I begged them not to rouse the house more than necessary, not to call Ella.

"Don't you speak a word. Lie quite still. We know exactly what is to be done.

Mrs. Lovegrove won't be disturbed, nor anybody if you will only do what you are told."

Benham's voice changed in an emergency; it was always a beautiful voice if a little hard; now it was gentle, soft, and her whole manner altered. She had me and the situation completely under her control, and that, of course, was what she always wanted. That night she was the perfect nurse. Lakeby obeyed her as if she had been a probationer. I often wonder I am not more grateful to Benham, failed to become quickly attached to her. I don't think perhaps that mine is a grateful nature, but I surely recognised already tonight, in this bad hour, her complete and wonderful competence. I was in high fever, very agitated, yet striving to keep command of my nerves.

"It looks bad, you know, but it is not really serious, it is only a symptom, not a disease. All you have to do is to keep very quiet. The doctor will soon be here."

"I'm not frightened."

"Hush! I'm sure you are not."

A hot bottle to my feet, little lumps of ice to suck; loose warm covering adjusted round me quickly, the blinds pulled up, and the window opened, there was nothing of which she did not think. And the little she said was all in the right key, not making light of my trouble, but explaining, minimizing it, helping me to calm my disordered nerves.

"I would give you a morphia injection only that Dr. Kennedy will be here any moment now."

I don't think it could have been long after that before he was in the room. In the meantime I was hating the sight of my own blood and kept begging the nurses or signing to them to remove basins and stained clothes.

Nurse Benham told him very quietly what had happened. He was looking at me and said encouragingly:

"You will soon be all right."

I was still coughing up blood and did not feel reassured. I heard him ask for hot water. Nurse and he were at the chest of drawers, whispering over something that might be cooking operations. Then nurse came back to the bed.

"Dr. Kennedy is going to give you a morphia injection that will stop the hæmorrhage at once."

She rolled up the sleeve of my nightgown, and I saw he was beside her.

"How much?" I got out.

"A quarter of a grain," he answered quietly. "You'll find it will be quite enough. If not, you can have another."

I resented the prick of the needle, and that having hurt me he should rub the place with his finger, making it worse, I thought. I got reconciled to it however, and his presence there, very soon. He was still in tweeds and they smelt of gorse or peat, of something pleasant.

"Getting better?"

There was no doubt the hæmorrhage was coming to an end, and I was no longer shivering and apprehensive. He felt my pulse and said it was "very good."

"The usual cackle!" I was able to smile.

"I shouldn't talk if I were you." He smiled too. "You will be quite comfortable in half an hour."

"I am not uncomfortable now." He laughed, a low and pleasant laugh.

"She is wonderful, isn't she?" he said to Benham. Benham was clearing away every evidence of what had occurred, and I felt how competent they both were, and again that I was in good hands. I was glad Ella was asleep and knew nothing of what was happening.

Dr. Kennedy was over at the chest of drawers again.

"I'll leave you another dose," he said, and they talked together. Then he came to say "good-bye" to me.

"Can't I sleep by myself? I hate any one in the room with me." I wanted to add, "it spoils my dreams," but am not sure if I actually said the words.

"You'll find you will be all right, as right as rain. Nurse will fix you up. All you have to do is to go to sleep. If not she will give you another dose. I've left it measured out. You are not afraid, are you?"

"No."

"The good dreams will come. I am willing them to you." I found it difficult to concentrate.

"What did you promise me before?"

"Nothing I shan't perform. Good-night...."

He went away quickly.

I was wider awake than I wished to be, and soon a desire for action was racing in my disordered mind. I thought the hæmorrhage meant death, and I had left so many things undone. I could not recollect the provisions of my will, and felt sure it was unjust. I could have been kinder to so many people, the dead as well as the living. It is so easy to say sharp, clever things; so difficult to unsay them. I remembered one particular act of unkindness ... even now I cannot bear to recall it. Alas! it was to one now dead. And Ella, Ella did not know I returned her love, full measure, pressed down, brimming over. Once, very many years ago, when she was in need and I supposed to be rich, she asked me to lend her five hundred pounds. Because I hadn't it, and was too proud to say so, I was ruder to her than seems possible now, asking why I should work to supply her extravagances. But she was never extravagant, except in giving. Oh, God! That five hundred pounds! How many times I have thought of it. What would I not give not to have said no, to have humbled my pride, admitted I could not put my hands on so large a sum? Now she lavishes her all on me. And if it were true that I was dying, already I was not sure, she would be lonely in her world. Without each other we were always lonely. Love of sisters is unlike all other love. We had slept in each other's bed from babyhood onward, told each other all our little secrets, been banded together against nurses and governesses, maintained our intimacy in changed and changing circumstances, through long and varied years. Ella would be lonely when I was dead. A hot tear or two oozed through my closed lids when I thought of Ella's loneliness without me. I wiped those tears away feebly with the sheet. The room was very strange and quiet, not quite steady when I opened my eyes. So I shut them. The morphia was beginning to act.

"Why are you crying?"

"How could you see me over there?" But I no longer wanted to cry and I had forgotten Ella. I opened my eyes when she spoke. The fire was low and the room dark, quite steady and ordinary. Margaret was sitting by the fireside, and I saw her more clearly than I had ever seen her before, a pale, clever, whimsical face, thin-featured and mobile, with grey eyes.

"It is absurd to cry," she said. "When I finished crying there were no tears in the world to shed. All the grief, all the unhappiness died with me."

"Why were you so unhappy?" I asked.

"Because I was a fool," she answered. "When you tell my story you must do it as sympathetically as possible, make people sorry for me. But that is the truth. I was unhappy because I was a fool."

"You still think I shall write your story. The critics will be pleased...." I began to remember all they would say, the flattering notices.

"Why were you crying?" she persisted. "Are you a fool too?"

"No. Only on Ella's account I don't want to die."

"You need not fear. Is Ella some one who loves you? If so she will keep you here. Gabriel did not love me enough. If some one needs us desperately and loves us completely, we don't die."

"Did no one love you like that?"

"I died," she answered concisely, and then gazed into the fire.

My limbs relaxed, I felt drowsy and convinced of great talent. I had never done myself justice, but with this story of Margaret Capel's I should come into my own. I wrote the opening sentence, a splendid sentence, arresting. And then I went on easily. I, who always wrote with infinite difficulty, slowly, and trying each phrase over again, weighing and appraising it, now found an amazing fluency come to me. I wrote and wrote.

De Quincey has not spoken the last word on morphia dreams. It is only a pity he spoke so well that lesser writers are chary of giving their experiences. The next few days, as I heard afterwards, I lay between life and death, the temperature never below 102 and the hæmorrhage recurring. I only know that they were calm and happy days. Ella was there and we understood each other perfectly, without words. The nurses came and went, and when it was Benham I was glad and she knew my needs, when I was thirsty, or wanted this or that. But when Lakeby replaced her she would talk and say silly soothing things, shake up my pillows when I wanted to be left alone, touch the bed when she passed it, coax me to what I would do willingly, intrude on my comfortable time. I liked best to be alone, for then I saw Margaret. She never spoke of anything but herself and the letters and diary she had left me, the rough notes. We had strange little absurd arguments. I told her not to doubt that I would write her story, because I loved writing, I lived to write, every day was empty that held no written word, that I only lived my fullest, my completest when I was at my desk, when there was wide horizon for my eyes and I saw the real true imagined people with whom I was more intimate than with any I met at receptions and crowded dinner-parties.

"The absurdity is that any one who feels what you describe should write so badly. It is incredible that you should have the temperament of the writer without the talent," she said to me once.

"What makes you say I write badly? I sell well!" I told her what I got for my books, and about my dear American public.

"Sell! sell!" She was quite contemptuous. "Hall Caine sells better than you do, and Marie Corelli, and Mrs. Barclay."

"Would you rather I gave one of them your MS.?" I asked pettishly. I was vexed with her now, but I did not want her to go. She used to vanish suddenly like a light blown out. I think that was when I fell asleep, but I did not want to keep awake always, or hear her talking. She was inclined to be melancholy, or cynical, and so jarred my mood, my sense of well-being.

Night and morning they gave me my injections of morphia, until the morning when I refused it, to Dr. Kennedy's surprise and against Benham's remonstrance.

"It is good for you, you are not going to set yourself against it?"

"I can have it again tonight. I don't need it in the daytime. The hæmorrhage has left off." Dr. Kennedy supported me in my refusal. I will admit the next few days were dreadful. I found myself utterly ill and helpless, and horribly conscious of all that was going on. The detail of desperate illness is almost unbearable to a thinking person of decent and reticent physical habits. The feeding cup and gurgling water bed, the lack of privacy, are hourly humiliations. All one's modesties are outraged. I improved, although as I heard afterwards it had not been expected that I would live. The consultants gave me up, and the nurses. Only Dr. Kennedy and Ella refused to admit the condition hopeless. When I continued to improve Ella was boastful and Benham contradictory. The one dressed me up, making pretty lace and ribbon caps, sending to London for wonderful dressing-jackets and nightgowns, pretending I was out of danger and on the road to convalescence, long before I even had a normal temperature. Benham fought against all the indulgences that Ella and I ordered and Dr. Kennedy never opposed. Seeing visitors, sitting up in bed, reading the newspapers, abandoning invalid diet in favour of caviare and foie gras, strange rich dishes. Benham despised Dr. Kennedy and said we could always get round him, make him say whatever we wished. More than once she threatened to throw up the case. I did not want her to go. I knew, if I did not admit it, that my convalescence was not established. I had no real confidence in myself, was much weaker than anybody but myself knew, with disquieting symptoms. It exhausted me to fight with her continually, one day I told her so, and that she was retarding my recovery. "I am older than you, and I hate to be ordered about or contradicted."

"But I am so much more experienced in illness. You know I only want to do what is best for you. You are not strong enough to do half the things you are doing. You turn Dr. Kennedy round your little finger, you and Mrs. Lovegrove. He knows well enough you ought not to be getting up and seeing people. You will want to go down next. And as for the things you eat!"

"I shall go down next week. I suppose I shall be exhausted before I get there, arguing with you whether I ought or ought not to go."

By this time I had got rid of the night nurse, Benham looked after me night and day devotedly. I was no longer indifferent to her. She angered me nevertheless, and we quarrelled bitterly. The least drawback, however, and I could not bear her out of the room. She did not reproach me, I must say that for her. When a horrible bilious attack followed an invalid dinner of melon and *homard à l'américaine* she stood by my side for hours trying every conceivable remedy. And without a word of reproach.

After my hæmorrhage I had a few weeks' rest from the neuritis and then it started again. I cried out for my forsaken nepenthe, but Peter Kennedy and Nurse Benham for once agreed, persuaded or forced me to codein. Dear half-sister to my beloved morphia, we became friends at once. Three or four days later the neuritis went suddenly, and has never returned. One night I took the nepenthe as well, and that night I saw Margaret Capel again.

"When are you going to begin?" she asked me at once.

"The very moment I can hold a pen. Now my hand shakes. And Ella or nurse is always here—I am never alone."

"You've forgotten all about me," she said with indescribable sadness. "You won't write it at all."

"No, I haven't. I shall. But when one has been so ill …" I pleaded.

"Other people write when they are ill. You remember Green, and Robert Louis Stevenson. As for me, I never felt well."

The next day, before Dr. Kennedy came, I asked Benham to leave us alone together. He still came daily, but she disapproved of his methods and told me that she only stayed in the room and gave him her report because she thought it her duty. They were temperamentally opposed. She had the scientific mind and believed in authority. His was imaginative, desultory, doubtful, but wide and enquiring. Both of them were interested in me, so at least Ella told me. She was satisfied now with my doctoring and nursing. At least a week had passed since she suggested a substitute for either.

Dr. Kennedy, when we were alone, said, as he did when nurse was standing there:

"Well! how are you getting on?"

"Splendidly." And then, without any circumlocution, although we had not spoken of the matter for weeks, and so much had occurred in the meantime, I asked him: "What did you do about that packet? I want it now. I am quite well enough."

"You have not seen her since?"

"Over and over again. She thinks I am shirking my responsibilities."

"Are you well enough to write?"

"I am well enough to read. When will you bring me the letters?"

"I brought them when I said I would, the day you were taken ill."

"Where are they?"

"In the first drawer, the right-hand drawer of the chest of drawers." He turned round to it. "That is, if they have not been moved. I put the packet there myself, told nurse it was something that was not to be touched. The morphia things are in the same place. I don't know what she thinks it is, some new and useless drug or apparatus; she has no opinion of me, you know. I used to see it night and morning, as long as you were having the injections."

"See if it is there now."

He went over and opened the drawer:

"It is there right enough."

"Oh! don't be like nurse," I said impatiently. "I am strong enough to look at the packet."

He gave it to me, into my hands, an ordinary brown paper parcel, tied with string and heavily, awkwardly, splotched and protected with sealing-wax. I could have sworn to his handiwork.

"Why are you smiling?" he asked.

"Only at the neatness of your parcel." He smiled too.

"I tied it up in a hurry. I didn't want to be tempted to look inside."

"So you make me guardian and executrix...."

"Margaret herself said you were to have them," he answered seriously.

"She didn't tell you so. You have only my word for it," I retorted.

"Better evidence than that, although that would have been enough. How else did you know they were in existence? Why were you looking for them?"

The parcel lay on the quilt, and all sorts of difficulties rose in my mind. I would not open it unless I was alone, and I was never alone; literally never alone unless I was supposed to be asleep. And, thanks to codein, when I was supposed to be asleep the supposition was generally correct! Thinking aloud, I asked Dr. Kennedy:

"Am I out of danger?"

He answered lightly and evasively:

"No one is ever really out of danger. I take my life in my hands every time I go in my motor."

"Oh, yes! I've heard about your driving," I answered drily.

He laughed.

"I am supposed to be reckless, but really I am only unlucky. With luck now...."

"Yes, with luck?"

"You might go on for any time. I shouldn't worry about that if I were you. You are getting better."

"I am not worrying, only thinking about Mrs. Lovegrove. She has two children, a large house, literary and other engagements. Will you tell her I am well enough to be left alone?" He answered quickly and surprised:

"She does not want to go, she likes being with you. Not that I wonder at that."

He was a strange person. Sometimes I had an idea he was not "all there." He said whatever came into his mind, and had other divergencies from the ordinary type. I had to explain to him my need of solitude. If Ella went back to town, Benham would soon, I hoped, with a little encouragement, fall into the way of ordinary nurses. I had had them in London and knew their habits. Two or three hours in the morning for their so-called "constitutionals," two or three hours in the afternoon for sleep, whether they had been disturbed in the night or not; in the intervals there were the meals over which they lingered. Solitude would be easily secured if Ella went away and there was no one to watch or comment on the amount of attention purchased or purchasable for two guineas a week. I misread Benham, by the way, but that is a detail. She was not like the average nurse, and never behaved in the same way.

My first objective, once that brown paper parcel lay on the bed, was to persuade Ella to go back to home and children. Without hurting her feelings. She would not have left the house for five minutes before I should be longing for her back again. I knew that, but one cannot work *and* play. I have never had any other companion but Ella. Still.... *Work whilst ye have the light.* One more book I *must* do, and here was one to my hand.

I made Dr. Kennedy put the parcel back in the drawer. Then I lay and made plans. I must talk to Ella of Violet and Tommy, make her homesick for them. Unfortunately Ella knew me so well. I started that very afternoon.

"How does Violet get on without you?"

"She is all right."

But soon afterwards Ella asked me quietly whether there was any one else I would like down.

"God forbid!" I answered in alarm, and she understood, understood without showing pang or offence, that I wanted to be alone. One thing Ella never quite realised, my wretched inability to live in two worlds at once, the real and the unreal. When I want to write there is no use giving me certain hours or times to myself. I want all the days and all the nights. I don't wish to be spoken to, nor torn away from my story and new friends. For this reason I have always had to leave London many months in the year, for the seaside or abroad. London meant Ella, almost daily, at the telephone if not personally.

"You don't write all day, do you? What are you pretending? Don't be so absurd, you must go out sometimes. I am fetching you in the car at...."

And then I was lured by her to theatres, dinners, lunches. She thought people liked to meet me, but I have rarely noticed any interest taken in a female novelist, however many editions she may run through. My strength was returning, if slowly. Ella of course had duties to those children of hers that sometimes I resented so unreasonably. I always wished her early widowhood had left her without ties. However, the call of them came in usefully now; it was not necessary for me to press it. I came first with her, I exulted in it. But since I was getting better....

I wished to be alone with that parcel. I did make a tentative effort before Ella left.

"I don't want to settle off to sleep just yet, nurse, I should like to read a little. There is a packet of letters...."

"No! No! I wouldn't hear of such a thing. Starting reading at ten o'clock. What will you be wanting to do next?"

"It would not do me any harm," I answered irritably. "I've told you before it does me more harm to be contradicted every time I make a suggestion."

"Well, you won't get me to help you to commit suicide. Night is the time for sleep, and you've had your codein."

"The codein does not send me to sleep, it only soothes and quiets me."

"All the more reason you should not wake yourself up by any old letters." She argued, and I.... At the end I was too tired and out of humour to insist. I made up my mind to do without a nurse as soon as possible, and in the meantime not to argue but to circumvent her. At this time, before Ella went, I was getting up every day for a few hours, lying on the couch by the window. I tested my strength and found I could walk from bed to sofa, from sofa to easy-chair without nurse's arm, if I made the effort.

"You *will* take care of yourself?" were Ella's last words, and I promised impatiently.

"I don't so much mind leaving you alone now, you have your Peter, and nurse won't let you overdo things."

"*You have your Peter.*" Can one imagine anything more ridiculous! My incurably frivolous sister imagined I had fallen in love, with that lout! I was unable to persuade her to the contrary. She argued, that at my worst and before, I would have no other attendant. And she pointed out that it could not possibly be Peter Kennedy's skill that attracted me. I defended him, feebly perhaps, for it was true that he had not shown any special aptitude or ability. I said he was quite as good as any of the others, and certainly less depressing.

"There is no good humbugging me, or trying to. You are in love with the man. Don't trouble to contradict it. And I am not a bit jealous. I only hope he will make you happy. Nurse told me you do not even like her to come into the room when he is here."

"Don't you know how old I am? It is really undignified, humiliating, to be talked to or of in that way...."

"Age has nothing to do with it. A woman is never too old to fall in love. And besides, what is thirty-nine?"

"In this case it is forty-two," I put in drily, my sense of humour not being entirely in abeyance.

"Well! or forty-two. Anyway you will admit I took a hint very quickly. I am going to leave you alone with your Corydon."

"Caliban!"

"He is not bad-looking really, it is only his clothes. And if anything comes of it you will send him to Poole's. Anyway his feet and hands are all right, and there is a certain grace about his ungainliness."

"Really, Ella, I can't bear any more. Love runs in your head; feeds your activities, agrees with you. But as for me, I've long outgrown it. I am tired, old, ill. Peter Kennedy is just not objectionable. Other doctors are. He is honest, simple...."

"I will hear all about his qualities next time I come. Only don't think you are deceiving me. God bless you, dear." She turned suddenly serious. "You know I would not go if you wanted me to stop or if I were uneasy about you any more. You know I will come down again at any moment you want me. I shall miss my train if I don't rush. Can I send you anything? I won't forget the sofa rug, and if you think of anything else...." Her maid knocked at the door and said the flyman had called up to say she must come at once. Her last words were: "Well, good-bye again, and tell him I give my consent. Tell him he gave the show away himself. I have known about it ever since the first night I was here when he told me what an interesting woman you were...."

"Good-bye ... thanks for everything. I'm sorry you've got that mad idea in your silly head...." She was gone. I heard her voice outside the window giving directions to the man and then the crunch of the fly wheels on the gravel as she was driven away.

CHAPTER IV

That night, the very night after Ella had gone, I tested my slowly returning strength. Benham gave me my codein, and saw that I was well provided with all I might need for the night; the lemonade and glycerine lozenges, a second codein on the table by my side, the electric bell to my hand. This bell had been put up since the night nurse left; it rang into Benham's bedroom. I waited for a quarter of an hour after she had gone, she had a habit of coming back to see if I had forgotten anything, or to show me how thick and abundant her hair was without the uniform cap. I should have felt like a criminal when I stole out of bed. But I did not, I felt like an invalid, and a feeble one at that. It was only a couple of steps from the bed to the chest of drawers and I accomplished it without mishap, then was back again in bed, only to remember the seals were still unbroken and the string firm. A pair of nail scissors were on the dressing-table. I was disinclined for the journey, but managed it all the same. I was then so exhausted I had to wait for a quarter of an hour before I was able to use them. Only then was my curiosity rewarded. A small number of letters, not more than fifteen or sixteen in all, a bound diary, a very cursory glance at which showed me the disingenuousness, and half a dozen pages of MS. notes or chapter headings with several trial titles, "Between the Nisi and the Absolute," "Publisher and Sinner," headed two separate pages. "The Story of an Unhappy Woman" the third. The notes were all in the first person, and I should have known them anywhere for Margaret Capel's.

Small as the whole *cache* was, I did not think it possible I could get through it all that night. Neither did it seem possible to get out of bed again. The papers must remain where they were, or underneath my pillow. I should be strong enough, I hoped, by the morning to put up with or confront any wrath or argument Benham would advance.

I had got up because I chose. That was the beginning and end of it. She must learn to put up with my ways, or I with a change of nurse.

The letters were in an elastic band, without envelopes, labelled and numbered. Margaret's were on paper of a light mauve, with lines, like foreign paper. Her handwriting, masculine and square, was not very readable. She rarely dotted an *i* or crossed a *t*, used the Greek *e* and many ellipses. Gabriel's letters were as easy to read as print. It was a pity therefore that hers were so much longer than his. Still, once I began I was sorry to leave off, and should not have done so if I could have kept my eyes open or my attention from wandering. I am printing them just as they stand, those that I read that night, at least. Here they are:—

No. 1.

211 Queen Anne's Gate, S.W.,
January 29th, 1902.

Dear Sirs:—

Would you care to publish a book by me on Staffordshire Pottery? What I have in my mind is a limited *édition de luxe*, illustrated in colours, highly priced. I may say I have a collection which I believe to be unique, if not complete, upon which I propose to draw largely. Of course the matter would have to be discussed both from your point of view and, mine. This is merely to ask if you are open.

My name is probably not unknown to you, or rather my pseudonym.

The critics have been kind to my novels, and I see no reason why they should be less so to a monograph on a subject I thoroughly understand. Although perhaps that will be hard for them to forgive. For it will be reviewed, if at all, by critics less well informed.

   Yours sincerely,
MARGARET CAPEL *("Simon Dare")*.
   Author of "The Immoralists,"
    "Love and the Lutist," etc.

Messrs. Stanton & Co.

No. 2.

117–118 Greyfriars' Square, E.C.,
January 30th, 1902.

Dear Madam:—

I have to thank you for your letter of yesterday with its suggestion for a book on Staffordshire Pottery.

The subject is outside my own knowledge, but I find there is no comprehensive work dealing with it, a small elementary booklet published in the Midlands some three years ago being the only volume catalogued.

In any case there can hardly be a large public for so special an interest, and it will probably be best, as you indicate, to issue a limited edition at a high price and appeal direct by prospectus to collectors. The success of the publication would be then largely dependent on the beauty of the illustrations and the general "get up" of the volume, for although I have no doubt your text will be excellent and accurate—it must be properly "dressed" to secure attention.

Indeed I have the privilege of knowing your novels well. They have always appealed to me as having the cardinal qualities of courage and actuality. Complete frankness combined with delicacy and literary skill is so rare with modern-day writers that your work stands out.

Could you very kindly make it convenient to call here so that we may discuss the details and plan for the Staffordshire book? This would save a good deal of correspondence.

I will gladly keep any appointment you make—please avoid Saturday, as I try to take that day off at this time of year to go to a little fishing I have in Hampshire.

Yours faithfully,

GABRIEL STANTON.

Mrs. Capel.
No. 3.
211 Queen Anne's Gate, S.W.,
February 1st, 1902.
Dear Sir:—

I am obliged by your courteous letter, and will be with you at four o'clock whichever day suits you. I propose to bring with me a short synopsis of "The Staffordshire Potters, Their Inspiration and Results," and also a couple of specimens from which you might make experiments for illustrations. I want to place the book definitely before writing it.

Domestic circumstances with which I need not trouble you, they are I fear already public property, make it advisable I should remain, if not sequestered, at least practically in retreat for the next few months. I find I cannot concentrate my mind on a novel at this juncture. But my cottages and quaint figures, groups and animals, jugs and plates, retain their attraction, and I shall do a better book about them now, when I am dependent on things and isolated from people, than I should at any other time.

It is good of you to say what you do about my novels, but I doubt if I shall ever write another. My courage has turned to cowardice, and under cross-examination I found my frankness was no longer complete. I have taken a dislike to humanity.

Yours sincerely,

MARGARET CAPEL.

No. 4.
211 Queen Anne's Gate, S.W.,
February 6th, 1902.
Dear Mr. Stanton:—

The agreement promised has not yet arrived; nor your photographer; but I have made a first selection for him, and I think you will find it sufficiently varied according to your suggestion. Thirty illustrations in colour and seventy in monochrome will give the cream of my collection, and be representative, although of course not exhaustive. I have 375 specimens, no two alike! Ten groups, with the dancing dogs for the half-title, six cottages, six single figures, and the rest animal pieces will all look well in the process you showed me. I propose the large so-called classical examples in monochrome; their undoubted coarseness will then be toned down in black or brown and none of their interest destroyed. Julia, Lady Tweeddale, has one piece of which I have never been able to secure a duplicate, and so has Mr. Montague Guest. Do you think it advisable to ask permission to photograph these for inclusion, or would it be better to use only my own collection, and keep to the personal note in the letterpress?

Our brief interview gave me the feeling that I may ask you for help in any difficulty or perplexity that occurs in the preparation of a work so new to me. You were very kind to me. I daresay I seemed to you nervous and uncertain of how I meant to proceed. I felt like a trembling amateur in that big office of yours. I have never interviewed a publisher before; my novels always went by post—and came back that way too, at first! I had a false conception of publishers, based on—but I must not tell you upon whom it was based. Although why not? Perhaps you will recognise the portrait. A little pot-bellied person, Jewish or German, with a cough, or a sniff, or a sneeze, a suggestion of a coming expectoration, speaking many languages badly and apparently all at once; impressed with his own importance, talking Turgenieff and looking Abimelech. Why Abimelech I don't know; but that is the hero of whom he reminds me. I met him at a literary garden party to which I was bidden after "The Immoralists" had been so favourably reviewed. It was given by a lady who seemed to know everybody and like no one, a keen two-bladed tongue leapt out among her guests, scarifying them. She told me Mr. Rosenstein was not only a publisher but an amorist. He looked curiously unlike it; but an introduction and a short interview turned me sceptic of my own impression, inclined me to the belief in hers.

I have wandered from my theme—your kindness, my nervousness. I shall try to do credit to your penetration. You said that you were sure I should make a success of anything I undertook! I wonder if you were right. And if my Staffordshire book will prove you so? I am going to try and make it interesting, not too technical! But my intentions vary all the time. A preliminary chapter on clays was in my first scheme, I now want instead to tell of the family history of half a dozen potters. From this I begin to dream of stories of the figures; the short-waisted husband and wife a-marketing with their basket of fruit and vegetables, the clergyman in the tithe piece, a benignant villain this, with a chucking-his-parishioners-under-the-chin expression. Dear Mr. Stanton, what will happen if it turns out that I cannot write a monograph, but am only a novelist? You said I could trust you to act as Editor and blue-pencil my redundancies. But what if it should be all redundancy? Put something about this in the agreement, will you? I want to make money, but not at your expense. I *am* nervous. I fear that instead of a book on Staffordshire Pottery I shall give you an illustrated volume of short stories published at five guineas!! What an outcry from the press! Already I have been called "precious." Now they will talk of "pretentiousness"; the "grand manner" without the grand brain behind it! Will you really help and advise me? I have never felt less self-confident.

Yours sincerely,

   MARGARET CAPEL.

No. 5.

118 Greyfriars' Square, E.C.,

   February 6th, 1902.

Dear Mrs. Capel:—

As we arranged at our interview yesterday I now enclose a draft contract for the book.

If there is any point not entirely clear to you please do not hesitate to tell me, and I shall be glad also of any suggestion or criticism that may occur to you in regard to possible alteration of the various clauses, and will do my best to meet your wishes. For I am more than anxious that we shall begin what I hope will prove a long and successful "partnership" with complete understanding and confidence.

Further enquiry makes me sanguine that the scheme is a good one, and we will do everything we can to produce a beautiful book.

May I say that it was a great pleasure and privilege to me to meet you here yesterday? I hope the interest you will find in this present work will afford you some relief during this time of trouble and anxiety you are passing through; and counteract to some extent at least the pettiness and publicity of litigation. I only refer to this with the greatest respect and sympathy.

There are many details, not only of the contract, but for the plan of the book, which we could certainly best arrange if we discussed them, rather than by writing.

Could you make it convenient to lunch with me one day next week? I shall be in the West End on Wednesday, and suggest the Café Royal at two o'clock.

It would be good of you to meet me there.

Yours sincerely,

   GABRIEL STANTON.

No. 6.

211 Queen Anne's Gate,

   February 7th, 1902.

Dear Mr. Stanton:—

Our letters crossed. Thanks for yours with agreement. The greater part seems to me to be merely technical, and I have no observations to make about it.

Par. 2: guaranteeing that the work is in no way "a violation of any existing copyright," etc. I think this is your concern rather than mine. You say there is a book existing on Staffordshire Pottery, perhaps you can get me a copy, and then I can see that ours shall be entirely different.

Par. 7: beginning "accounts to be made up annually," etc., seems to give you an exceptionally long time to pay me anything that may be due. But perhaps I misunderstand it.

Therefore, and perhaps for other reasons, I very gladly accept your kind invitation to lunch with you on Wednesday at the Café Royal, and will be there at two, bringing the agreement with me.

With kind regards,

        Yours very truly,

                MARGARET CAPEL.

No. 7.

118 Greyfriars' Square, E.C.,

        February 13th, 1902.

Dear Mrs. Capel:—

I am breaking into the commonplace routine of a particularly tiresome business day, to give myself the pleasure of writing to you, and you will forgive me if I purposely avoid business—for indeed it seems to me today that life might be so pleasant without work. That little grumble has done me good. I want to say what I fear I did not express to you yesterday—how greatly I enjoyed our talk. It was good of you to come and more good of you to tell me something of your present difficulties. I wish I could have been more helpful—but please believe I am more sympathetic than I was able to let you know, and I do understand much of what must be trying and unhappy for you during these weeks. Counsels of perfection are poor comfort, but perhaps that some one is most genuinely in accord with you—and anxious to help in any way possible—may be of some little value.

I beg you to believe that this is so, and I should welcome the chance of being of any service to you. This all reads very formal I fear, but your kindness must interpret the spirit rather than the letter.

Last evening I went into an old curiosity shop to try and find a wedding-present for a niece who is also my god-daughter, and I secured six beautiful Chippendale chairs. Curiously enough the man showed me what he said was the best specimen of Staffordshire he had ever had. A group of musicians—seeming to my inexperienced eye good in colour and design. I know not what impulse persuaded me to buy the piece. Today I am fearing that my purchase is not genuine. May I bring it to you on Sunday for approval or condemnation? Don't trouble to answer if you will be at home—I will call at five o'clock.

Now I must return to less pleasant business affairs—the telephone is insistent.

Yours very sincerely,

                GABRIEL STANTON.

No. 8.

211 Queen Anne's Gate, S.W.,

        14th February, 1902.

Dear Mr. Stanton:—

Thank you so much for your kind letter, it made a charming savoury to that little luncheon you ordered. Did I tell you how much I enjoyed it? If not, please understand I am doing so now. The *mousse* was a dream of delight, the roses were very helpful. I have a theory about flowers and food, and how to blend them. Which reminds me that my father wants to share with me in the pleasure of your acquaintance and bids me ask if you will dine with us on the 24th at eight o'clock. This of course must not prevent your coming Sunday afternoon with your pottery "find." I am more than curious, I am devoured with curiosity to see it. I don't know a Staffordshire "group of musicians," it sounds like Chelsea! Bring it by all means, but if it is Staffordshire and not in my collection, I warn you I shall at once begin bargaining with you, spending my royalties in advance! Yes! I think I hate business too, as you say, and should like to avoid it. We were fairly successful, by the way, in the Café Royal! Our talk ranged over a large field, became rather personal—I think I spoke too freely; it must have been the Steinberger! or because I am really very worried and depressed. Depression is the old age of the emotions, and garrulousness its distressing symptom.

Yours sincerely,
> MARGARET CAPEL.

No. 9.

118 Greyfriars' Square, E.C.,
> 15th February, 1902.

Dear Mrs. Capel:—

I am so glad to have your letter and look forward to Sunday. Should my little pottery "find" prove authentic I have no doubt we can arrange for its transfer to you, on business or even un-business lines!

I accept with pleasure your invitation to dinner on the 24th. I have heard often of your father from my friend Wilfrid Henning, who attends to what little investments I make—and who meets your father in connection with that big Newfoundland scheme for connecting the traffic from the Eastern ports to Lake Ontario. I should value the opportunity to hear of it, firsthand.

Yours most sincerely,
> GABRIEL STANTON.

No. 10.

211 Queen Anne's Gate, S.W.,
> 16th February, 1902.

Dear Mr. Stanton:—

I am no longer puzzled about the "musicians"; it is Staffordshire, I was convinced of that from the first but had to confirm my impression. I will tell you all about it when we meet again (on the 24th), I am sure you will be interested. I want you to let me have it. Whatever you paid for it I will give you, and any profit you like. I won't bargain with you, but I really feel I can never part with it again. It was a wonderful chance that you should find it. Wasn't Sunday altogether strange? Such a crowd, and so difficult to talk. I shall have to get out of London, I have a sense of fatigue all the time, of restless incoherent fear. I dread sympathy, and scent curiosity as if it were carrion. In that little talk I had among the tea-things I said none of the things I meant. I believe you understood this, although you only said yes, and yes again to my wildest suggestions. I am only epigrammatic when I am shy; it is the form taken by my mental stammer. Epigrams come to me too, when I have a scene in my head too big to write. I find my hand shaking, heart beating, tremulous. Then my queer brain relieves the pressure on my feelings and stammers out my scene in short cryptic sentences. That is why, although I am an emotional thinker, I am what you are pleased to call an intellectual writer.

And now for the agreement, in which I have ventured to make alterations, and even additions. Will you return it to me with comments if you think I have been too difficult or exacting. My father tells me I have inherited his business ability. He means to pay me a compliment, but I gather your point of view is that business ability is but deformity in an intellectual woman? I'm sorry for this deformity of mine, realising the unfavourable impression it may create. Try and forgive me for it, won't you? You need not even remember it when you are telling me what I am to give you for the Staffordshire piece!

With kind regards,
> Yours very sincerely,
>> MARGARET CAPEL.

No. 11.

118 Greyfriars' Square, E.C.,
> 17th February, 1902.

Dear Mrs. Capel:—

What good news about the little "Staffordshire" piece! I am really delighted. Please don't mar my pleasure in thinking of it happily housed with you by questions of price or bargaining. Rather add to my pride in my "find" by accepting it as a small recognition of my great good fortune in having made your acquaintance.

Out of the chatter and clatter of the tea on Sunday the things you said remain with me; if they were epigrams they were vivid and to me very real.

I hated everything that interrupted—and hated going away. Quite humbly I say that I think I did understand, and was longing to tell you so. But I have never had the tongue of a ready speaker, and as I left your beautiful home I was choked with unspoken words a cleverer man would have found more quickly.

How much I wished I could have expressed myself. I wanted to say that I had no hateful curiosity, but only an overwhelming sympathy and desire for your confidence, a bedrock craving for your friendship. May I be your friend? May I? Or am I presuming on your kindness and too short an acquaintanceship?

Anyhow, I can't write on business, the contract is to go through with all your alterations.

Looking forward to the 24th, I need only sign,

Au revoir,

    Yours very truly,

               GABRIEL STANTON.

No. 12.

211 Queen Anne's Gate, S.W.,

       18th February, 1902.

Dear Mr. Stanton:—

I don't know what to say about "The Musicians," that is why I have not already written to say it! I have not put the group into my collection, it is on my bedroom mantelpiece. I see it when I first wake in the morning, it is the last thing upon which my tired eyes rest before I turn off the light at night. Sometimes I think those musicians are playing the prelude to the friendship of which you speak.

I wonder why you are so curiously sympathetic to me, and why I mind so little admitting it. Friendship has been rare in my life. You offer me yours, and I am on the point of accepting it; thinking all the time what it may mean, what I can give you in return. An hour now and again of detached talk, a great deal of trouble with my literary affairs ... there is not much in that for you; is there? Are the Musicians really a gift? They must go on playing to me softly then, and the prelude be slow and long-drawn-out. I am afraid even of friendship, that is the truth. I'm disillusioned, disappointed, tired. Nothing has ever happened to me as I meant it. When I first came from America with my father, I was full of the wildest hopes, and now I have outlived them all. It is not an affectation, it is a profound truth, and at twenty-eight I find myself worn out, dimmed, exhausted. I have had fame (a small measure of it, but enough for comparison), wealth, and that horrid nightmare, love.

My father spoiled me when I was small, believed too much in me. He thought me a genius, and I ... perhaps I thought so too. I puzzled and perplexed him, and he felt overweighted with his responsibilities, with character-studying an egotistic girl of sixteen. The result was a stepmother. Can you imagine what I suffered! She began almost immediately to suffocate me with her kindness. She too admitted I was a genius. Do you know we had the idea, these besotted parents of mine and I, that I was to be a great pianist! I practised many hours a day, sustained by jellies, and beef-tea and encouragement. I had the best teachers, a few weeks in Dresden with Lentheric, my father poured out his money like water. The end of that period was a prolonged fainting fit, the first of many, the discovery I had a weak heart, that the exertion of piano-playing affected it unfavourably. I came back from Dresden at eighteen, was presented the same year, the papers said I was beautiful; father put himself out of the way to be nice to pressmen; he had acquired the habit in America whilst he was building up his fortune. That I was accounted beautiful and could play Chopin and was to have a fortune, made me appear also brilliant. My father paid for the printing of my first book. My first one-act play was performed at a West End theatre. Then I met James Capel. Mr. Justice Jeune knows the story of my married life better than any one else. I was high-spirited before it began. At the end of a year I was physically, mentally, morally a wreck. I don't know which of us hated the other more, my husband or I. Anyway, he made no objection to my returning to my father. My stepmother's suffocating kindness descended upon me again, and now I found it healing. When I was healed I wrote "The Immoralists." Then my father's pride in me revived. He and my stepmother kept open house and collected celebrities to show the dimness of their light as a background for my supposed more brilliant shining! Society was pleased to come, my father growing always richer.... I wrote "The Farce of Fearlessness" and "Love and the Lutist" about this time, and my other play. When my husband made it imperative by his proved and public blackguardism I resorted to the law, and acting under advice, fought him in the arena he chose, and have now won my freedom, but at an incredible, hardly yet to be realised cost, all my wounds exposed in the market-place.

I wonder why I am recapitulating all this. I think it is to show you I am in no mood for friendship. There are times when I am savage with pain, and times when I am exhausted from it, times when I feel bruised all over, so tender that the touch of a word brings tears, times when my overwhelming pity for myself leaves me incapable of realizing anything beyond my wrongs. I say I have won my freedom, but even this is untrue: at present I have only won six months of probation, during which I am still James Capel's wife. Sometimes I think I shall never live through them, the stain of my connection with him is like mortification.

The prelude played by the Musicians is a prelude to a dream.

And still I am grateful you gave them to me.

Yours very truly,

    MARGARET CAPEL.

When I had read as far as this the codein exerted its influence. My eyelids drooped, I slept and recovered myself. The sense of what I was reading began to escape, I knew it was time to put the bundle away. There were not very many more letters. I put all the papers on the table by my side, then dropped off. Margaret betrayed herself completely in her letters. Gabriel Stanton was still a strange unrealisable figure.

CHAPTER V

The few words I had with Nurse Benham the next morning cleared the air and the situation between us. The strange thing was that at first she did not notice the parcel at all, still loose and untidy in the paper in which Dr. Kennedy had enwrapped it. Not until I told her to be careful not to spill the tea over it did it strike her to wonder how it came there.

"Did Suzanne give you that?" she asked suspiciously.

"She has not been in my room since you left me."

"That's the very parcel you asked for the other night. How ever did you get hold of it?"

"After you left me I got out of bed and fetched it."

"You got out of bed!" She grew red in the face with rage or incredulity.

"Yes, twice. Once for the parcel and once for the scissors!"

She did not speak at once, standing there with her flushed face. So I went on:

"It is absurd for you to insist on me doing this or that, or leaving it undone. You are here to take care of me, not to bully and tyrannise over me."

"I am no good to you at all. I'd better go. You *will* take matters into your own hands. I never knew such a patient, never. One would think you'd no sense at all, that you didn't know how ill you were."

"That is no reason why I should not be allowed to get better. Believe me, the only way for that to come about is that I should be allowed to lead my own life in my own way."

"To get up in the middle of the night with the window wide open, to walk about the room in your nightgown!"

"I should not have done so, you know, if you had passed me the things when I asked you for them."

"You don't want a nurse at all," she repeated.

"Yes, I do. What I don't want is a gaoler."

I was on the sofa when Dr. Kennedy called, the papers on the table beside me. He asked eagerly what I thought of them:

"I see you have got at them. Are you disappointed, exhilarated? Are they illuminative? Tell me about them; I want so much to hear."

He had forgotten to ask how I was.

"I will tell you about them presently. I haven't read them all. Up to now they are certainly disappointing, if not dull! They are business letters, to begin with. But it is obvious she is trying to get up something like a flirtation with him."

"Oh, no!"

"Oh, yes! I have watched Ella, my sister Mrs. Lovegrove, for years. She is past mistress of the art of flirtation. Sentiment and the appeal of her femininity, a note of unhappiness and the suggestion the man's friendship may assuage it...."

"Mrs. Lovegrove is a very charming woman. But Margaret Capel was not in the least like her."

"Or any other woman?"

"No."

"You have put yourself out of court. No woman is unlike any other. Your 'pale fair Margaret' admits, from the first, that Gabriel Stanton attracts her. And this at a moment when she should allow herself to be attracted by no man. When she has just gone through the horrors of the Divorce Court."

"You are not bringing that up against her?"

"I am not bringing anything up against her. But you asked me about the letters. I have only read a dozen of them, and that is how they strike me. A little dull and, on her part, flirtatious."

"I hope you won't do the book at all if you don't feel sympathetic."

"Believe me I shall be sympathetic if there is anything with which to sympathise. Do you know her early life, or history? It is hinted at, partly revealed here, but I should like to see it clearly."

"Won't she tell you herself?" He smiled. I answered his smile.

"She has left off coming since I have begun to get well. I shall have to write the book, if I write it at all, without further help. By the way, talking about getting better, I know that doctoring bores you, but I want to know how much better I am going to get? I am as weak as a rat; my legs refuse to carry me, my hand shakes when I get a pen in it. I shall get the story into my head from these papers," I added, with something of the depression that I was feeling: "But I don't see how I am to get it out again. I don't see how I shall ever have the strength to put it on paper."

"That will come. There is no hurry about that. As a matter of fact I believe letters are copyright for fourteen years. It isn't twelve yet."

It was not worth while to put him right on the copyright acts.

"You'll be going downstairs next week, you'll be at your writing-table, her writing-table in the drawing-room. You ask me about her early life. I only know her father was a wealthy American absolutely devoted to her. He married for the second time when she was fifteen or sixteen and they both concentrated on her. She was remarkable even as a child, obviously a genius, very beautiful."

"She outgrew that," I said emphatically.

"She was a very beautiful woman," he insisted. And then said more lightly, "You must remember you have only seen her ghost." The retort pleased me and I let the subject of Margaret Capel's beauty drop. She interested me less when I felt well, and notwithstanding my active night I felt comparatively well this morning. Since I could not get him to take my weakness seriously I told him my grievance against nurse.

"When she hears I am to go down next week she will have a fit. I wish for once you would use your medical authority and tell her I am on no account to be contradicted or thwarted."

"I'll tell her so if you like, but I never see her. She runs like a rabbit when I come near."

"You are not professional enough for her taste, there are too few examinations and prescriptions. How is my unsatisfactory lung, by the way? Give a guess, something scientific to retail. I must keep Ella informed."

"There has not been time for the physical signs to have cleared up yet. I'll listen if you like, but after seeing all those specialists I should have thought you were tired of saying '99'."

"They varied it sometimes. '999' seems to be the latest wheeze."

"I wish you had not left off seeing Margaret," he sighed.

"It is a pity," I laughed at him. "You should not have dropped giving me the morphia so soon."

"You wouldn't have it."

"It was dulling my brain. I felt myself growing stupid and more stupid."

"You only had one-quarter grain twice a day for the inside of a week, and there was atropin in it. If it had really had a deadening effect upon you you would not have refused it, but just gone on. Not that I believe anything would ever dull *your* brain."

I wished Ella could have heard him, it would have confirmed her in her folly and made for my amusement. He left shortly after paying me that remarkable compliment, but stopped on his way out to speak to Benham. The immediate effect of his words was to make her silent and perhaps sullen for a few hours. After which, but still under protest, she gave me whatever I asked for, and began to be more like other nurses in the time she took off duty for exercise, sleep, and meals. She even yawned in my face on the rare occasions when I summoned her in the night. I tried to chaff her back into good humour, but without much success.

"Do you find me any worse for having got out of leading strings?" I asked her. "Have pencils and MS. paper sent up my temperature?"

"You are not out of the wood yet," she retorted angrily.

"No, but I am enjoying its umbrageous rest," I returned. "Reading my papers in the shadows."

"Shadow enough!"

"That's right. Mind you go on keeping up my spirits." She did smile then, but she was obviously dissatisfied, both with me and Dr. Kennedy. I was taking no drugs, doing a little more each day, in the way of moving about. And yet I could not call myself convalescent. My legs were stiff and my back heavy. I had no feeling of returning vigour. What little I did I forced myself to do. I had hardly the energy to finish the letters. Had it not been for Dr. Kennedy I don't believe, at this stage, I should have finished them! Although the next two or three set me thinking, and I was again visualising the writers. Not that Gabriel Stanton betrayed himself in his letters, as Margaret did in hers. I had to reconcile him with the donnish master of Greek roots, whom I had met and been ignored by, in Greyfriars' Square. This was his answer to her last effusion.

No. 13.

118 Greyfriars' Square,
      19th February, 1902.

Dear Mrs. Capel:—

I have read your letter ten—twenty times; my business day was filled and transformed by it. Now it is midnight and I am alone in the stillness of my room, the routine of the day and the evening over, and my brain, not always very quick, alight with the wonderment of your words, and my restless anxiety to respond. Don't, I implore you, belittle the possibility of friendship!

Surely the value of it is only proved by its needs?

May I not say that in this crisis in your life friendship may be much to you. Can I hope that my privilege may be to fill the need?

You have been so splendidly frank and outspoken. *I* have suffered all my life from a sort of stupid reticence, probably cowardly. But tonight, and to you, I want to throw off the habit of years and not miss, before it is too late, the luxury of being natural.

Well, I am hot with hatred that you should have been hurt, and yet I am happy that you have told me of your wounds. Tonight I pray that it may be given to me to heal them.

I am writing this because I must—though conventionally the shortness of our acquaintance does not justify me. But I have been conventional so long—circumstance has ruled and limited my doings. And tonight it comes to me that chance and fate are, or should be, greater than environment. The Gods only rarely offer gifts, and the blackness and blankness of despair follow their refusal. So I cling to the hope that they have now offered me a precious gift, and that in spite of all your pain—all the past which now so embitters you, to me may come the chance in some small way of proving to you that in friendship there is healing, and in sympathy and understanding, at least the hope of forgetfulness.

I shall hardly dare to read over what I have written, for I should either be conscious that it is inadequate to express what I have wanted to say to you—or that I have presumed too much in writing what is in my mind.

Look upon those Musicians as playing a prelude, not to a dream but to a happier future, and then my pleasure in the little gift will be enormously increased.

It has been a sort of joke in my family that I am over-cautious and too deliberate, but for tonight at least in these still quiet hours I mean to conquer this, and go out to post this letter myself; just as I have written it, with no alteration; yet with confidence in the kindness you have already shown me.

And I shall see you at dinner on Thursday.

Yours very sincerely,

    GABRIEL STANTON.

A little over a fortnight passed before there was any further correspondence. Meanwhile the two must have met frequently. Her letters were often undated, and her figures even more difficult to read than her handwriting generally. The hieroglyphic over the following looks like 5, but I could not be sure. The intimacy between them must have grown apace, and yet the running away could have been nothing but a ruse. There could have been little fear of so sedate a lover as Gabriel Stanton. I found something artificial in the next letter of hers, recapitulative, as if already she had publication in her mind. Of course it is more difficult for a novelist or a playwright to be genuine and simple with a pen than it is for a person of a different avocation, but I could not help thinking how much better than Margaret Ella would have acted her part, and my sympathy began to flow more definitely toward the inexperienced gentleman, no longer young, to whom she was introducing the game of flirtation under the old name of Platonic friendship.

No. 14.

Carbies,

  Pineland,

March 5th, 1902.

I have run away, you realise this, don't you, simply turned tail and run. That long dinner which seemed so short; the British Museum the next day, and your illuminating lecture so abruptly ended—that dreadful lunch ... boiled fish and ginger beer! Ye Gods! Greek or Roman, how could you appear satisfied, eat with appetite? I sickened in the atmosphere. Thursday at the National Gallery was better. Our taste in pictures is the same if our taste in food differs. But perhaps you did not know what you were given in the refreshment room of the British Museum? I throw out this suggestion as an extenuating circumstance, for I find it difficult to forgive you that languid cod and its egg sauce. Our other two meals together were so different. That first lunch at the Café Royal was perfect in its way. As for our dinner, did I not myself superintend the ménu, curb the exuberance of the chef and my stepmother; dock the unfashionable sorbet; change Mayonnaise sauce into Hollandaise; duck and green peas into an idealised animal of the same variety, stuffed with foie gras, enriched and decorated with cherries? For you I devoted myself to the decoration of the table, interested myself in the wine list my father produced, discussed vintages with our pompous and absurd butler. I must tell you a story about that butler. You said he looked like an Archdeacon. Can you imagine an Archdeacon in the Divorce Court? No! No! No! Nothing to do with mine. Had it been I could not have written of it, the very thought sets me writhing again. Poor Burden was with the Sylvestres, you remember the case. Everybody defended and it was fought for five interminable days. The papers devoted columns to it, nothing else was discussed in the Clubs, the whole air of London—Mayfair end—was fœtid and foul with it. Burden was a witness, he had seen too much, and his evidence sent poor silly Ann Sylvestre to hide her divorced and disgraced head in Monte Carlo. And can a head properly *ondulé* be said to be divorced? Heavens! how my pen runs on, or away, like me. And I haven't come to the story, which now I come to think of it is not so *very* good. I will tell you it in Burden's own words. He applied for our situation through a registry office, and stood before my stepmother and me, hat in hand, sorrowful, but always dignified, as he answered questions.

"My last situation was with a Mrs. Solomon. I'm sorry, milady, to have to ask you to take up a character from such people. I'd always been in the best service before that.... I was hallboy with the Jutes, third and then second with His Grace the Duke of Richland, first footman under the Countess Foreglass. I was five years with the Sylvestres; you know, Ma'am, he was first cousin to the Duke of Trent, near to the Throne itself, as one might say. I'd never lowered myself to an untitled family before. But after the divorce I couldn't get nothing. Ma'am, I hope you'll believe me, but from the moment I accepted Mr. Solomon's place all I was planning to do was to get out of it. They was Jews, if I may mention such a thing to you. I took ten pounds a year less than I'd had at his Lordship's, but Mr. Solomon, he said in his facetious way that being in the witness box 'ad knocked at least ten pounds off my value, an' he ground me down. But I'll have to ask you to take up my character from him. That's the worst of it, Ma'am, milady."

We had to break it to him that we were without titles, but he said sorrowfully that having been in a witness box in the divorce court made it impossible for him to stand out.

Burden and I have always been on good terms. I understand him, you see, his point of view, and his descent in the social scale when he went to live with Jews. What I was going to tell you was, that notwithstanding our friendship he resented my interference in his department when I insisted on selecting the wine for your—our—dinner party. I am almost sorry I quarrelled with him on your account. He looks at me coldly now, he is remembering my American blood, despising it. And to think I have lost the priceless regard of Burden for a man who can eat boiled and tired cod, masked with egg sauce, washed down with ginger beer!

Where was I? The sculpture at the British Museum; then the next day at the National Gallery. Our spirits kneeled there; we grew small. No, we didn't, I'm disingenuous. We said so, not meaning it in the least. After twenty minutes we forgot all about the pictures. Rumpelmayer's, St. James's Park, out to Coombe.

Did you realise we were seeing each other every day, how much time we spent together?

Am I eighteen or twenty-eight? You've a reputation for knowing more about Greek roots than any other Englishman. Should I have run away down here if you had talked about Greek roots? I'm excited, exhausted, bewildered. For three nights sleep failed me. Nothing is so wonderful as a perfect friendship between a man of your age and a woman of mine. Why did you change your mind, or your note, so quickly yesterday? *I* knew all the time what was happening to us. I think there is something arrogant in your humility. I am naturally so much more outspoken than you, although my troubles have made me more fearful. You are a strange man. I think you may send me a portrait. When I try to recall you, you don't always come whole, only bits of you, inconsistent bits, a gleam of humour in your eyes, your stoop, the height that makes us so incongruous together. I like you, Gabriel Stanton, and I've run away from you; that's the truth. That disingenuous aggressive humility of yours is a subtle appeal to my sympathies. I don't want to sympathise with you overmuch, with the loneliness of your life, or anything about you. We were meeting too often, talking too freely. I curl up and want to hide when I think of some of the things we have said (*I* have said!!!). I know I am too impulsive.

I'm going to settle down here and start seriously on my Staffordshire Potters. I've taken the house for three months. If I had not already written the longest letter ever penned I'd describe it to you. Perhaps I'll write again if you encourage me. Think of me as a novelist out of work, using up my MS. paper. Down here everything has become unreal. You and I, but especially "*us*"! I *want* everything to be unreal, I'm not strong enough for more reality. Keep unsubstantial. I don't suppose you will understand me (I am not sure that I understand myself). But you begged me to "let myself go," "pour myself out on you." Can I take your strength and lean upon it, the tenderness you promise me and revel in it, all that I believe you are offering me, and give you nothing? I am mean, afraid of giving. It all came so quickly, so unexpectedly. I have never had a real companion. Never, never, never even as a child been wholly natural with anybody, posing always. The only daughter of a millionaire with more talent than she ought to have, a shy soul behind a brazen forehead, is in a difficult position. To undrape that shy soul of mine as you so nearly make me do, unwillingly—but it might happen—makes me shiver. That's why I ran away, I want to be isolated, to stand alone. Here is the truth again, not at the bottom of a well, but at the end of an interminable letter. I am afraid of pain, and this intimacy presages it. You cannot be all I think you. I don't want to be near enough to see your clay feet.

I am going to get some picture postcards with small space for writing; this MS. paper demoralises me.

Sincerely,

       MARGARET CAPEL.

No. 15.

Will you ever know what your dear wonderful letter has given me? I passed through moments of doubt, of bewildered unbelief into a golden trance of joy and hope. And as again and again I read it some of your far braver personality fills me, and I refuse to think this new spring of hope is a mere dream, and take courage and tell myself I *am* something to you—something in your life, and that to me, Gabriel Stanton, has come at last the chance of helping, tending, caring for against all the world if need be, such a woman as Margaret Capel.

Let me revel in this new strange happiness. You are too kind, too generous to destroy it! For it is all strange and marvellous to me—I've lived so much alone—have missed so much by circumstance and the fault of what you call my "aggressive humility." I *can* help you! As I write I feel I want nothing else in life. Oh! my wonderful friend, don't let us miss a relationship which on my part I swear to you shall be consecrated to your service, to your happiness in any and every way you decide or will ask. Let me come into your life, give me the chance of healing those wounds which have bruised you grievously, but can never conquer your brave spirit. You must let me help.

You have gone away, but your dear letter is with me—it is so much your letter—so much you that I am not even lonely any more. And yet I long to see you—hear you talk, be near you. Thoughts—hopes— ideas, crowd upon me tonight, things to tell you——It is like having a new sense—I've wakened up in a new and so beautiful country. Do you wish for those weeks of solitude? Only what you wish matters. But I confess I've looked up the trains to Pineland. I will come on any day at any moment you say. There is no duty that could keep me should you say "come." Give me at least one chance of seeing you in your new home. Then I will keep away and respect your solitude if you wish it.

The joy of your letter and the golden castles I am building help the hours until I hear from you.

G. S.

It is my opinion still that she only ran away in order to bring him after her, to secure a greater solitude than they could enjoy in places of public resort, or in her father's house. I don't mean that she deliberately planned what followed, but had that been her intention she could have devised no better strategy than to leave him at the point at which they had arrived without a word of farewell other than that letter. As for me, when I had finished reading it and the answer, I had recourse to the diary and MS. notes. They would, however, have been of but little use had not a second dose of codein that night brought me again in closer relation with the writer.

CHAPTER VI

As I said, I took two codein pills instead of one that night, and in an hour or so was conscious of the comfort and phantasmagoria of morphia. I was no longer in the bedroom of which I had tired, nor in the rough garden without trees or shade. I had escaped from these and in returning health was beside the sea, happily listening to the little waves breaking on the stones, no soul in sight but those two, Margaret Capel and Gabriel Stanton, in earnest talk that came to me as I sat with my back against a rock, the salt wind in my face. How it was they did not see me and moderate their voices I do not know, morphia gives one these little lapses and surprises.

Margaret looked extraordinarily sedate and yet perverse, her thin lips pink and eyes dancing. I saw the incandescent effect of which Peter Kennedy had told me. It was not only her eyes that were alight but the woman herself, the luminous fair skin and the fairness of her hair stirred and brightened by the sun and the sea-wind. She talked vividly, whilst he sat at her feet listening intently, offering her the homage of his softened angularities, his abandoned scholarship, his adoring eyes.

"Why did you come? I told you not to come. Of course I meant to wire in answer to your letter that you were to stay in London. What was the use of my running away?"

I saw that he fingered the hem of her skirt, and watched her all the time she spoke.

"Tomorrow I shall have no expectation in the post. I hate not to care whether my letters come or not. And Monday too. You have spoiled two mornings for me."

"I am not as satisfying as my letters to you." Even his voice was changed, the musical charming Stanton voice. His had deepened and there was the note of an organ in it. She looked at him critically or caressingly.

"Not quite, not yet. I understand your letters better than I do you. And you are never twice alike, not quite alike. We part as friends, intimates. Then we come together again and you are almost a stranger; we have to begin all over again."

"I am sorry." He looked perplexed. "How do I change or vary? I cannot bear to think that you should look upon me as a stranger."

"Only for a few moments."

"When you met me at the station today?"

"I was at the station early, and then was vexed I had come, looking about me to see if there were any one I knew or who knew me. I took refuge at the bookstall, found 'The Immoralists' among the two-shilling soiled." She left off abruptly, and her face clouded.

"Don't!" he whispered.

"How quick you are!" Now their hands met. She smiled and went on talking. "I heard a click and saw that the signals were down. The train rounded the curve and came in slowly. People descended; I was conscious of half a dozen, although I saw but one. No, I didn't see you, only your covert coat and felt hat. I felt a pang of disappointment." Their hands fell apart. I saw he was hurt. She may have seen it too, but made no sign.

"It was not your fault, you had done nothing … you just were not as I expected you. You had cut yourself shaving, for one thing." He put his hand to his chin involuntarily, there was barely a scratch. "As we walked back from the station my heart felt quite dead and cold. I hated the scratch on your cheek, the shape of your hat, everything." He turned pale. "I wondered how I was going to bear two whole days, what I should say to you."

"We talked!"

"I know, but it was outside talk, forced, laboured. You remember, 'How warm the weather was in London'; and that the train was not too full for comfort. You had papers in your hand, the *Saturday Review*, the *Spectator*. You spoke of an article by Runciman in the first."

"You seemed interested."

"I was thinking how we were going to get through the two days. What I had ever seen in you, why I thought I liked you so much."

He was quite dumb by now, the sunken eyes were full of pain, the straight austere mouth was only a line; he no longer touched the hem of her dress.

"You left me in the garden of the hotel when you went to book a room, to leave your bag. I sat on a seat in the garden and looked at the sea, the blue wonder of the sea, the jagged coast-line, and one rock that stood out, then hills and always more hills, the sky so blue, spring in the air. Gabriel …" she leaned forward, touched him lightly on the shoulder. A deep flush came over his face, but he did not move nor put up his hand to take hers. "You were only gone ten minutes. I could not have borne for you to have been away longer. There were a thousand things I wanted to say to you, that I knew I could say to no one but you. About the spring and my heart hunger, what it meant."

"And when I came out I suppose all you remembered was that I had cut myself shaving?"

She seemed astonished at the bitterness of his tone.

"You are not angry with me, are you?"

"No! Not angry. How could I be?"

"When you came out and I felt rather than saw you were moving toward me across the grass I thought of nothing but that you were coming; that we were going to have tea together, on the ricketty iron table, that I should pour it out for you. That after that we should walk here together, and then you would go home with me, dine together at Carbies, talk and talk and talk...."

He could not help taking her hand again, because she gave it to him, but his face was set and serious.

"Tell me, is it the same with you as it is with me? Am I a stranger to you sometimes? Different from what you expect? Do I disappoint you, and leave you cold, almost as if you disliked me? Don't answer. I expect, I know it is the same with you. You find me plain, gone off, you wonder what you ever saw in me."

He answered with a quiet yet passionate sincerity:

"When I see you after an interval my heart rushes out to you, my pulses leap. I feel myself growing pale. I am paralysed and devoid of words. Margaret! My very soul breathes *Margaret*, my wonderful Margaret. I cannot get my breath." Her eyes shone and exulted.

"It is not like that always?" she whispered, leaning towards him.

"It is like that always. But today it was more than that. I had not seen you for a week, a whole long week. Sometimes in that week I had not dared look forward."

"And then you saw me." She was hanging upon his words. He got up abruptly and walked a few paces away from her, to the edge of the sea. She smiled quietly to herself when he left her like that. He was suffering, he could not bear the contrast between what she had thought of him and he of her.

"Gabriel!" she called him back presently, called softly and he came swiftly.

"I had better go back to town by the next train. I disappoint you."

"Silly!" She was amazingly, alluringly smiling into his dour eyes, not satisfied until he smiled too. "It is my sense of style. I am like grammar; all moods and tenses. You want me to tell you everything, don't you?"

"Am I the man for you? that is what I want you to tell me. I don't know what you mean by that sense of strangeness—I cannot bear it."

"Don't you vary? wonder, doubt?"

"I always knew from the first afternoon when you were shown into my room in Greyfriars', your black fur framing your exquisite porcelain face, your eyes like wavering stars, that you were the only woman in the world. Since then the conviction of it grows deeper and deeper, more certain. You are never out of my mind. I know I am not good enough for you, too old and grave. But you have let me hope. Oh! you wonderful child." For still she was smiling at him in that dazzling alluring way. He was at her feet and the hem of her dress again against his lips. "Don't you understand, can't I make you understand? I adore you, I worship you. I want nothing from you except that you let me tell you so sometimes."

"It is so much nicer when you write it," she murmured.

"Don't." She cajoled him.

"I can't take it lightly," he burst out. "Pity me, forgive me, but don't laugh at me."

"I am not laughing."

"I know. You are an angel of sweetness, goodness. Margaret, let me love you!"

I was back again in bed, very drowsy and comfortable, wondering how I had got there, what had happened, what time it was. I took a drink of lemonade and thought what a bad night I was having. I remembered my dream; it had been very vivid, and I was sorry for Gabriel Stanton and tried to remember what had become of him, when I had heard of or seen him last; it must have been a long time ago. Margaret was a minx. If ever I wrote about them it would be to tell the truth, to analyse and expose the spirit and soul of a woman flirt. And again when I lay down I thought of what the critics would say of this fine and intimate study, this human document that I was to give the world. Phrases came to me, vivid lightning touches ... I hoped I should be able to remember them, but hardly doubted it, for others came, even better than these, and then in consequence, sleep....

Benham said in the morning:

"Whatever did you take another pill for? Was anything the matter with you? You could have called me up."

"But you might have argued with me."

"I am sure I don't know what good a nurse is to you at all!"

"You would be invaluable if you would only get it into your head that I am not a mental case. Don't you realise that I am a very clever woman, quite as clever as you?"

"I don't call it clever to retard your own recovery."

"Am I going to recover?" I asked quickly.

"Your beloved Dr. Kennedy says you are."

"By the way, is he coming today?"

"It isn't many days he misses."

"He comes to protect me from you, to see I have some few privileges and ameliorations of my condition, that my confinement is not too close, my gaoler too vigilant."

We understood each other better now, and I could chaff her without provoking anything but a difficult smile. I, of course, was a bad patient. I found it difficult to believe that I ought not to try and overcome my weakness and inertia, that it was my duty to leave off fighting and sink into invalidism as if it were a feather bed.

That afternoon she helped me to the writing-table in the drawing-room, and I sat there trying to recapture the conversation I had heard. But although I could remember every word I found it hard to write. I could lie back in the chair and look at the gorse, the distant hills, the sea, the dim wide horizon, but to lean forward, take pen in hand, dip it in the ink, write, was almost beyond that still slowly ebbing strength. I whipped myself with the thought of what weak women had done, and dying men. "*My head is bloody but unbowed....*" Mine was bowed then, quickly over the writing-table; tears of self-pity welled hot, but I would not let them fall. It was not because Death was coming to me. I swear that then nor ever have I feared Death. But I was leaving so much undone. I had a place, and it was to know me no more. And the world was so lovely, the promise of spring in the air. When I lifted my bowed head Peter Kennedy was there, very pitiful as I could see by his eyes, and with a new gift of silence. Silence as to essentials, at least. He did not ask what ailed me, but spoke of a breakdown to the motor, of the wonder of the April weather. I soon regained my self-possession.

"How soon after Margaret Capel came here did you make her acquaintance?" I asked him suddenly, and *à propos* of nothing either of us had said.

"It must have been a week or two, not more. I knew the house had been taken, but not by whom. And at first the name meant nothing to me. I am not a reading man; at least I don't read novels."

"Don't apologise. I have heard of the *Sporting Times*, *Bell's Life*."

"Go on, gibe away, I like it. She was just the same only kinder, much kinder."

I laughed.

"I knew she would be kind, and soft, and womanly. Didn't she say she was lonely?"

"Yes."

"And then say quickly: 'But of course you are quite right. Reading is a waste of time, living everything, and you are doing a fine work, a man's work in the world.' She said she envied you. I can hear her saying it." He looked ecstatic.

"So can I. Ella says the same thing."

"Why are you so bitter?"

I could not tell him it was because I had heard other women, many women, who were all things to all men, and that I despised, or perhaps envied them, lacking their gift and so having lived lonely save for Ella and Ella's love. Until now, when it was too late. And then I looked at him, at Dr. Kennedy, and laughed.

"Why do you laugh? You are so like and so unlike her. She would laugh for nothing, cry for nothing...."

"Tell me all about her from the beginning." It was an excuse to rest on the cushions in the easy-chair, to cease whipping my tired conscience.

"There is little or nothing to tell. It was about a week after she came here we had the first call. *Urgent*, the message said. So I got on my bicycle and spun away up here. I did not even wait to get out the car."

"What day of the week was it?" I asked, interrupting him.

"What day of the week?" he repeated in surprise.

"Yes, what day?"

"As a matter of fact it was on a Monday. What's the point? I remember because it happens to have been my Infirmary day. I had just come home, dog-tired, but of course when the call came I had to go. I actually thought what a bore it was as I pedalled up. It's nearly all uphill from our house to Carbies. The maid looked frightened when she opened the door."

"Oh, sir, I am so glad you are here. Will you please come into the drawing-room? Mrs. Capel, she fainted right away. Miss Stevens has tried hartshorn an' burnt feathers, everything we could think of."

"Everything that had a smell?"

"Yes, sir. I perceived it as I approached the drawing-room—this room. She was on the sofa," he looked over to it, "very pale and dishevelled, only partly conscious."

"Who was Miss Stevens?"

"Her maid. Quite a character. Something like your nurse, only more so."

"What did you do?"

"I felt her pulse, her heart, thought of strychnine."

"You are not a great doctor, are you?" I scoffed lightly.

"Oh! I know my work all right; it's simple enough. You try this drug or the other...."

"Or none, as in my case."

"That's right."

"And then if the patient does not get better or her relatives get restive, you call in some one else, who makes another shot." There was a twinkle in his eye. I always thought he knew more about medicine than he pretended. "And what did you do for Margaret?" I went on.

"Opened the window, and her dress; waited. The first thing she said was, 'Has he gone?' I did not know to whom she referred, but the maid told me primly: 'Mrs. Capel's publisher has been down for the week-end. He left this morning. She don't know what she's saying.' Margaret opened her eyes, her sweet eyes, dark-irised, the light in them wavered and grew strong. She seemed to recall herself with difficulty and slowly. 'Did I faint? I'm all right now. Is that you, Stevens? What happened?'

"'I came in to bring your afternoon tea and you were in a dead faint, at the writing-table, all in a heap. I rang for cook and we carried you to the sofa, and tried to bring you round. Then cook telephoned for Dr. Lansdowne.'

"'Are you Dr. Lansdowne?'

"'He was out. I'm his partner, Dr. Kennedy. How are you feeling?' I asked her.

"'Better. Stevens, you can go away. Bring me some more tea. Dr. Kennedy will have a cup with me.' She struggled into a sitting position and I helped her. Then she told me she had always been subject to these attacks, ever since she was a child, that she was to have been a pianist, had studied seriously. But the doctors forbade her practising. Now she wrote. She admitted that her own emotional scenes overcame her. Then we talked of the emotions...."

Dr. Kennedy looked at me as if enquiringly.

"Do you want to hear any more?"

"You saw her often after that?"

"Nearly every day, all the time she was here."

"And talked about the emotions?"

"Sometimes. What are you implying? What are you trying to get at? Whatever it is, you are wrong. I was in her confidence, she liked talking to me. I did her good."

"With drugs or dogma?" I asked.

"With sympathy. She had suffered terribly, more than any woman should be allowed to suffer. And she was ultra-sensitive, her nerves were all exposed, inflamed. You have sometimes that elusive, strange resemblance to her. But she had neither strength nor courage and as for hardness ... she did not know the meaning of the word."

"You are wrong. Last night I heard her talk to Gabriel Stanton."

"Did you?" His eyes lightened. "Tell me. But he was not the man for her, never the man for her. Not sufficiently flexible. He took her too seriously."

"Can a man take a woman too seriously?"

"An emotional, nervous, delicate woman. Yes. You've been through all the letters?"

"No. There are a few more."

They were on the table, and I put my hand on them. I was sure that no one but I must see them.

"The first two or three times that Gabriel Stanton came down he stayed at 'The King's Arms.' She was always ill after he left, always. She made a brave effort, poor girl. Day after day I have come in and seen her sitting as you are, paper before her, and ink. I don't think anything ever came of it. She would play too, for hours."

"You stayed away when he was here, I suppose?"

"No! Not always. I was sent for once or twice. She had those heart attacks."

"Hysteria?"

"Heart attacks. He did not know how to treat or calm her."

"Poor Gabriel Stanton!"

"Poor Margaret Capel!" he retorted. "I wouldn't try to write the story if I were you. You misjudge her, I am sure you do. She was delicate-minded."

"Why did she have him down here at all? She knew the risk she ran. Why did she not wait until the decree *was* made absolute?" For by now, of course, I knew how the trouble came about.

"She was in love with him."

"She did not know the meaning of the word. She was philandering with you at the time." He grew red.

"She was not. I was her doctor."

"And are not doctors men?"

"Not with their patients."

I looked at him thoughtfully and remembered Ella. He answered as if he read my thoughts.

"You are not my patient, you are Lansdowne's." He gave a short uncertain laugh when he had said that. That seemed amusing to me, for I did not care whether he was a man or not, feeling ill and superlatively old and sexless, also that he lacked something, had played this game with Margaret, the game she had taught him, until his withers were all unwrung, until she had bereft him of reason, leaving him empty, as it were hollow, filled up with words, meaningless words that were part of the fine game, of which he had forgotten or never known the rules.

After he left I read her next letter, the one written after Gabriel Stanton had been to Pineland for the first time, and she had told him how she felt about him.

Carbies, Pineland.

I have been writing to you and tearing up the letters ever since you left. I look back and cannot believe you were here only two days. The two days passed like two hours, but now it seems as if we must have been together for weeks. You told me so much and I ... I exposed myself to you completely. You know everything about me, it is incredible but nevertheless true that I tried all I knew to show you the real woman on whom you are basing such high hopes. What are you thinking of me now, I wonder. That I am a little mad, not quite human? What is this genius that separates me from the world, from all my kind? My books, my little plays, my piano-playing! There is a little of it in all of them, is there not, my friend, my companion, the first person to whom I have ever spoken so frankly. Is it not true that I have a wider vision, intenser emotions than other women? Love me therefore better, and differently than any man has ever loved a woman. You say that you will, you do, that I am to pour myself out on you. I like that phrase of yours—you need never use it again, you have already used it twice.

"I shall remember while the light is yet,
And when the darkness comes I shall not forget."

It went through me, there is nowhere it has not permeated. And see, I obey you. I no longer feel a pariah and an outcast, with all the world pointing at me. The degradation of my marriage is only a nightmare, something, as you say, that never happened. I look out on the garden and the sea beyond, on the jagged coast-line and the green tree-clad hills, all bathed in sunshine, and forget that I have suffered. I am glad to know you so intimately that I can picture each hour what you are doing. You are not happy, and I am almost glad. What could I give you if you were happy? But as it is when you are bored and wearied, with your office work, depressed in your uncongenial home, I can send you my thoughts and they will flow in upon you like fresh water to a stagnant pool. I have at times so great a sense of strength and power. At others, as you know, I am faint and fearful. Nobody but you has ever understood that I am not inconsistent, only a different woman at different times. I know I see things that are hidden from other people, not mystic things, but the great Scheme unfolded, the scheme of the world, why some suffer and some enjoy, what God means by it all. In my visions it is blindingly brilliant and clear, and I understand God as no human being has ever understood Him before. I want to be His messenger, to show the interblending marvel. I know it is for that I am here. Then I write a short story that says nothing at all, or I sit at the piano and try to express, all alone by myself, that for which I cannot find words. Afterwards I go to bed and know I am a fool, and lie awake all night, miserable enough at my futility. I have always lived like this save during those frenzied months when I thought love was the expression for which I had waited, and with my eyes on the stars, blundered into a morass. Notwithstanding we have hardly spoken of it, you know the love I ask from you has nothing in common with the love ordinary men and women have for each other, nothing at all in common. The very thought of physical love makes me sick and ill. That is still a nightmare, nothing more nor less. I want my thoughts held, not my hands. How intimate we must be for me to write you like this, and the weeks we have known each other so few.

You won't read this in the office, you will take it home with you to the bookish and precise flat in Hampstead, and hoard it up until the little round-backed sister with her claim and her querulousness has left you in peace. She is part of that great scheme of things which evades me when I try to write it. Why should you sacrifice your freedom to make a home for her? Poor cripple, with her cramped small brain; your companion to whom you are tied like a sound man to a leper, and with whom you cannot converse and yet must sometimes talk. You cannot read or write very well in the atmosphere she creates for you, but must listen to gossip and answer fittingly, wasting the precious hours. Nevertheless you will find time to answer this letter. I shall not watch for the coming of the post and be disappointed. She does not care for you overmuch I fear, this poor sister of yours, only for herself. I am sorry she is hunchbacked and ailing. But I am sorrier still that she is your sister and burdens you. Life has given you so little. Your dreary orphaned childhood in your uncle's large hospitable family, of which you were always the one apart, you and that same suffering sister; your strenuous schooldays. You say you were happy at Oxford, but for the cramping certainty that there was no choice of a career; only the stool at Stanton's, and so repayment for all your uncle had done for you. My poor Gabriel, it seems to me your boyhood and your manhood have been spent. And now you have only me. Me! with hands without gifts and arid lips, an absorbing egotism, and only my passionate desire for expression. I don't want to live; I want to write, and even for that I am not strong enough! My message is too big for me. Hold me and enfold me, I want to rest in you; you are unlike all other men because you want to give and give and give, asking nothing. And therefore you are my mate, because I am unlike all other women, being a genius. You alone of all men or women I have ever known will not doubt that I have a message, although I may never prove it. You don't want to be proud of me, only to rest me.

Which reminds me—that book on Staffordshire Pottery will never be written. How will you explain it to your partners, and the wasted expense of the illustrations? I shall send you a business letter withdrawing; then I suppose you will say that you had better run down and discuss the matter with me. But, oh! it's so wonderful to know that you, you yourself will know without any explaining that I cannot write about pottery just now. I *have* written a few verses. I will send them to you when they are polished and the rhythm is perfect. There will be little else left by then! Write and tell me that one day you will come again to Pineland. One day, but not yet. I could not bear it, not to think of you concretely here with me again, this week or next. I want you as a light in the distance, my eyes are too weak to see you more closely.... I won't even erase that, although it will hurt you. Sometimes I feel I am not going to bring you happiness, only drain you of sympathy.

MARGARET.

Church Row, Hampstead.

My dear, dear love, you wonderful, wonderful

Margaret:—

I wish I could tell you, I wish I could begin to tell you all you mean to me, what our two days together meant to me. You ask me what I am thinking of you. If only I could let you know that, you would know everything. For your sufferings I love you, for your crucified gift and agonies. You say I am to love you better and differently than any man has ever loved woman. My angel child, I do. Can't you feel it? Tell me you do. That is all I want, that you tell me you do know how I worship you, that it means something to you, helps you a little.

What am I to answer to your next sentence? You say you ask of me a love that has nothing in common with the love ordinary men and women have for each other, that physical love makes you sick and ill. Beloved, everything shall be as you wish between us. I would not so much as kiss the hem of your dress if you forbade it by a look, nor your delicate white hands. I love your hands. You let me hold them, you must let me hold them sometimes. Dear generous one, I will never trouble you. I am for you to use as you will, that you use me at all is gift enough. This time will pass this trying dreadful time. Until then, and afterwards if you wish it, I will be only your comrade—your very faithful knight. I love your delicacy and reserve, all you withhold from me. I yearn to be your lover, your husband; all and everything to you. Don't hate and despise me. You say when radiant love came to you, your eyes were on the stars, and you blundered into a morass. But, sweetheart, darling, if I had been your lover—husband, do you think this would have happened? Think, *think*. I cannot bear that you should confuse any love with mine. I want to hold you in my arms, teach you. I can't write any more, not now. Thank you for your letter, for my sleepless nights, for my dreams, for everything. You are my whole world.

GABRIEL.

Greyfriars'.

I fear I wrote you a stupid letter last night. I had had a long evening with my sister. She insisted on reading to me from a wonderful book she has just bought. It was on some new craze with the high-sounding name of Christian Science. The book was called "Science and Health." More utter piffle and balderdash I have never heard. There were whole sentences without meaning, and many calling themselves sentences were without verbs. I swallowed yawn after yawn. Then she left off reading and asked my opinion. I suggested the stuff might have emanated from Earlswood. She made me a dreadful scene. It seemed she had already consulted a prophetess of this new religion and had been promised she should be made whole if only she had sufficient faith! Now I was trying to "shake her faith and so retard her cure"; she sobbed. Poor woman! I tried reasoning with her, went over a few passages and asked her to note inconsistency after inconsistency, stupidity after stupidity, blasphemy and irrelevance. She cried more. Then my own unkindness struck me. She too had had a vision, seen the marvellous sun rise. To be made whole! She who had been thirty years a cripple and in pain always. I tried to withdraw all I had said, to find a strange and mystic sense and meaning in the stuff. I think I comforted her a little. I insisted she should go on with her induction, or initiation, or whatever they call it. There are paid healers; the prophets play the game for cash. I gave her money. I could not bear her thanks or to remember I had been unkind, I, with my own overwhelming happiness. If I were able I would make happiness for all the world. When at last I was alone I sat a long time with your letter in my hand, your dear, dear letter. I don't know what I wrote; dare not recall my words. Forgive me, whatever it was. If there was a word in my letter that should not have been there forgive me. Bear with me, dear. You don't know what you are to me, I am bewildered with the mystery.

About the book on Staffordshire Pottery. Don't give it another thought. I can arrange everything here without any trouble. You need not write. But if you do, and suggest, as you say, that I shall come down and discuss the matter with you, why then, then—will you write? I want to come. I promise not to cut myself shaving this time. Although is it not natural my hand should have been unsteady? It shakes now. I must come and discuss the pottery book or anything. *Let me.* It is much to ask, but I won't be in your way. I've some manuscripts to go through. I'll never leave the hotel. But I want to be in the same place.

For ever and ever,

  Y<small>OUR</small> G<small>ABRIEL</small>.

CHAPTER VII

Of course she let him come. Not only that week-end but many others, until the early spring deepened into the late, the yellow gorse grew more golden, and the birds sang as they mated. It was the same time of year with me now, and I saw Margaret Capel and Gabriel Stanton often together in the house or garden, lying on the stones by the sea, walking toward the hills. My strength was always ebbing and I was glad to be alone, drowsily listening to or dreaming of the lovers, drugging myself with codein, seeing visions. I fancy Benham began to suspect me, counted the little silver pills that held my ease and entertainment. I circumvented her easily. Copied the prescription and sent it to my secretary in London to be made up, replaced each extra one I took. I was not getting better, although I wrote Ella in every letter of returning strength, and told her that I was again at work. My conscience had loosened a little, and I almost believed it to be true. Anyway I had the letters, and knew that when the time came it would be easy to transcribe them. Meanwhile I told myself disingenuously that I hoped to become better acquainted with my hero and heroine. I was wooing their confidence, learning their hearts. Now Gabriel's was clear, but Margaret's less distinct. I saw them sometimes as in a magic-lantern show, when the house was quiet, and I in the darkness of my bedroom. On the circle in the white sheet that hung then against the wall, I saw them walk and talk, he pleading, she coquetting. Whilst the slide was being changed Peter Kennedy acted as spokesman:

"Week-end after week-end Gabriel Stanton came down, and all the hours of the day they passed together. Four months of the waiting time had gone by and her freedom was in sight. Her nerves were taut and fretted. She often had fainting attacks. He never questioned me about her but once. I told him the truth, that she had suffered, was suffering more than any woman can endure, any young and delicate woman. And her love for him grew...."

I did not want to stop the show, the moving figures and changing slides, yet I called out from my swaying bed:

"No, no, she never loved him." And Peter Kennedy turned his eyes upon me, his surprised and questioning eyes.

"Why do you say that? Do you know a better way of loving?"

"Yes, many better ways."

"You have loved, then?"

"Read my books."

"The love-making in your novels? Is that all you know?" A coal fell from the fire; I frowned and said something sharply. He did not go on, and I may have slept a little. When I looked up again there was no more sheet nor Peter. Instead Margaret herself sat in the easy-chair and asked me how I was getting on with her story.

"Not very well. I don't understand why you took pleasure in making Gabriel miserable by your scenes and vapours. That first day now. What did you mean by telling him of your reaction on seeing him, that it might have been because he had cut himself shaving, or because of the shape of his hat; the hang of his coat disappointed you. Either you loved the man or you did not. Why hurt his feelings, deliberately, unnecessarily? Why did you tell him not to come and then telegraph him? Why should I write your story? I don't know the end of it, but already I am out of sympathy with you."

"You were that from the first," she answered unhappily. "Don't think I am ignorant of that. In a way, I suppose you are still jealous of me."

"I! jealous! And of you?"

"Why did you pretend you did not know my books, and send for them to the London Library? You knew them well enough and resented my reputation. The *Spectator*, the *Saturday Review*, the *Quarterly*; you were dismissed in a paragraph where I had a column and a turn."

"At least you never sold as well as I did."

"That is where the trouble comes in, as you would say—although you are a little better in that way than you used to be. You wanted to 'serve God and Mammon,' to be applauded in the literary reviews whilst working up sentimental situations with which to draw tears from shopgirls...."

"I am conscious of being unfairly treated by the so-called literary papers," I argued. "I write of human beings, men and women; loving, suffering, living. You wrote of abstractions, making phrases. The sentences of one of your characters could have been put in the mouths of any of the others. Life, it was of life I wrote. Now that I am dying...."

"You are not dying, only drugged. And you are jealous again all the time. Jealous of Gabriel Stanton, who despised your work and could not recall your personality, however often he met you. Jealous of the literary critics who ignored you and praised me. And jealous of Peter, Peter Kennedy, who from the first would have laid down his great awkward body for me to tread upon."

I half woke up, raised myself on my arm, and drank a little water, looked over to where Margaret sat, but she was no longer there. I did not want to go to sleep again, and lay on my back thinking of what had been told me. "Jealous!" Why should I be jealous of Margaret Capel's dead fame, of her dying memory? But perhaps it was true. I had a large public, made a large income, but had no recognition, no real reputation, was never in the "Literary Review of the Year," was not jeered at as other popular writers, but only ignored. Well, I did not overrate my work. I never succeeded in pleasing myself. I began every book with unextinguishable hope, and every one fell short of my expectations. People wrote to me and told me I had made them laugh or cry, helped them through convalescence, cheered their toilsome day.

"I love your 'Flash of the Footlights.'"

To repletion I had had such letters, requests for autographs, praise, and always: "I love your 'Flash of the Footlights.'" Fifty-eight thousand copies had been sold in the six-shilling edition. I wonder what were the figures of Margaret Capel's biggest seller. Under four thousand I knew. Little Billie Black told me, cherubic Billie, the publisher, with his girlish complexion and his bald head, who knew everybody and everything and told us even more.

I was getting drowsy again, figures, confused and confusing, passing over the surface of my mind. Billie Black and Sir George Stanton, Gabriel, then Ella, a dim glance of my long-lost husband, Dennis, a smiling flash in the foreground; my eyes were hot with tears because of this short glad sight of him. Then Peter Kennedy again; awkward in his tweed cutaway morning coat. What did she mean by saying I was jealous of Peter Kennedy? I smiled in my deepening somnolence. Then there was an organ and children dancing, a monkey, a policeman, and the end of a string of absurdities in a long narrow vista. Sleep and unconsciousness at the end.

I observed Dr. Kennedy with more interest the next few times he came to see me. A personable man without self-consciousness, some few years younger than myself, the light in his eyes was strange and fitful, and he talked abruptly. He was not well-read, ignorant of many things familiar to me, yet there was nothing of the village idiot about him such as I have found in many country apothecaries. He looked at me too long and too often, but at these times I knew he was thinking of Margaret Capel, comparing me with her. And I did not resent it, she was at least fourteen years younger than I, and I never had any pretensions to beauty. Dr. Kennedy had good hands, long-fingered, muscular; dark hair interspersed with grey covered his big head.

"What are you thinking about me?" he asked.

"What sort of doctor you are!" I answered with a fair amount of candour. "Here have I been without any one else for three or is it five weeks? You don't write me prescriptions, nor tell me how I shall live, what to eat, drink, or avoid. You call constantly."

"Not as often as I should like," he put in promptly. Then he smiled at me. "You don't mind my coming?"

"Have you found out what is the matter with me?"

"I know what is the matter with you!"

"Do you know I get weaker instead of stronger?"

"I thought you would."

"Tell me the truth. Is there no hope for me?"

"Patients ask so often for the truth. But they never want it."

"I am not like other patients. Haven't I got a dog's chance?" He shook his head.

"How long?"

"Months. Very likely years. No one can tell. You are full of vitality. If you live in the right way...."

"Like this?"

"More or less."

"And nothing more can be done for me?"

"Rest, open air, occupation for the mind." I thought over what he had just told me. I had known or guessed it before, but put into words it seemed different, more definite. "Not a dog's chance."

"You think Margaret Capel and Gabriel Stanton will do me good? They are part of your treatment?" I asked him.

"They and I," he said. I was silent after that, silent for quite a long time. He was sitting beside me and put his shapely hand on mine. I did not withdraw it, my thoughts were fully occupied. "You know I shall do everything I can for you; you are a reincarnation." He spoke with some emotion. "Some day I shall want to ask you something; you will know more about me soon. You are in touch with her."

"Do you really believe it?" I asked him. We were in the upstairs room. Today I had not adventured the stairs.

"May I play?" he asked. It was not the first time he had played to me. I rather think he played well, but I know nothing of music. If he were talking to me through the keys he was talking to a deaf mute. I lay on the sofa and thought how tired I was, may even have slept. I was taking six grains of codein in the twenty-four hours when the prescription said two, and often fell asleep in the daytime without preparation or expectation.

"I will tell you why I would do anything on earth for you," he said, turning round abruptly on the piano stool. "If you want to know." I was wide-awake now and surprised, for I had forgotten of what we had talked before I went off. "It is because you are so brave and uncomplaining."

"It isn't true. Ask Ella. She has had an awful time with me, grumbling and ungrateful."

"Your sister adores you, thinks there is no one like you."

"That is merely her idiosyncrasy."

"Well! there is another reason. You asked for it and you are going to be told. The love of my life was Margaret Capel." He stared at me when he said it. "You remind me of her all the time." I shut my eyes. When I opened them again his back was all I saw and he was again playing softly; talking at the same time. "When I came here, the first time, the first day, and saw you sitting in her chair, at her table, in her attitude, as I said, it was a reincarnation." He got up from the music stool and came over to me. He said, without preliminary or excuse, "You are taking opium in some form or other."

"I am taking my medicine."

"I am not blaming you. You've read De Quincey, haven't you? You know his theory?"

"Some of it."

"Never mind; perhaps you've missed it, better if you have. In those days it was often thought that opium cured consumption."

"Then it is consumption?"

"What does it matter what we call it? Pleurisy, as you have had it, generally means tubercle. But you will hang on a long time. The life of Margaret Capel must be written and by you. She always wanted it written. From what you tell me she still wants it. I poured my life at her feet those few months she was here, but she never gave me a thought, not until the end. Then, then at the last, I held her eyes, her thoughts, her bewildered questioning eyes. Bewildered or grateful? Shall I ever know? Will you tell me, I wonder, hear it from her, reassure me...." He stopped. "I suppose you think I am mad?"

"I have never thought you quite sane. But," I added consolingly, "that is better than being merely stupid, like most doctors. So you regard me," I could not help my tone being bitter, "as a clairvoyante, expectantly...."

"Does any man ever care for a woman except expectantly, or retrospectively?"

"How should I know?" He sat down by my side.

"No one should know better. Tell me more about yourself, I have only heard from Mrs. Lovegrove."

"She told you, I suppose, that I had a great and growing reputation, had faithful lovers sighing for me, that I was thirty-eight...."

"She told me a great deal more than that."

"I have no doubt. Well! in the first place I am not thirty-eight, but forty-two. My books sell, but the literary papers ignore them. I make enough for myself and Dennis."

"Dennis?" His tone was surprised.

"Ella never mentioned Dennis to you?"

"No."

I did not want to talk about Dennis. Since he had left me I never wanted to talk of him. His long absence had meant pain from the first, then agony. Afterwards the agony became physical, and they called it neuritis. Now it has pierced some vital part and I don't even know what they call it. Decline, consumption, tuberculosis? What does it matter? In the two years he had been away my heart had bled to death. That was the truth and the whole truth. No one knew my trouble and I had spoken of it to nobody save once, in early days, to Ella. Ella indignantly had said the boy was selfish to leave me, and so closed my confidence. It is natural our children should wish to leave us, they make their trial flights, like the birds, joyously. My son wanted to see the world, escape from thraldom, try his wings. But I had only this one. And it seemed to me from his letters that he was never out of danger, now with malaria, and in Australia with smallpox. The last time I heard he had been caught in a typhoon. After that my health declined rapidly. But it was not his fault.

"And Dennis?"

"Since you know so much you can hear the rest. I married at eighteen. I forget what my husband was like. I've no recollection of his ever having interested me particularly. Married life itself I abhorred, I abhor. But it gave me Dennis. My husband died when I was two-and-twenty. Ever since Ella has been trying to remarry me. But when one writes, and has a son——" I could talk no more.

"You are tired now."

"I am always tired. Why do you say years? You mean months, surely?"

"You will write one more book."

"Still harping on Margaret?"

"Let me carry you into your room; I have so often carried her."

"Physically at least I am a bigger woman than she was."

"A little heavier, not much."

"Well, give me your arm, help me. I don't need to be carried." I leaned on his arm. "We will talk more about your Margaret another day. I daresay I shall write her story. Not using all the letters, people are bored with letters. I am myself. And I am not sure about the copyright acts!"

"You will give them back to me when you have done with them?"

"Why not?"

Benham bullied him for having let me sit up so late. My illness was deepening upon me so quietly, so imperceptibly that I had forgotten I once resented her overbearing ways. Now I depended on her for many things. Suzanne had gone, finding the house too *triste*, and seeing no possibility of further emolument from my neglected wardrobe. Benham did everything for me; yawningly at night, but willingly in the day.

I was desperately homesick for Ella this evening. I wondered what she would say when she knew what Dr. Kennedy had told me. I cried again a little because he said I had not a dog's chance, but was quickly ashamed. Why should I cry? I was so hopelessly tired. The restfulness of Death began to appeal to me. Not to have to get up and go to bed, dress and undress daily, drag myself from room to room. I had not done all my work, but like an idle child I wanted to be excused from doing any more. I was in bed and my mind wandered a little. Why was not Ella here? It seemed cruel she should have left me at such a time. But of course she did not know that I was going to die. Well! I would tell her, then she would come, would stay with me to the end. I forgot Margaret and Gabriel Stanton, two ghosts who walked at night. No extra codein for me any more. I no longer wanted to dream, only to face what was before me with courage. My writing-block was by my side and pencils, one of Ella's last gifts, and I drew them toward me. I had to break to her that if she would be lonely in the world without me, then it was time for her to prepare for loneliness. I wanted to break it to her gently, but for the life of me I could not think, with pencil in my hand and writing-block before me, of any other way than that of the man who, bidden to break gently to a woman that her husband was dead, had called up to the window from the garden: "Good-morning, Widow Brown." So I started my farewell letter to Ella:

"Good-morning, Widow Lovegrove."

I never got any further. The hæmorrhage broke out again and I rang for Benham. She came yawning, buttoning up her dressing-gown, pushing back her undressed hair, but when she saw what was happening her whole note changed. This time I was neither alarmed nor confused, even watching her with interest. She rang for more help, got ice, gave rapid instructions about telephoning for a doctor.

"Will you wait for an injection until he comes, or would you like me to give it to you?"

"You."

"Very well, lie quite quiet, I shan't be a minute."

I lay as quietly as circumstances would allow whilst she brewed her witches' broth.

"What dreams may come."

"Hush, do keep quiet."

"Mind you give me enough."

"I shall give you the same dose he does, a quarter of a grain."

"It won't stop it this time."

"Oh, yes! it will."

She gave the injection as well, or better than Dr. Kennedy. I hardly felt the prick, and when she rubbed the place, so cleverly and gently, she almost made a suffragist of me. Women who did things so well deserved the vote.

"Do you want the vote?" I asked her feebly.

"I want you to lie quite still," was her inappropriate answer. I seemed to be wasting words. The room was slowly filling with the scent of flowers. When I shut my eyes I saw growing pots of hyacinth, then lilies, floating in deep glass bowls, afterwards Suzanne came in, and began folding up my clothes, in her fat lethargic way.

"I thought Suzanne went away."

"So she did."

"Who is in the room, then?"

"No one. Only you and I."

"And Dr. Kennedy?"

"No."

"You have sent for him?"

"I thought you wouldn't care for me to give you a morphia injection."

"Why not? You give it better than he does. I want to see him when he comes."

"You may be asleep."

"No! I shan't. Morphia keeps me awake, comfortably awake. De Quincey used to go to the opera when he was full up with it."

Peter Kennedy came in, and I followed the line of my own thoughts. I was feeling drowsy.

"I don't want you to play for me," I said, a little pettishly perhaps. "I should never have gone to the opera."

"All right, I won't." He asked nurse in a low voice, "How much did you give her?"

"A quarter of a grain, the same as before." The bleeding had not left off. Benham straightened me amongst the pillows and fed me with ice.

"I shall give her another quarter," he said abruptly after watching for a few minutes. I smiled gratefully at him. Benham made no comment, but got more hot water. He made the injection carefully enough, but I preferred nurse's manipulation.

"For Margaret?" I asked him.

"Partly," he answered. "You will dream tonight."

"I shall die tonight. I want to die tonight. Give me something to hurry things, be kind. I don't mind dying, but all this!"

"Don't. I can't. Not again. For God's sake don't ask me!" There was more than sympathy in his voice. There was agitation, even tears. "You will get better from this."

"And then worse again, always worse. I want it ended. Give me something."

"Oh! God! I can't bear this. Margaret!"

"Don't call me Margaret. My name is Jane. What is that stuff that criminals take in the dock? Italian poisoners keep it in a ring. I see one now, with pointed beard, melancholy eyes, a great ruby in the ring. Is anything the matter with my eyes? I can't see."

"Shut them. Be perfectly quiet. The Italian poisoner will pass."

"You will give me something?"

"Not this time."

I must have slept. When I woke he was still there. I was very comfortable and pleased to see him. "Why am I not asleep?"

"You are, but you don't know it."

"You won't tell Ella?"

"Not unless you wish it."

"I've written to her. See it goes." I heard afterwards he searched for a letter, but could only find four words "Good-morning, Widow Lovegrove …" which held no meaning for him.

"Don't let me wake again. I want to go."

"Not yet, not yet…."

There followed another week of morphia dreams and complete content. I was roused with difficulty, and reluctantly, to drink milk from a feeding-cup, to have my temperature taken, my hands and face washed, my sheets changed. There was neither morning nor evening, only these disturbances and Ella's eyes and voice in the clouded distance, vague yet comforting.

"You will soon be better, your temperature is going down. Don't speak. Only nod your head. Shall I cable for Dennis?"

I shook it, went on slowly shaking it, I liked the motion, turning from side to side on the pillow, continuing it. Ella, frightened, begged me to leave off, summoned nurse, who took my cheeks gently between her hands. That did not stop it, at least I recollect being angry at the slight compulsion and making up my mind, my poor lost feeble mind that I should do what I liked, that I would never leave off moving my head from side to side.

That night I dreamed of water, great masses of black water, heaving; too deep for sound or foam. Upon them I was borne backwards and forwards until I turned giddy and sick, very cold. The Gates of Silence were beyond, but I was too weak to get there, the bar was between us. I saw the Gates, but could not reach them. The waters were cold and ever rising. Sometimes, submerged, my lips tasted their dank saltness and I knew that my strength was all spent. Soon I should sink deeper. I wished it was over.

Then One came, when I was past help, or hope, drowning in the dark waters, and said:

"Now I will take you with me." We were going rapidly through air currents, soft warm air-currents and amazing space, a swift journey, over plains and mountains. At last to the North, and there I saw snow-mountains and at the foot the cold sea, frozen and blue, heaving slowly. Swimming in that slow frozen sea, I saw a seal, brown and beautiful, swimming calmly, with happy handsome eyes. They met mine. One who was beside me said:

"That is your sister Julia. See how happy she looks, and content...."

Then everything was gone and I woke up in my quiet bedroom, the fire burning low and Ella in the chair by my side.

"Do you want anything?" She leaned over me for the answer.

"I have just seen Julia."

She hushed me, tears were in her reddened eyes. Our sister Julia had been dead two years, to our unextinguishable sorrow.

"Don't cry, she is very happy."

I told her my dream. She said it was a beautiful dream, and I was to try and sleep again.

"Why are you sitting up?" I asked her.

"It is not late," was her evasive reply.

Many nights after that I saw her sitting there, I forgot even to ask her why, I was too far gone, or perhaps only selfish. I did not know for a long time whether it was night or day. I always asked the time when I woke, but forgot or did not hear the answer, drank obediently through the feeding-cup,—the feeding-cup was always there; enormously large, unnaturally white, holding little or nothing, unsatisfactory. Once I remember I decided upon remaining awake to tell poor Ella how much better I felt....

I told it to Margaret instead, and she had no interest in the news, none at all.

"I knew you were not going to die yet. Not until you had written my story."

"It seems not to matter," I answered feebly, "to be small and trivial."

"*Work whilst ye have the light,*" she quoted. The words were in the room, in the air.

"It is not light, not very light," I pleaded.

"There has been no biography of me. How would you like it if it had been you? And all the critics said I would live...."

"Must I stay for that?"

"You promised, you know."

"Did I? I had forgotten."

"No, no. You could not forget, not even you. And you will make your readers cry."

"But if I make myself cry too?"

"Write."

And I wrote, sick with exhaustion, without conscious volition or the power to stop. I wonder whether any other writer has ever had this experience. I could not stop writing although my arm swelled to an unnatural size and my side ached. I covered ream after ream of paper. I never stopped nor halted for word or thought. I was wearied, aching from head to foot, shaking and even crying with fatigue and the pain in my swollen arm or side, but never ceasing to write, like a galley slave at his oar. Sometimes in swimming semi-consciousness I thought this was my eternal punishment, that because I had swept so much aside that I might write, and yet had written badly, now I must write for ever and for ever, words and scenes and sentences that would be obliterated, that would not stand. I knew in these semi-conscious moments that I was writing in water and not in ink. But I was driven on, and on, relentlessly.

CHAPTER VIII

Here is the story I wrote under morphia and in that strange driving stress, set down as well as I can recall it, but seeming now so much less real and distinct. I have not tried to polish, only to remember. There was then no effort after composition, no correction, transposition nor alteration, and neither is there now; nor conscious psychology nor sentiment. The scenes were all set in the house where I lay, and there was no pause in the continuity of the drama. I saw every gesture and heard every word spoken. The letters were and are before me as confirmatory evidence. My own intrusive illness minimised the interest of the circumstances to my immediate surroundings. But to me it seems that the consecutive actuality of the morphia dream or dreams is unusual if not unique, and gives value to the narrative.

I refer to the MS. notes and diary for the beginning of the story, but have had to make several emendations and additions. There were too many epigrams, and the impression the writer wished to convey was only in the intention, and not in the execution. What she left out I have put in. It should be easy to separate my work from hers. And she carried her story very little way. From the beginning of the letters the autobiography stopped. It started abruptly, and ended in the same way.

There were trial titles in the MS. notes. "Between the Nisi and the Absolute" competed in favour with "The Love Story of a Woman of Genius."

Margaret Belinda Rysam was the daughter of a New Yorker on the up-grade. Her father began to make money when she was a baby and never left off, even to take breath, until she was between thirteen and fourteen. Then his wife died, not of a broken heart, but of her appetites fed to repletion, and an overwhelming desire for further provender. Her poor mouth, so much larger than her stomach, was always open. He piled a great house on Fifth Avenue into it and a bewilderment of furniture, modern old Masters and antiquities, also pearls and other jewellery. She never shut it, although later there were a country house to digest and some freak entertainments, a multiplicity of reporters and a few disappointments. The really "right people" were difficult to secure, the nearly "right people" were dust and ashes. A continental tour was to follow and a London season.... Before they started she died of a surfeit which the doctors called by some other name and operated upon, expensively.

In the pause of the hushed house and the funeral Edgar B. Rysam began to think that perhaps he had made sufficient money. He really grieved for that poor open mouth and those upturned grasping hands, realising that it was to overfill them that he had worked. He gave up his office and found the days empty, discovered his young daughter, and, nearly to her undoing, filled them with her. During her mother's life she had been left to the happy seclusion of nursery or schoolroom; subsidiary to the maelstrom of gold-dispensing. Now she had more governesses and tutors than could be fitted into the hurrying hours, and became easily aware of her importance, that she was the adored and only child of a widowed millionaire. Forced into concentrating her entire attention upon herself she discovered a remarkable personality. Bent at first on astonishing her surroundings she succeeded in astonishing herself. She found that she acquired knowledge with infinite ease and had a multiplicity of minor talents. She wrote verses and essays, sang, and played on various instruments. Highly paid governesses and tutors exclaimed and proclaimed. The words prodigy, and genius, pursued and illuminated her. At the age of sixteen no subject seemed to her so interesting as the consideration of her own psychology.

Nothing could have saved her at this juncture but what actually occurred. For she had no incentive to concentration, and every battle was won before it was fought. To be was almost sufficient. To do, superfluous, almost arrogant.

Edgar B. Rysam had, however, forgotten to safeguard his resources. That is to say, his fortune was invested in railroad bonds and stocks. In the great railway panic of 1893 prices came tumbling down and public confidence fell with them. Edgar B. in alarm, for he had forgotten the ways of railway magnates and financiers, sold out and lost half his capital. He reopened his office, and by dint of buying and selling at the wrong time, rid himself of another quarter. When he woke to his position, and retired for the second time, he had only sufficient means to be considered a rich man away from his native land. The sale of the mansion in Fifth Avenue, the country house, and the yacht damned him in the sight of his fellow-citizens. He found himself with a bare fifty thousand dollars a year, and no friends. Under the circumstances there was nothing for it but emigration, and he finally decided upon England as being the most hospitable as well as the most congenial of abiding-places. His linguistic attainments consisted of a fair fluency in "Americanese."

During the year he had spent in ruining himself, his young daughter became conscious of a pause in the astonished admiration she excited. She bore it better than might have been expected, because it synchronised with her first love affair. She had become passionately enamoured of the "cold white keys" and practised the piano innumerable hours in every day.

When Edgar B. remembered her existence again she had grown pale and remote, enwrapped in her gift and in her egotism, not doubting at all she would be the greatest pianist the world had ever seen, and that all those friends and acquaintances who had ignored or cold-shouldered her during the last year would wither with self-disdain at not having perceived it earlier. Not by her father's millions would she shine, but by reason of her unparalleled powers. The decision to visit Europe and settle in England, for a time was not unconnected with these visions. She insisted she required more and better lessons. Edgar B. was awed by her decision, by her playing, by her astonishingly perverse and burdened youth. He was grateful to her for not reproaching him for his failure to grapple with a new position, and contrasted her, favourably, notwithstanding an uneasy fear of disloyalty, with her mother.

"What do we want of wealth?" she asked in her young scorn. And spoke of the vulgarity of money and their scampered friends of the Four Hundred. In those early days, when she hoped to become a pianist, she had many of the faults of inferior novelists or writers. She used, for instance, other people's words instead of her own, and said she wished to "scorn delight and live laborious days." Edgar B., who knew no vision but money against a background of rapacious domestic affection, gaped at and tried to understand her. It was not until they were on board the "Minotaur" and he had come across an amiable English widow, that he learnt his daughter was indeed a genius, ethereal, a wonder-child. But one who needed mothering!

Even genius must eat, sleep for reasonable hours, wear warm clothes in cold weather. Margaret's absorbed self-consciousness left her no weapons to fight Mrs. Merrill-Cotton's kindness. She accepted it without surprise. It seemed quite natural to her; the only wonder was that the whole shipload had eyes or ears for any one else once they had heard her play the piano! Mrs. Merrill-Cotton brought her port wine and milk, shawls and rugs, volubly admiring her reticence, her unlikeness to other girls, her dawning delicate beauty. In truth Margaret at that period was girlishly angular and emaciated, from midnight and other labours, too much introspection and too little exercise, other than digital. She was desultorily interested in her appearance and a little uncertain as to whether the mass of her fair hair accorded with her pallid complexion. Her eyes were hazel and seemed to her lacking in expression. She did not think herself beautiful, but admitted she was "mystic" and of an unusual type.

Mrs. Merrill-Cotton found the more appropriate words. "Dawning delicate beauty." They led her to the looking-glass so often that she had no time nor thought for what was happening elsewhere. Meanwhile Mrs. Merrill-Cotton and Mr. Rysam foregathered on deck, and at mealtimes, at the bridge table and in the saloon. Margaret was assured of a stepmother long before she realised the possibility of her father having a thought for anybody but herself. And then she was told that it was only for her sake that the engagement had been entered into! Mrs. Merrill-Cotton, it appeared, was the centre of English society, had a large income and a larger heart. She, Margaret, would be the chief interest of the two of them.

Margaret's indifference to mundane things was sufficient to make her presently accept the position, if not enthusiastically, yet agreeably. And, strangely enough, Mrs. Merrill-Cotton proved to be as alleged. She had never had a daughter, and wished to mother Margaret: she had no other ulterior motive in marrying the American. Her income was at least as much as she had said, and she knew a great many people. That they were city people of greater wealth than distinction made no difference to her future husband. He wanted a domestic hearth and some one to share the embarrassment of his exceptional daughter.

The first thing they did after the wedding was to take Margaret to Dresden for those piano lessons she craved. She broke down quickly,—had not the health, so the doctors said, for her chosen profession. They said her heart was weak, and that she was anæmic. So father and stepmother brought her back to England, and installed her as the centre of interest in the big house in Queen Anne's Gate.

At eighteen she published her first novel, at her father's expense. It was new in method and tone. Word was sent round by the publisher that the authoress was a young and beautiful American heiress, and the result was quite an extraordinary little success.

The Lady Mayoress presented her to her Sovereign, after which the social atmosphere of the house quickly changed. Margaret began to understand, and act. Into the thick coagulated stream of city folk for whom the new Mrs. Rysam had an indefinable respect there meandered journalists, actors, painters, musicians. The whole tone of the house unconsciously but quickly altered. Culture was now the watchword. Money, no longer a topic of conversation, was nevertheless permitted to minister to the creature comfort of men and women of distinction in art and letters. The two elderly people accustomed themselves easily to the change, they were of the non-resistant type, and Margaret led them. When in her twentieth year her first play was produced at a West End theatre, and she came before the curtain to bow her acknowledgment of the applause, their pride was overwhelming. The next book was praised by all the critics who had been entertained and the journalists who hoped for further entertainment. Another and another followed. Open house was kept in Queen Anne's Gate, and there was an idea afloat in lower Bohemia that here was the counterpart of the Eighteenth-century salon.

This was the high-water tide of Margaret's good fortune. She had (as she told Gabriel Stanton in one of her letters) everything that a young woman could desire. The disposition of wealth, a measure of fame, the reputation of beauty, lovers and admirers galore. Why, out of the multiplicity of these, she should have selected James Capel, is one of those mysteries that always remain inexplicable. It is possible that he wooed her perfunctorily, and set her aflame by his comparative indifference! She imbued him with diffidence and a hundred chivalrous qualities to which he had no claim.

James Capel, at the piano, his head flung back, his dark and too long locks flowing, his dark eyes full of slumbrous passions, singing mid-Victorian love songs in a voluptuous manner and rich vibrating voice, was irresistible to many women, although his lips were thick and his nose not classic. A woman like Margaret should have been immune from his virus. Alas! she proved ultra-susceptible, and the resultant fever exacted from her nearly the extremest penalty.

James Capel accepted all his tributes and seemed to dispense his favours equally, kissing this one's hands and casting languorous glances on the others. He made love to Margaret with the rest, knowing no other language nor approach. Probably he liked the Rysams' establishment, their big Steinway Grand and the fine dinners, the riot of wealth and the unlimited hospitality!

He said afterwards, and every one believed it, all the women at least, that the last thing in the world he contemplated was marriage, that the whole situation and final elopement were of Margaret's contriving. Be that as it may, one cannot but pity her. She was only twenty, ignorant of evil, with the defects of her qualities, emotional, highly strung. She contracted a secret marriage with the musician. What she suffered in her quick disillusionment can easily be realised. James Capel was ill-bred, and of a vanity at least as great as hers. But hers had justification and his none.

Margaret may have been inadequate as a wife, she had been used to every consideration and found herself without any. James Capel was beneath her in everything, in culture and education, refinement. He said openly that men like himself were not destined for one woman. Their short married life was tragedy, a crucifixion of her young womanhood. She had, with all her faults, delicacy, physical reserve, a subtlety of charm and brilliant intellect. She had given herself to a man who could appreciate none of these, who was coarse from his thick lips to his language, from his large spatulate hands to his lascivious small brain. He burned her with his taunts of how she had pursued him, torn him from other women, forced her love upon him. There was just enough truth in it to make her writhe in her desecrated soul and modesties. Of course she thought he had feared to aspire. Now he made it evident he considered it was she who had aspired!!! He told her of duchesses who had sought his songs and his caresses, and gloatingly of unimaginable incidents. He tortured her beyond endurance.

She left him for the shelter of her father's home within a few months of their marriage. There she was nursed back into moral and physical health, welcomed, comforted, pitied, and she slowly emerged from this mud bath of matrimony. Her press, theatrical and lettered friends rallied round her; wealth and foreign travel ameliorated the position. She wrote again and with greater success than before. Suffering had deepened her note, she was still without sentiment, but had acquired something of sympathy.

Years passed. She had almost forgotten the degradation and humiliation of her marriage, when an escapade of her husband's, brazenly public, forced her to take definite steps for legal freedom. She was now sufficiently famous for the papers to treat the news as a *cause célèbre*. James Capel unexpectedly defended himself, and fought her with every weapon malice and an unscrupulous solicitor could forge. Part of the evidence was heard *in camera*, the rest should have been relegated to the same obscurity. All the bitterness and misery of those terrible months were revived. Now it seemed there was nothing for her but obliteration. She thought it impossible she could ever again come before the public, for her story to be recalled. She was all unnerved and shaken, refusing to go out or to see people. She thought she desired nothing but obscurity.

Yet she had to write.

The book on pottery was a sudden inspiration. It would be something entirely new and unassociated with her in the public mind. There were dreadful months to be got through, the waiting months during which, in law at least, she was still James Capel's wife, a condition more intolerable now than it had ever been.

Whatever she may have thought about herself it is obvious that in essentials she was unaltered. Her egotism had re-established itself under her father and good stepmother's care, and her amazing self-consciousness. To her it seemed as if all the world were talking about her. There was some foundation for her belief, of course. In so much as she was a public character, she was a favourite of that small eclectic public. She may have overrated her position, taken as due to herself alone that which was equally if not more essentially owing to her father's wealth and habit of keeping open house. Her letters are eminently characteristic. Her self is more prominent in them than her lover. She seems to have bewildered Gabriel Stanton, who knew little or nothing of women, and carried him off his feet. He may have begun by pitying her, she appealed to his pity, to his chivalry. As she said herself, she "exposed herself entirely to him." Young, rich, beautiful, famous, she was, nevertheless, at the time she first met Gabriel Stanton as a bird in flight, shot on the wing and falling; blood-stained, shrinking, terrified, the stain spreading. Into Gabriel Stanton's pitiful powerless hands, set on healing, she fell almost without a struggle. This at least is her own phrasing, and the way she wished the matter to appear. As it did appear to him, and perhaps sometimes to herself. To others of course it might seem she was the fowler, he the bird!

Certainly after the first visit to Greyfriars', when she opened the matter of the ill-fated book on Staffordshire Pottery there were constant letters, interviews and meetings, conventional and unconventional. Perhaps it was only her dramatic brain, working for copy behind its enforced and vowed inactivity, that made her act as she did. Her letters all read as if they were intended for publication. In her disingenuous diary and short MS. notes, there were trial titles, without a date, and forced epigrammatic phrases. "Publisher and Sinner" occurred once. There is a note that "Between the Nisi and the Absolute" met the position more accurately.

She told Gabriel Stanton, she must have convinced Peter Kennedy and herself, that she never knew the danger she ran until it was too late. But the papers she left disproved the tale.

CHAPTER IX

The early letters have already been transcribed. Also the description of when and how I first saw Margaret and Gabriel Stanton together, on the beach when she told him that his coming had been a disappointment.

Recalling the swift and painful writing of the story it would seem I saw them again two days later, and that she was occupied in making amends. They had talked and grown in intimacy, and now it was Sunday evening. They were in the music room at Carbies, and she had been playing to him while he sat spellbound, listening to and adoring her. She was in that grey silk dress with the white muslin fichu finished with a pink rose, her pale hair was parted in the middle and she wore her Saint Cecilia expression. She left off playing presently, came over to him with swift grace and sank on the footstool at his feet.

"What are you thinking about? You are not vexed with me still?"

"Was I ever vexed with you?"

"Yesterday afternoon, when I said I was disappointed in you."

"Not vexed, surely not vexed, only infinitely grieved, startled."

"Have you enjoyed your visit, notwithstanding that strange slow beginning? Tell me, have you been happy?"

"Have you?"

"I don't know. I don't quite know. I have been so excited, restless. I have not wanted any one else. It is difficult for me to know myself. Are you still sorry for me, like you were in London?"

"My heart goes out to you. You have suffered, but you have great compensations; great gifts. I would sympathise with you, but you make me feel my own limitations. I fear to fail you. You have the happier nature, the wider vision...."

"Then you have not been happy?"

"Yes, I have, inexpressibly happy. I wish I could tell you. But I matter so little in comparison with you."

"I don't want you to be humble."

"I am not humble, I am proud."

"Because?"

"Because you have taken me for your friend."

He never touched her whilst she sat there at his feet, but his eyes never left her and his voice was deep and tender. They talked of friendship, all the time, they only spoke of friendship. And he was unsure of himself, or of her, more deeply shy than she, and moved, though less able to express it.

"Next week you will come again. Will it be the same between us?"

"I will come whenever you let me. With me it will always be the same, or more. Sometimes I cannot believe that it is to me this is happening. To me, Gabriel Stanton! What is it you find in me? Sometimes I think it is only your own sweet goodness; that what you expressed in seeing me this time you will find again and again—disappointment; that I am not the man you think me, the man you need."

"Am I what you thought I would be? Are you satisfied with me?"

"I am overpowered with you."

She stole a look at him. His close and thin-lipped mouth had curves that were wholly new, his sunken eyes were lit up. She was secretly enraptured with him.

"I thought you very grave and severe when I first came to the office. What did you think of me?"

"What I do now, that you were wonderful. After you left I could not settle to work ... but I have told you this."

"Tell me again. Why didn't you say something nice to me then? You were short, sharp, noncommittal. I went away quite downcast, I made sure you did not want my poor little book, that you would write and refuse it, in set businesslike terms."

"I knew I would not. If George had said no, I should have fought him. I was determined upon that book of Staffordshire Pottery. Were you disappointed with my letter when it came?"

"I loved it. I have always loved your letters. You never disappoint me then."

Because they had grown more intimate he was able to say to her gently, but with unmistakable feeling:

"Dear, it hurts me so when you say that. I know I shall think of it when I am alone, wonder in what way I fail you, how I can alter or change. Can you help me, tell me? I came down with such confidence."

"But you had cut yourself shaving."

"Be a little serious, beloved. Tell me."

"You thought I cared for you ... that we should begin in Pineland where we left off in London?"

"I hoped...."

"But I had run away from you!"

They smiled at each other.

"You will come again next week?" she asked him inconsistently.

"And if I should again disappoint you?"

"Then you must be patient with me, good to me until it is all right again. I am a strange creature, a woman of moods." She was silent a moment. "I have been through so much." He bent toward her. She rose abruptly, there had been little or no caressing between them. Now she spoke quickly:

"Don't hope too much ... or ... or expect anything. I am a megalomaniac: everything that happens to me seems larger, grander, finer, more wonderful than that which happens to any one else."

She paused a moment. "This ... then, between us is friendship?" she went on tentatively.

He answered her very steadily:

"This, between us, is what you will."

"You know how it has been with me?" Her voice was broken. He was deeply moved and answered:

"God gave it to me to comfort you."

There was a long pause after that. It was getting late, and they must soon part. He kissed her hands when he went away, first one and then the other.

"Until next week."

"Until next week, or any time you need me."

Then there were letters between them, letters that have already been transcribed.

He came the next week and the next. A man of infinite culture, widely read and with a very real knowledge of every subject of which he spoke, it was not perhaps strange that she fell under the spell of his companionship, and found it ever more satisfying.

Her own education was American and superficial, but her intelligence was really of a high order and browsed eagerly upon his. The only other she was seeing at this time was Dr. Peter Kennedy, a man of very different calibre. Peter Kennedy, country born and bred, of a coarsening profession and provincial experience.

Margaret was not made to live alone, for all her talk of resources, her piano and her books, her writing materials. The house, Carbies, was soon obnoxious to her. She had taken it for three months against the advice of her people, who feared solitude for her. She could not give in so soon, tell them they were right. But it was and remains ugly, ill-furnished, with its rough garden. She had some sort of heart attack the Monday after Gabriel Stanton's first visit, and it was then Dr. Kennedy told her about her house, wondered at her having taken it.

After he told her that it had been a nursing-home she began to dislike the place actively, said the rooms were haunted with the groans of people who had been operated upon, that she smelt ether and disinfectants. She did not tell Gabriel Stanton these things. To Gabriel, Carbies was enchanted ground, he came here as to a shrine, worshipping. He used to talk to her of the golden bloom of the gorse, and the purple of the distant sea, of the way the sun shone on his coming. When with him she made no mention of distaste. For five successive weeks that spring the weather held, and each week-end was lovelier than the last. From Friday to Monday she may have felt the charm of which he spoke. From Monday to Friday she lamented to her doctor about the groans and the smell of disinfectants, and he consoled her in his own way, which was not hers, and would not have been Gabriel's, but was the best he knew.

Peter Kennedy at this time was recently qualified, not very learned in his profession, nor in anything else for that matter. He became quickly infatuated with his new patient. She told him she had heart disease, and he looked up "Diseases of the Heart" in Quain's "Dictionary of Medicine" and gave her all the prescribed remedies, one after another.

He heard of her reputation; chiefly from herself, probably. And that she was rich. Mr. and Mrs. Rysam came down once, with motors and maids, and made it clear; they told him what a precious charge he had. He took Edgar Rysam out golfing, golfing had been Peter Kennedy's chief interest in life until he met Margaret Capel. And Edgar found him very companionable and most considerate to a beginner. Edgar Rysam had taken to golf because he was putting on flesh, because his London doctor and some few stock-broking friends advised it. He had practised assiduously with a professional, learnt how to stand, but forgotten the lessons in approach and drive and putt.

He had succeeded in acquiring a bag of fine clubs and some golfing jargon. He never knew there was any enjoyment in the game until Peter Kennedy walked round the Pineland course with him and handicapped him into winning a match. After that he wanted to play every day and always, talked of prolonging his stay, of coming down again. Margaret reproached Peter for what he had done.

"I did it to please you.... I thought you wanted them to be amused."

"If that was all I wanted I would have stayed in London," she retorted. She was extraordinarily and almost contemptuously straightforward with Peter Kennedy. She knew that with a man of his limited experience it was unnecessary to be subtle. She may have sometimes encouraged his approaches, but the greater part of the time snubbed him unmercifully.

"You don't put yourself on the same level as Gabriel Stanton, do you?" she asked him scornfully one day when he was gloomily complaining that "a fellow never had a chance."

"If I were not more of a man than that I'd kick myself!"

"More of a man!"

"You wouldn't get *me* to stay at the hotel." She flushed and said:

"Well, you can go now. I've had enough of you, you tire me."

"You'll send for me to come back directly you are ill?"

"Very likely. That only means I like your drugs better than you."

He seized her hand, her waist, not for the first time, swore that he would kill himself if she despised and flouted him. Probably she liked the scenes he made her, for she often provoked them. They were mere rough animal scenes, acutely different from those she was able to bring about with Gabriel. But she did not do the only obvious and correct thing, which was to dismiss him and find another doctor.

In these strange days, waiting for her freedom, seeing Gabriel Stanton from Saturday to Monday and only Peter Kennedy all the long intervening week, she may have liked the excitement of being attended by a doctor who was madly in love with her. She excused herself to me on the ground that she was a novelist and he a strange and primitive creature of whom she was making a study. Also, curiously enough, he was genuinely musical. Something of an executant and an enthralled listener.

He himself suggested more than once that she should have other advice about her heart and he brought his partner to see her. But never repeated the experiment. Dr. Lansdowne purred and prodded her, talking all the time he used his stethoscope, smiling between whiles in a superior way as if he knew everything. Particularly when she tried to tell him her symptoms, or what other doctors had diagnosed.

"You have a nurse?" he asked her. "I had better see her nurse, Kennedy."

"A nurse,—why should I have a nurse? I have a maid."

"You ought never to be without a nurse. You ought never to be alone," he told her solemnly. "Now do, my dear child, be guided by me." He smiled and patted her. "I will tell Dr. Kennedy all about it, give him full instructions. I will see you again in a few days. Come, Kennedy, I can give you a lift; we will decide what is to be done." He smiled his farewell.

"See me again in a day or two! Not if I know it. Not in a day or two, or a week or two, or a month or two."

She was furious with him, and with Dr. Kennedy for having brought him. Peter Kennedy had acted well, according to his lights. He did not wish to turn his beloved patient over to his all-conquering partner, but the more infatuated he became about her the less he trusted his own knowledge.

"A bad case of angina, extensive valvular disease. Keep her as quiet as possible, she ought not to be contradicted. Get a nurse or a couple of nurses for her. Daughter of Edgar Rysam, the American millionaire, isn't she? Seems to have taken quite a fancy to you. Extraordinary creatures these so-called clever women! You ought to make a good thing out of the case."

Kennedy went back to Carbies after Dr. Lansdowne dropped him, made his way back as quickly as possible. Margaret had bidden him return to tell her what had been said.

"Not that I believe in him or in anything he may have told you. He did not even listen to my heart, he was so busy talking and grinning and reassuring me. What did he tell you? That he heard a murmur? I am so sick of that murmur. I have been hearing of it ever since I was a child."

Peter slurred over everything Lansdowne had said to him, except that she must be kept quiet; she must not allow herself to get excited. He implored her to keep very quiet. She laughed and asked whether he thought he had a calmative influence? He put his arms about her for all that she resisted him and blubbered over her like the great baby he was.

"I adore you, I want to take care of you, and you won't look at anybody but him."

She pushed him away, told him she could not bear to be touched.

"If it hadn't been for him? Tell me, if it hadn't been for Gabriel Stanton it would have been me, wouldn't it? You do like me a little, don't you?"

It was impossible to keep him at a proper distance.

"Like you! not particularly. Why should I? You are very troublesome and presumptuous."

She could not deal with him as she did with Gabriel. To this young country doctor, ten years before I knew him and he had acquired wisdom, men and women were just men and women, no more and no less. He had fallen headlong in love with Margaret, and when he saw he had, as he said, no chance, he could not be brought to believe that Gabriel Stanton was not her lover. He was demonstratively primitive, and many of his so-called medical visits she spent in fighting his advances. He knew that what she had to give she was giving to Gabriel Stanton, because she told him so, made no secret of it, but was for ever asking "If it hadn't been for him? If you'd met me first?" One would have thought that Margaret, Gabriel's "fair pale Margaret," would have resented or at least tired of this rough persistent wooing, but if this were so there was nothing in her conduct to show it.

She said or wrote to Gabriel Stanton: "the very thought of physical love is repugnant to me, horrible." Yet Peter kissed her hands, her feet, attempted her lips, made her fierce wild scenes. She called him a boy, but he was a year older than herself. Gabriel brought her books and the most reverent worship, was mindful of her slightest wish. He hoped that one day she would be his wife, but scarcely dared to say it, since once she put the matter aside, almost imploringly, growing pale, seeming afraid.

"Don't talk to me of marriage, not yet. How can you? At least, wait!"

She spoke of her sensitiveness. But her sensitiveness was as a mountain to a mist compared with his.

She would tell him her most intimate thoughts, sit with him by dying fire or in gathering twilight, holding herself aloof. If, because he was so different from Peter Kennedy, she did sometimes try her woman's wiles on him, she never moved him to depart from the programme or the principles she herself had laid down.

Another Sunday evening,—it was either the third or fourth of his coming,— sitting in the lamplight, after dinner, in the music room, after a long enervating day of mutual confidences and ever-growing intimacy, she tried to break through his defences. They had been talking of Nietzsche, not of his philosophy, but his life. She had been envying Nietzsche's devoted sister and her opportunities when, suddenly and disingenuously, she startled Gabriel by saying:

"You are not a bit interested in what I am saying, you are thinking of something else all the time."

"Of you ... only of you!"

"Of the intellectual me or the physical me? Do I please you tonight?"

She nearly always wore grey, a ribbon or a flower, material or cut, diversified her wardrobe. Tonight the grey material was the softest crêpe de chine; and she wore one pink rose in a blue belt. This treatment gave value to her *blonde cendré* hair and fair complexion, she gave the impression of a most delicate, slightly faded, yet modern miniature.

"You always please me."

"Please, or excite you?"

"My dear one!"

He was startled, thought she did not know what it was she was saying. His blood leaped, but he had it under control. What was growing perfectly between them was love. She would soon be a free woman.

"I want to know. Sometimes I wonder if I were more beautiful...."

"You could not be more beautiful."

"More like other women, or perhaps if you were more like other men...."

"There is no difference between me and other men," he answered quickly. And then although he thought she did not know what she was implying, or where the conversation might carry them, he went on even more steadily: "I want to carry out your wishes. If I had the privilege of telling you all that is in my heart...."

"I am admiring your self-control."

It was true she hardly knew what was impelling her to this reckless mood. "My wishes! What are my wishes? Sometimes one thing and sometimes another. Tonight for instance...."

He was in the corner of the sofa, she on the high fender stool in the firelight. There were only oil lamps in the room, and she and the fireside shone more brightly than they.

When she said softly, "Tonight for instance," she got up; her eyes seemed to challenge him. He rose too, and would have taken her in his arms, but that she resisted.

"No, no, no, you don't really want to ... talking is enough for you."

"You strange Margaret," he said tenderly.

"I sometimes wonder if you care for me or only for my talk," she said with a nervous laugh.

"If you only knew." His arms remained about her.

"If I only knew!" she exclaimed. "Tell me," she whispered coaxingly.

"How I long for this waiting time to be at an end. To woo you, win you. You say anything approaching physical love is hateful and abhorrent to you. Yet, if I thought ... Margaret!"

She did not repel him, although his arms were around her. And now, reverently, softly, he sought and found her unreluctant lips. One of the lamps flickered and went out. His arms tightened about her; she had not thought to be so happy in any man's arms. Her heart beat very fast and the blood in her pulses rose.

"How much do you care for me?" she whispered; her voice trembled.

"More than for life itself," he whispered back.

"And I ... I...." He felt her trembling in his arms as if with fear. He loved and hushed her with ineffable tenderness, his control keeping pace with his rising blood. "My love, my love, I will take care of you. Trust yourself to me. I love you perfectly, beloved."

He had an exquisite sense of honour and a complete ignorance of womanhood. A flash of electricity from him and all would have been aflame. But she had said once that until the decree was made absolute she did not look upon herself as a free woman.

"My little brave one, beloved. *It will not be always like this between us.* Tell me that it will not. I count the days and hours. You will take me for your husband?"

She could feel the beating of his pulses, her cheek lay against his coat. But her heart slowed down a little. How steadfast he was and reliable, the soul of honour. But she was a woman, difficult to satisfy. She had wanted from him this evening, this moment, something of that she won so easily from Peter Kennedy. The temperament she denied was alight and clamorous.

"Gabriel."

"Heart of my innermost heart."

"I am so lonely in this house."

"Sweetheart."

"So lonely; it is haunted, I think. I can never sleep, I lie awake … for hours. *Don't go.*"

Her own words shook and shocked her. She was still and supine in his encompassing arm. There was perhaps a relaxation of his moral fineness, a faint disintegration. But of only a moment's duration, and no man ever held a woman more reverently or more tenderly.

"My wife that will be … that will be soon. How I adore you."

Their hands were interlocked, they felt the dear sweetness of each other's breath; their hearts were beating fast.

Silence then, a long-drawn silence.

"It is not long now. I am counting the days, the hours. You won't say again I disappoint you, will you? You will bear with me?"

She clung closer to him. Tonight he moved her strangely.

"You really do love me?" she whispered.

"I want to take care of you always. My dear, darling, how good you are to let me love you! One day I will be your husband! I dare hardly say the words. Promise me!" And again his lips sought hers. "Your husband and your lover…."

An extraordinary chill came upon her. She could not herself say what had happened, the effect, but never the cause.

She disengaged herself from him. When he saw she wanted to go he made no effort to hold her.

"It is very late, isn't it?" He made no answer, and she repeated the question. "It's very late, isn't it?"

"I don't know."

"I wish you would look."

He took out his watch.

"Barely ten. You are tired?"

"Yes, a little."

"Margaret, you say you are lonely in this house, nervous. Would you feel better if I patrolled the garden, if you felt I was at hand?"

"Oh, no, no. I didn't know what I was saying."

All her mood had changed.

"I must have forgotten Stevens and the other maids."

Then she moved away from him, over to the round table where the dead lamp still gave an occasional flicker.

She tried it this way and that, but there was no flame, only flicker.

"You always take me so seriously, misunderstand me."

He came near her again.

"I don't think I misunderstand you," he said tenderly.

"I am sorry," she answered vaguely. "It was my fault."

"Fault! You have not a fault!"

"But now—I want you to go."

His eyes questioned and caressed her.

"Until next week then."

He took her in his arms, but her lips were cold, unresponsive, it was almost an apology she made:

"I am really so tired."

When he had gone, lying among the pillows on the sofa, she said to herself:

"Greek roots! He is supposed to be more learned in Greek roots than any one in England. But the root word of this he missed entirely. REACTION. That is the root word. I don't know what came over me. Why is he so unlike other men? What if such a moment had come to me with Peter Kennedy!"

She smiled faintly all by herself in the firelight. How impossible it was that she should have played like this with Peter Kennedy. He moved her no more than a log of wood. Then she was suddenly ashamed, her cheeks dyed red in the darkness.

CHAPTER X

She was surprised at what had happened to her, thought a great deal about it, magnifying or minimising it according to her mood. But in a way the incident drew her more definitely toward Gabriel Stanton. She began to admit she was in love with him, to do as he had bidden her, "let herself go." In imagination at least. Had she been a psychological instead of an epigrammatic novelist, she would have understood herself better. To me, writing her story at this headlong pace, it was nevertheless all quite clear. I had not to linger to find out why she did this or that, what spirit moved her. I knew all the time, for although none of my own novels ever had the success of "The Dangerous Age" I knew more about what the author wrote there than he did himself, much more. The Dangerous Age comes to a woman at all periods. With Margaret Capel it was seven years after her marriage and over six from the time when she had left her husband. She was impulsive, and for all her introspective egotism, most pitifully ignorant of herself and her emotional capacity. Fortunately Gabriel Stanton was almost as ignorant as she. But, at least after that Sunday evening, there was no more talk of friendship between them. There was coquetting on her side and some obtuseness on his. Rare flashes of understanding as well, and on her part deepening feeling under a light and varying surface.

She was rarely twice alike, often she merely acted, thinking of herself as a strange character in a drama. She was genuinely uncertain of herself. Her love flamed wild sometimes. Then she would pull herself up and remember that something like this she had felt once before, and it had proved a will o' the wisp over a bog. She wanted to walk warily.

"Supposing I am wrong again this time?" she asked him once with wide eyes.

"You are not. This is real. Trust me, trust yourself." She liked to nestle in the shelter of his arm, to feel his lips on her hair, to torment and adore him. The week-ends seemed very short; the week-days long. Week-days during which she was restless and excitable, and Peter Kennedy and his bag of tricks, medical tricks, often in request. She was very capricious with Peter, calling him ignorant, and a country yokel. As a companion he compared very badly with Gabriel. As an emotional machine he was easier to play upon. She spared him nothing, he was her whipping-boy. Watching him one noticed that he grew quieter, improved in many ways as she secured more and more mastery over him. When there were scenes now they were of her and not of his making. He was wax in her hands, plastic to her moulding. Sometimes she was sorry for him and a little ashamed of herself. Then she gave him a music lesson or lectured him gravely on his shortcomings. But from first to last he was nothing to her but a stop-gap. His devotion had the smallest of reward.

The weeks went by. Gabriel Stanton coming and going, staying always at the local hotel. Ever more secure in his position with her, but never taking advantage of it.

"He is naturally of a cold nature," she argued. And once her confidant was Peter Kennedy and she compared the two of them. This was in early days, before her treatment of Peter had subdued him.

"What's he afraid of?" Peter asked brusquely.

"Until the decree has been made absolute I am not free."

"So what he is afraid of is the King's Proctor?"

"Don't."

"His precious respectability, the great house of Stanton."

"You take it all wrong, you don't understand. How should you?"

"Don't I? I wish I'd half his chances."

"You are really not in the same category of men. It is banal—I have never fully realised the value of a banal phrase before, but you are 'not fit to wipe the mud off his shoes.'"

"Because I am a country doctor."

"Because you are—Peter Kennedy."

She knew then how comparatively thick-skinned he was; that if he had some sense or senses *in excelsis*, in others he was lacking, altogether lacking and unconscious. It is not paradoxical but plain that the more she saw of Gabriel Stanton the less heed she took of Peter Kennedy's freedom of speech and ways. The two men were as apart as the poles, that they both adored her proved nothing but her undoubted charm. She was not quite looking forward, like Gabriel Stanton, through the "decree absolute" to marriage. She lived in the immediate present; in the Saturdays to Mondays when she tortured Gabriel Stanton and in a way was tortured by him. For she had never met so fine a brain, nor honour and simplicity so clean and clear, and she was upborne by and with him. And the Tuesdays to Fridays she had attacks or crises of the nerves and Kennedy alternately doctored and clumsily courted her.

There came a time when she wrote and asked Gabriel to bring his sister next time he came, and that both of them should stay in the house with her, at Carbies. It was clear, if it had not been put into actual words, that they would marry as soon as she was free, and she thought it would please him that she should recognise the position.

"I want to know her. Tell her I am a friend of yours who is interested in Christian Science, then she won't think it strange that I should invite her here." She was not frank enough to say "since she is to be my sister-in-law."

Gabriel, nevertheless, was translated when the letter came, and answered it rapturously. The invitation to his sister seemed to admit his footing, to make the future more definite and domestic.

But if you want me to stay away I will stay away. Remember it is your wishes not mine that count. I tired you, perhaps? Did I tire you? God bless you!

I can never tell you half that is in my heart. You are an angel of goodness, and I am on my knees before you all the time. I will tell Anne as little as possible until you give me permission, yet I am sure she must guess the rest. My voice alters when I speak of you, although I try to keep it even and calm. I went to her when I got your letter. "A friend of mine wants to know you." I began as absurdly as that. She looked at me in surprise, and I went on hurriedly, "She wants you to go down with me to her house in Pineland at the end of the week...."

"You have been there before?" she asked suspiciously, sharply. "Is that where you have been each week lately?"

"Yes," I answered, priding myself that I did not go on to tell her each week I entered Paradise, lingered there a little while. She began to question, probe me. Were you old, young, beautiful; the questions poured forth. Somehow or other, in the end these questions froze and silenced me. I could not tell her, you were you! She would not have understood. Nor was I able to satisfy her completely on any point. I could not describe you, felt myself stammering like a schoolboy over the colour of your hair, your eyes. How could I say to her "This sweet lady who invites you to make her acquaintance is just perfection, no more nor less; all compound of fire and dew, made composite and credible with genius"? As for giving a description of you, it would need a poet and a painter working together, and in the end they would give up the task in despair. I did not tell Anne this.

She is now reviewing her wardrobe. And I ... I am reviewing nothing ... past definite thought. Do you know that when I left you on Sunday I feared that I had vexed or disappointed you again? You seemed to me a little cold—constrained. Monday and Tuesday I have examined and cross-examined myself—suffered. My whole life is yours—but if I fail to please you! I was in a hotel in the country once, when a man was brought in from the football field, very badly hurt. His eyes were shut, his face agonised; he moaned, for all his fortitude. There was a doctor in the crowd that accompanied him, who gave what seemed to me a strange order: "Put him in a hot bath, just as he is, don't delay a moment; don't wait to undress him." My own bath was just prepared and I proffered it. They lowered him in. He was a fine big fellow, but suffering beyond self-restraint. Within a minute of the water reaching him, clothes on and everything, he left off moaning. His face grew calm. "My God! I am in heaven!" he exclaimed.

"The relief must have been exquisite. I thought of the incident when your letter came, when I had submerged myself in it. I had forgotten it for years, but remembered it then. I too had passed in one moment from exquisite agony to a most wonderful calm. Dear love, how can I thank you! I am not going to try. Anne and I will come by the train arriving at Pineland at 4.52. I will not ask your kindness for her; I see you diffusing it. She will be grateful, and the form her gratitude will take will be the endeavour to convert you to Christian Science. My sweet darling, you will listen gravely, patiently. And I shall know it will be for me. I have done nothing to deserve you, am nothing, only your worshipper. Some day perhaps you will let me do something for you. Dear heart, I love you, love you, love you, however I write."

G. S.

Friday, Margaret decided it was better that she should entertain her guests alone. She had to learn the idiosyncrasies of this poor sister of her lover's, to acclimatise herself to a new atmosphere between herself and Gabriel. She invited Peter Kennedy to dine with them on Saturday, but bade him not to speak lightly of Christian Science.

"What's the game?" he asked her.

"I think it is probably some form of mesmerism; I don't quite know. Anyway Mr. Stanton's sister is an invalid and thinks Christian Science has relieved her. You are not to laugh at or argue with her."

"I am to dine here and talk to her, I suppose, whilst you and that fellow ogle and make love to each other." She turned a cold shoulder to him.

"I withdraw my invitation, you need not come at all."

"Of course I shall come. And what is the name of the thing? Christian Science? I'll get it up. You know I'd do anything on earth you asked me, though you treat me like a dog."

"At least you snatch an occasional bone," she smiled as he mumbled her hand.

Margaret sent for Mary Baker Eddy's "Science and Health; with a Key to the Scriptures," and spent the emptiest two hours she could remember in trying to master the viewpoint of the book, the essential dogma. Failing completely she flung it to Peter Kennedy, who read aloud to her sentence after sentence as illuminative as these:

"'Destructive electricity is not the offspring of infinite good.' Who the devil said it was?"

"Hush, go on. There must be something more in it than that." He turned to the title-page, "'Printed and published at Earlswood'? No, my mistake—at Boston. 'Christian Science rationally explains that all other pathological methods are the fruits of human faith in matter, in the working, not of spirit, but of the fleshly mind, which must yield to Science.' Don't knit your brows. What's the good of swotting at it? Let's say Abracadabra to her and see what happens."

"What an indolent man you are. Is that the way you worked at your examination?"

"I qualified."

"I suppose that was the height of your ambition?"

"You don't give a man much encouragement to be ambitious."

"But this was before I knew you."

"Don't you believe it. I never lived at all before you knew me."

"Absurd boy!"

"I'm getting on for thirty."

"You can't expect me to remember it whilst you behave as if you were seventeen. Take the book up again, let us give it an honest trial."

He read on obediently, and she listened with a real desire for instruction. Then all at once she put her fingers in her ears and called a halt.

"That will do. Ring for tea, I can't listen to any more...."

He went on nevertheless: "'*Mind is not the author of Matter.*' I say, this is jolly good. You can read it the other way too. '*Matter is not the author of mind. There is no matter ... put matter under the foot of mind.*' Put Mrs. Eddy under the foot of a militant suffragette. Oh! I say ... listen to this...."

"No, I won't, not to another word. Poor Gabriel...." He threw the book away.

"Always that damned fellow!" he said.

When Friday came and the house had been swept and garnished Margaret drove to the station to receive her guests. The room prepared for Anne was on the same corridor as her own, facing south, and with a balcony. Margaret herself had seen to all the little details for her comfort. A big sofa and easy-chair, pen and ink and paper, the latest novel: flowers on the mantelpiece and dressing-table, a filled biscuit box, and small spirit stand. Then, more slowly, she had gone into the little suite prepared for Gabriel, bedroom and bathroom, no balcony, but a wide window. She only stayed a moment, she did not give a thought to his little comforts. She was out of the room again quickly.

She arrived late at the station, and Gabriel was already on the platform; he never had the same happy certainty as the first time, nor knew how she would greet him. The first impression she had of Anne was of a little old woman, bent-backed, fussing about the luggage, about some bag after which she enquired repeatedly and excitedly, of whose safety she could not be assured until Gabriel produced it to her from among the others already on the platform.

"Shall we go on and leave him to follow with the luggage?" Margaret asked.

"Oh, no, no, I couldn't think of moving until it is found. So tiresome...."

"I am sure you are tired after your journey."

"I don't know what it is to be tired since I have taken up Christian Science. You know we are never tired unless we think we are," Anne said, when they were in the carriage, bowling along the good road toward the reddening glow of the sunset. Margaret and Gabriel, sitting opposite, but not facing each other —embarrassed, shy with the memory of their last parting,—were glad of this intervening person who chattered of her non-fatigue, the essential bag, and the number of things she had had to see to before she left home. All the way from Pineland station to the crunching gravel path at Carbies Anne talked and they made a feint of listening to her. The feeling between them was a great height. They were almost glad of her presence, of her fretting small talk. Margaret said afterwards she felt damp and deluged with it, properly subdued. "I felt as if I had come all out of curl," she told him. "No wonder you speak so little, are reserved."

"I am not reserved with you," he answered.

"I think sometimes that you are."

"There is not a corner or cranny of my mind I should not wish you to explore if it interested you," he replied passionately.

All that evening Anne's volubility never failed. She was of the type of woman, domestic and frequent, who can talk for hours without succeeding in saying anything. Most of it seemed simultaneous! Anne Stanton, who was ten years older than Gabriel and had an idea that she "managed" him, prided herself also on her good social quality and capacity for carrying off a situation. She thought of this invitation and introduction to the young lady with whom her brother had evidently fallen in love as "a situation" and she felt herself of immense importance in it. Gabriel must have kept his secret better than he knew. She believed that he was seeking her opinion of his choice, that the decision, if there was to be a decision, rested with her. One must do her the justice to admit that she did not give a thought to any possible alteration in her own position. She had always lived with Gabriel, she knew he would not cast her off. Conscious of her adaptability she had already said to him on the way down:

"I could live with anybody, any nice person, and, of course, since I have been so well everything is even easier. I do hope I shall like her...."

She did like her, very much, Margaret saw to that, behaving exquisitely under the stimulus of Gabriel's worshipping eyes; listening as if she were absorbedly interested in a description of the particular Healer who had Anne's case in hand.

"At first you see I was quite strange to it, I didn't understand completely. Mr. Roope is a little deaf, but he says he hears as much as he wants to ... so beautifully content and devout."

"Has Mrs. Roope any defect?" Margaret got a word or two in edgeways before the end of the evening, her sense of humour helping her.

"She has a sort of hysterical affection. She goes 'Bupp, bupp,' like a turkey-cock and swells at the throat. At least that is what I thought, but I am very backward at present. Some one asked her the cause once, when I was there, and she said she had no such habit, the mistake was ours. It is all very bewildering."

"Are there any other members of the family?"

"Her dear mother! Such a nice creature, and quite a believer; she has gall-stones."

"Gall-stones!"

"Not really, you know, they pass with prayer. She looks ill, very ill sometimes, but of course that is another of my mistakes. I am having absent treatment now."

"They know where you are?" Gabriel asked, perhaps a little anxiously.

"Oh! dear, yes. I am never out of touch with them."

After she had retired for the night, for notwithstanding her immunity from fatigue and pain, she retired early, explaining that she wanted to put her things in order, Gabriel lingered to tell Margaret again what an angel she was, and of his gratitude to her for the way she was receiving and making much of his sister.

"I like doing it, she interests me. I suppose she really believes in it all."

"I think so. You see her illness is partly nervous, partly her spine, but still to a certain extent, nervous. She is undoubtedly better since she had this hobby. The only thing that worries me is this family of whom she speaks, these Roopes. Of course they will get everything she has out of her, every penny. If it only stops at that...."

"You have seen them?"

"Not yet. I hear the man is an emaciated idler, not over-clean, his wife has evidently a bad form of St. Vitus's dance. The woman leads them all, the old mother, all of them. I expect they live upon what she makes. I've heard a story or two ... I had not realized about this absent treatment, that Anne tells them where she goes. You don't mind?"

"Why should I mind?"

"She may have told them I come here...."

"Oh! that! I had forgotten."

It was true, she had forgotten that she must walk circumspectly. She had spoken of and forgotten it. Now she remembered, because he reminded her; reddened and wished she had not invited Anne. Anne, with her undesirable acquaintances and meandering talk, who would keep her and Gabriel company on their walks and drives for the next two days.

But Providence, or a broken chain in the sequence of the Roope Christian Science treatment, came to her aid. On Saturday Anne was prostrated with headache.

"She has never been able to bear a railway journey."

"Does she explain?"

"I went in to see her. 'If only I had faith enough,' she moaned, and asked me to send Mrs. Roope a telegram. I persuaded her to five grains of aspirin, but I could see she felt very guilty about it. She will sleep until the afternoon."

"We can leave her?"

"Oh, yes! I doubt if she will be well awake by dinner, certainly not before."

"Let us get away from here, from Carbies and Pineland...."

"Right to the other side of the island. We could lunch at Ryde. I'll get a car."

Nothing suited either of them so well today as a long silent drive. The car went too fast for them to talk. Retrospect or the comparison of notes was practically impossible. They sat side by side, smiling rarely, one at the other as the spring burst into life around them. The tall hedges were full of may blossom, with here and there a flowering currant, the trees wore their coronal of young green leaves, great clumps of primroses succeeded the yellow gorse of which they had tired, fields were already green with the autumn-sown corn, there was nothing to remind them of Carbies. For a long time the sea was out of sight. Never had they been happier together, for all they spoke so little.

At Ryde he played the host to her, and she sat on the verandah whilst he went in to give his orders. A few ships were aride in the bay, but the scene was very different from what she had ever seen it before, in Regatta time, when it was gay with bunting and familiar faces. Today they had it to themselves, the hotel she only knew as overcrowded, and the view of the town, so strangely quiet. And excellent was the luncheon served to them. A lobster mayonnaise and a fillet steak, a pie of early gooseberries, which nevertheless Margaret declared were bottled. They spoke of other meals they had had together, of one in the British Museum in particular. On this occasion it pleased her to declare that boiled cod, not crimped, but flabby and served with lukewarm egg sauce, was the most ambrosial food she knew.

"I don't know when I enjoyed a meal so much," she said reflectively.

"You wrote and reproached me for it." His eyes caressed and forgave her for it.

"Impossible!"

"You did indeed. I can produce your plaint in your own handwriting."

"You don't mean to say you keep my letters!"

"I would rather part with my Elzevirs."

This was the only time they approached sentiment, approached and sheered off. There was something between them, in wait for them, at which at that moment neither wished to look.

The sun sparkled on the waters, a boatload of smart young naval officers put off from a strange yacht in the bay. Gabriel and Margaret wished that their landing at the pier should synchronise with their own departure. Nothing was to break the unusualness of their solitude in this whilom crowded place. He showed his tenderness in the way he cloaked her, tucked the rugs about her, not in any spoken word. She felt it subtly about her, and glowed in it, most amazingly content.

When they got back to Carbies, after having satisfied herself that her guest had recovered and would join them at dinner, she astonished her maid by demanding an evening toilette. She wore a gown of grey and silver brocade, very stiff and Elizabethan, a chain of uncut cabochon emeralds hung round her neck, and a stomacher of the same decorated her corsage. The mauve osprey upstanding in her hair was clasped by a similar encrusted jewel. She carried herself regally. Had she not come into her woman's Kingdom? Tonight she meant that he should see what he had won.

It was a strange evening, nevertheless, and they were a strangely assorted quartette. There was a little glow of colour in Margaret's cheeks, such as Peter Kennedy had never seen there before, her eyes shone like stars, and she wore this regal toilette. Peter was introduced to Anne. Anne, yellowish and subdued after the migraine, dressed in brown taffeta, opening at the wizened throat to display a locket of seed pearls on a gold chain; her brown toupée had slipped a little and discovered a few grey hairs, her hands, covered with inexpensive rings, showed clawlike and tremulous. Margaret's unringed hands, so pale and small, were like Japanese flowers. Peter had to take in Anne. Gabriel gave his arm to Margaret. The poverty of the dining-room furniture was out of the circle of the white spread table, where the suspended lamp shone on fine silver and glass. Flowers came constantly to Carbies from London. Tonight red roses scented the room; hothouse roses, blooming before their time, on long thornless stems. Margaret drew a vase toward her, exclaimed at the wealth of perfume.

"I only hope they won't make your headache worse."

Anne tried to insist she had no headache. Peter advised a glass of champagne. She began to tell him something of her new-found panacea for all ills, but ceased upon finding he was what she called a "medical man," one of the enemies of their creed. Before the dinner had passed the soup stage he hardly made a pretence of listening to her. Both men were absorbed in this regal Margaret. All her graciousness was for Gabriel, but she found occasion now and again for a smile and a word for Peter. Poor Peter! guest at this high feast where there was no food for him. But he made the most of the material provender, and proved fortunately to be an excellent trencherman. Otherwise Margaret's good cook had exerted herself in vain. For none of them had appetite but Peter; Margaret because she talked too much, and Gabriel because he could do nothing but listen; Anne because she was feeling the after-effects, and regretting she had yielded to the temptation of the aspirin.

The men sat together but a short time after the ladies left them. They had one subject in common of which neither wished to speak. Gabriel smoked only a cigarette. Peter praised the port, which happened to be exceptionally bad; the weather was a topic that drew blank. Fortunately they struck upon Pineland and its health-giving qualities, upon which both were enthusiastic. Peter Kennedy was in Gabriel's secret, but Gabriel had no intuition of his.

"Mrs. Capel seems to have derived great benefit from her stay. Probably from your treatment also," he said courteously. His thoughts were so full of her; how could he speak of anything else?

"I can't do much for her," Peter said gloomily. He had had the greater part of a bottle of champagne, and the port on the top of it. "She doesn't do a thing I tell her. She doesn't care whether I'm dead or alive."

"I am sure you are wrong," Gabriel reassured him earnestly. "She has, I am sure, the highest possible opinion of your skill. She carries out your régime as far as possible. You think she should rest more?"

"She should do nothing but rest."

"But with an active mind?"

"It is not only her mind that is active."

"You mean the piano-playing, writing...."

"She ought just to vegetate. She has a weak heart, one of the valves...."

Gabriel rose hurriedly, it was not possible for him to listen to a description of his beloved's physical ailments. He was shocked with Peter for wishing to tell him, genuinely shocked. It was a breach of professional etiquette, of good manners. They arrived upstairs in the music room completely out of tune.

"He wouldn't even listen when I told him how seedy you were, that you ought to be kept quiet. Selfish owl. You've been out with him all day."

"I rested for half an hour before dinner. Do I look tired or washed out?" She turned a radiant face to Peter for investigation. "I am going to play to you presently, when you will see if I am without power."

"Power! Who said you were without that? You'd have power over the devil tonight."

"Or over my eccentric physician." She smiled at him. "Have you been behaving yourself prettily downstairs?"

"I haven't told him what I think of him, if that's what you mean!"

"Will you play first?" she asked him. Peter Kennedy was a genuine music lover, and he played well, very much better since Margaret Capel had come to Pineland. He sang also, but this accomplishment Margaret would never let him display. She had no use for a man's singing since James Capel had lured her with his love songs.

Gabriel was talking to his sister whilst Margaret and Peter had this little conversation. He was persuading her to an early retreat.

"Did you send my telegram to Mrs. Roope? I am sure I am getting better, I have been thinking so all the evening. She must have been treating me."

"I am sure, but are not the vibrations stronger between you if you are alone, if there is nothing to disturb your thoughts?..." Even Gabriel Stanton could be disingenuous when the occasion demanded. She hesitated.

"Wouldn't Mrs. Capel be offended? One owes something to one's hostess. She has promised to play. You told me she played beautifully. I do think she is very sweet. But, Gabriel, have you thought of the flat? I shouldn't like to give it up. The gravel soil and air from the heath, and everything. Isn't she ... isn't she...."

"A size too big for it?" He finished her sentence for her.

"Too grand, I meant."

"Yes, too grand. Of course she is too grand." He turned to look at her. This time their eloquent eyes met. She indicated the piano stool to Peter Kennedy and came swiftly to the brother and sister.

"Has he made you comfortable?" She adjusted the pillows, and stole a glance at Gabriel. Whenever she looked at him it seemed that his eyes were upon her. They were extraordinarily conscious of each other, acting a little because Anne and Peter were there. Peter Kennedy, over on the music stool, struck a chord or two, as if to lure her back.

"One can always listen better when one is comfortable," she said to Anne. Then went over to the fender stool, where Gabriel joined her, after a moment's hesitation.

"Isn't it too hot for you?" she asked him innocently.

"It might have been," he answered, smiling, "only the fire is out."

"Is it?" she turned to look. "I had not noticed it. Hush! He is going to play the *Berceuse*. You haven't heard him before, have you? He plays quite well."

So they sat there together whilst Peter Kennedy played, and every now and then Anne said from the sofa:

"How delicious! Thank you ever so much. What was it? I thought I knew the piece."

Peter got up from the piano before Gabriel and Margaret had tired of sitting side by side on the fender stool, or Anne of ejaculating her little complimentary, grateful, or enquiring phrases.

"I suppose you've had enough of it," he said abruptly to Margaret.

"No, I haven't. You could have gone on for another hour."

"I daresay."

Gabriel thought his manner singularly abrupt, almost rude. This was only the second or third time he had met Margaret's medical attendant, and he was not at all favourably impressed by him. As for Peter:

"Damned dry stick," he said to Margaret, when he had persuaded her to the redemption of her promise, and was leading her to the piano.

"What a boor you really are, notwithstanding your playing," she answered calmly, adjusting the candles, the height of the piano stool, looking out some music. "I really thought you were going to behave well tonight. And not a word about Christian Science," she chaffed him gently, "after all the coaching."

She too tried a few chords.

"I say, don't you play too long tonight. Don't you go overdoing it." Her chaff made no impression upon him, he was used to it. But he was struck by some alteration or intensification of her brilliancy. How could he know the secret of it? The love of which he was capable gave him no key to the spell that was on those two tonight.

Anne slipped off to bed presently, at Gabriel's whispered encouragement, and Margaret went on playing to the two men. Peter commented sometimes, asked for this or the other, went over and stood by her side, turning over the music, sat down beside her now and again. Gabriel remained on the corner of the sofa Anne had vacated, and listened. Therefore it was Peter who caught her when she fell forward with a little sigh or moan, Peter who caught her up in his arms and strode over with her to the sofa. Gabriel would have taken her from him, but Peter issued impatient orders.

"Open the window, pull the blind up, let us have as much air as possible. Ring for her maid, ring like blazes ... she has only fainted." Within a minute she was sitting up, radiantly white, but with shadows round her pale mouth and deep under her eyes.

"It is nothing, it is only a touch of faintness. Not an attack. Gabriel, you were not frightened?" she asked, and put out her hand to him.

Peter said something inarticulate and got up from where he had been kneeling beside her.

"I'll get you some brandy."

"Shall I go?" Gabriel asked, but was holding her hand.

"No, no. You stay. Dr. Kennedy knows where it is."

Gabriel knelt beside her now.

"Were you frightened?" she asked, still a little faintly.

"Love, lover, sweet, my heart was shaken with terror."

"It is really nothing. We have had such a wonderful day I was trying to play it all to you. Then the glory spread, brightened, overwhelmed me...."

"Beloved!"

"Hush! he is coming back. You won't believe anything he tells you?"

"Not if you tell me you are not really ill? Oh! my darling! I could not bear it if you were to suffer. Let me get some one else...."

Peter was back with the brandy, a measured dose, he brushed Gabriel aside as if now at least he had the mastery of the position. For all Gabriel's preoccupation with Margaret, Dr. Kennedy managed to attract from him a wondering moment of attention. Need he have knelt to administer the draught? What was it he was murmuring? Whatever it was Margaret was unwilling to hear. She leaned back, closing her eyes. When the maid came, torn reluctantly from her supper, she was able, nevertheless, to reassure her.

"Nothing of consequence, Stevens, not an attack. I am going across to my bedroom. One of you will lend me an arm," they were both in readiness, "or both." She took an arm of one and an arm of the other, smiled in both their faces. "What a way to wind up our little evening! You will have to forgive me, entertain each other."

"I'll come in again and see you when you are comfortable," the doctor said, a little defiantly, Gabriel thought.

"No, don't wait. Not on any account. Stevens knows everything to do for me. Show Mr. Stanton where the cigars are."

They were not in good humour when they left her.

"I don't smoke cigars," Gabriel said abruptly when Dr. Kennedy made a feint of carrying out her wishes. Peter shrugged his shoulders.

"She told me to find them for you."

"Has she had attacks like this before?" Gabriel asked, after a pause. Peter answered gloomily:

"And will again if she is allowed to overtire herself by driving for hours in the sun, and then encouraged to sit through a long dinner, talking all the time."

"She ought not to have played?" Peter Kennedy threw himself on to the sofa, desecrating it, bringing an angry flush to Gabriel's brow. But when he groaned and said:

"If one could only do anything for her!"

Gabriel forgave him in that instant. Gabriel had lived all his life with an invalid. Attacks of hysteria and faintness had been his daily menu for years.

"But surely an attack of faintness is not very unusual or alarming? My sister often faints...."

"She isn't Margaret Capel, is she?"

"You ... you knew Mrs. Capel before she came to Carbies?"

"No, I didn't. But I know her now, don't I?"

Gabriel was silent. He had seen a great many doctors too, before the Christian Scientists had broken their influence, but such a one as this was new to him. Margaret was so sacred and special to him that he did not know what to think. But Peter gave him little time for thinking. He fixed a gloomy eye upon him and said:

"A man's a man, you know, although he's nothing but a country practitioner." Gabriel was acutely annoyed, a little shocked, most supremely uncomfortable.

"But ought you to go on attending her?" he got out.

"I shan't do her any harm, shall I, because I am madly in love with her, because I could kiss the ground she walks on, because I'd give my life for hers any day?" Gabriel's face might have been carved. "She treats me like a dog...."

Gabriel made a gesture of dissent, Margaret could not treat any one like a dog.

"Oh, yes, she does, she says I'm not fit to wipe the mud off your shoes...."

Then Margaret knew. He was a little stunned and taken by surprise to think Margaret knew her doctor was in love with her, knew and had kept him in attendance. But of course she was right, everything she did was right. She had not taken the matter seriously.

"I suppose I'd better go." Peter dropped his feet to the ground, rose slowly. "She won't see me again if she says she won't. She's got her bromide. You might ring me up in the morning and tell me how she is, if she wants me to come round. That's not too much to ask, is it?" he said savagely.

"Not at all," Gabriel answered coldly. "I should of course do anything she wished." Peter paused a moment at the door.

"I say, you're not going to try and put her off me, are you? Just because I've let myself go to you?"

"I am not authorised to interfere in Mrs. Capel's affairs." Gabriel was quite himself again and very stiff.

"But I understand you will be."

"I would rather not discuss the future with you."

"Then you do intend to try and out me?"

Gabriel was suddenly a little sorry for him, he looked so desperately miserable and anxious, and after all he, Peter Kennedy, was leaving the house. Gabriel was remaining, sleeping under the same roof.

"I will see her maid if possible. You shall be called up if you are needed. Nothing but her well-being, her own wish will be thought of.... Anyway you shall have a report."

"As her doctor she trusts me. I can ease her symptoms." It was almost a plea. "She need not suffer."

"Of course you will be sent for. They have your telephone number?"

Peter held out his hand.

"Good-night. You're a good fellow. She is quite right. I suppose I ought not to have told you how it is with me…?"

"It is of no consequence," Gabriel answered, intending to be courteous.

CHAPTER XI

Sunday morning the church bells were chiming against the blue sky in the clear air. Both invalids were better. The reports Gabriel received whilst he sat over his solitary breakfast were to the effect that Miss Stanton had slept well and was without headache, she sent word also of her intention to go to church if it were possible. Stevens herself told him that Mrs. Capel would be coming down at eleven o'clock or half-past, having had an excellent night. He was not to stay in for her.

"Can you tell me how far off is the nearest church?"

Stevens was fully informed on the matter. There were two almost within equal distance.

"Not more than a quarter of an hour to twenty minutes away. The nearest is the 'ighest...." Stevens was a typical English maid, secretly devoted to her mistress, well up in her duties but with a perpetual grievance or list of grievances. "Not that I get there myself, not on Sunday mornings, since I've been here."

Gabriel was sympathetic. Contempt, however, was thrown upon his suggestion of the afternoon.

"Children's services and such-like, no thank you!"

As for the evenings Stevens said "they was mostly hymns." He detained her for a few minutes, for was she not Margaret's confidential maid, compensating her, too, for her lack of religious privileges. He told her to tell her mistress he would walk to church with his sister and then return, that he looked forward to seeing her if she were really better. Otherwise she was not to think of rising.

"She'll get up right enough. I'm to have her bath ready at 'alf-past ten."

When Anne came down he walked with her over the common-land, bright with gorse and broom that lay between Carbies and the higher of the two churches, heard how Anne had lain awake and then how she had slept, sure of the intervention of Mrs. Roope. Her headache had completely disappeared.

"You did send that telegram, didn't you?"

Gabriel assured her that the telegram had been duly despatched.

"She must have started on me at once. She is a good creature. I wish you were more sympathetic to it. You've never once been with me to a meeting."

"But I have not put anything in the way of your going."

"Oh, yes! I know how good you are. Which reminds me, Gabriel, about Mrs. Capel. We must talk things over when we get home. You must not do anything in a hurry. I heard about her fainting away last night. It is not only that she is a widow, and terribly delicate, her maid tells me, but she takes no care of herself, none at all…. What a rate you are walking at; I'm sure we have plenty of time, the bells are still going. I can't keep up with you." He slowed down. "As I was saying, I shouldn't like you to be more particular with her until we have talked things over together. Of course as far as her delicacy is concerned, we might persuade her to see Mrs. Roope."

"I have already asked Mrs. Capel if she will do me the honour of becoming my wife," her brother said in a tone she found curious, peculiar, not at all like himself.

"Oh, dear! how tiresome! You really are so impulsive. Of course I like her very much, very much indeed, but there are so many things to be thought of. How long has her husband been dead? You know she is more than half an American, she told me so herself, and such strange things do happen with American husbands."

"Mrs. Capel divorced her husband!" He spoke quickly, abruptly, hurrying her on toward the church, through the gate and up the path where a little stream of people was already before them, people carrying prayer-books, or holding by the hand a stiffly dressed unwilling child; one or two women with elderly husbands.

Anne gave a little subdued scream when Gabriel told her that Mrs. Capel had divorced her husband, a little gasp.

"Oh dear, oh dear!" It was impossible to say more under the circumstances, she could not make a scene here.

"You will be able to find your way back all right?" he asked her. The bells were clashing now almost above their heads, clashing slowly to the finish.

"I'm sure I don't know whether I am standing on my head or my heels."

"You will be all right when you are inside."

"I haven't even got my smelling-salts with me, I promised to leave off carrying them." She was almost crying with agitation.

"You will be all right," he said again. He waited until she had gone through the door, the little bent figure in its new coat and skirt and Victorian hat tied under the chin. Then he was free to return on swift feet to Carbies to await Margaret's coming. He walked so swiftly that although it had taken them twenty minutes to get there he was barely ten in coming back. He hurried faster when he saw there was a figure at the gate.

"It is too fine to be indoors this morning. I am going down to the sea. I yearn for the sea this morning. Go up to the house, will you? Fetch a cushion or so. Then we can be luxurious." He executed his commission quickly, and when he came up to her again had not only a cushion but a rug on his arm. She said quickly:

"What a wonderful morning! Isn't it a God-given morning?"

"All mornings are wonderful and God-given that bring me to you," he answered little less soberly, walking by her side. "Won't you lean a little on me, take my arm?"

"Do I look decrepit?" She laughed, walking on light feet. Spring was everywhere, in the soft air, and the throats of courting birds, in the breeze and both their hearts. They went down to the sea and he arranged the cushions against that very rock behind which I had once sat and heard them talk. She said now she must face the sea, the winds that blew from it.

"Not too cold?" he asked her.

"Not too anything. You may sit on the rug too, there is a bit to spare for you. What book have you in your pocket?"

"No book today. I carried Anne's prayer-book."

"'Science and Health'?"

She was full of merriment and laughter.

"No; the ordinary Church Service. There was nothing else available."

"Oh, yes, there was. I sent for a copy of Mrs. Eddy's lucubrations."

"No!"

"Of course I did. I had to make myself acquainted with a subject on which I should be compelled to talk."

"What a wonderful woman you are."

"Not at all. If she had been a South Sea Islander I'd have welcomed her with shells or beads. Tell me, have I made a success? Will she give her consent?"

"Have you given yours, have you really given yours? You have never said so in so many words."

"Well, the implication must have been fairly obvious." The eyes she turned on him were full of happy laughter, almost girlish. Since yesterday she had had this new strange bloom of youth. "Don't tell me your sister has not guessed."

"I told her."

"You told her! Well! I never! as Stevens would say. And you were pretending not to know!"

"I only said you had never put it into words. Say it now, Margaret, out here, this wonderful Sunday."

"What am I to say?"

"Put your little hand in mine, your sweet flower of a hand." He took it.

"Not a flower, a weed. See how brown they have got since I've been here." He kissed the weed or flower of her hand.

"Say, 'Gabriel, you shall be my husband. I will marry you the very first day I am free!'" Her brows knitted, she took her hand away a little pettishly.

"I *am* free. Why do you remind me?"

"Say, 'I will marry you on the last day in May, in six weeks from today.'"

"May marriages are unlucky."

"Ours could not be."

"Oh, yes! it could. I am a woman of moods."

"Every one more lovely than the last."

"Impatient and irritable."

"You shall have no time to be impatient. Anything you want I will rush to obtain for you. If you are irritable I will soothe you."

"And then I want hours to myself."

"I'll wait outside your door, on the mat, to keep interruptions from you."

"I want to write … to play the piano, to rest a great deal."

"Give me your odd half-hours." She gave him back her hand instead.

"Let's pretend. We are to sail away into the unknown; to be happy ever afterwards. Where shall we go, Gabriel? Can we have a yacht?"

"I am not rich."

"Pretend you are. Where shall we go? To Greece, where every stone is hallowed ground to you. All the white new buildings shall be blotted out and you may turn your back on the museum...."

"I shall only want to look at you."

"No, on rocks and the blue Ægean Sea. No, we won't go to Greece at all. You will be so learned, know so much more than I about everything. I shall feel small, insignificant."

"Never. Bigger than the Pantheon."

"We will go to Sicily instead, go down among the tombs."

"I bar the tombs."

"Contradicting me already. How dare you, sir?"

So the time passed in happy fooling, but often their hands met, the undercurrents between them ran swift and strong, deep too. Then it was time for lunch. It was Margaret who suggested they would be in time to meet Anne, walk up to the house with her. Nothing had been said about Dr. Kennedy. Gabriel had meant to broach the subject, only touch it lightly, suggest if she still needed medical attendance some one older, less interested might perhaps be advisable.

But he never did broach the subject, it had been impossible on such a morning as this, she in such a mood, he in such accord with her. Anne, when they met her, dashed them both a little. She twittered away about the service and the sermon, but it was nervous and disjointed twitter, and her eyes were red. She responded awkwardly to all Margaret's kind speeches, her enquiries after her headache; she was even guilty of the heinous offence, heinous in her own eyes when she remembered it afterwards, of saying nothing of the other's faintness. Her landmarks had been swept away, the ground yawned under her feet. Divorce! She did not think she could live in the house with a divorced person. She knew that some clergymen would not even marry divorced people, nor give them the sacrament. She was miserably distressed, and longing to be at home. She felt she was assisting at something indecorous, if not worse; she thought she ought not to have waited for the sermon, she ought not to have left them so long alone together. All her mingled emotions made her feel ill again. She told Gabriel crossly that he was walking too fast.

"Perhaps Mrs. Capel likes fast walking? Don't mind me if you do," she said to Margaret, "I can manage by myself."

When they had adapted their pace to hers she was little better satisfied; querulous, and as Margaret had pictured her before they met. Luncheon was a miserable meal, or would have been but that nothing could have really damped the spirits of these other two. First Anne found herself in a draught, and then too hot. She never eat eggs, and explained about her digestion, the asparagus tops could not tempt her. A lobster mayonnaise was a fresh offence or disappointment. And she could not disguise her disapproval. After all she prided herself she did know something about housekeeping.

"I never give Gabriel eggs except for breakfast."

"I do hope I have not upset your liver." Margaret's eyes were full of laughter when she questioned him.

"In my young days, in my papa's house, nor for the matter of that in my uncle's either, did we ever have lobster salad except for a supper dish."

Gabriel suggested gently that the whole art of eating had altered in England.

"Cod and egg sauce," put in Margaret.

"Nectar and ambrosia."

"We never gave either of them," said poor hungry Anne.

Fortunately a spatchcock with mushrooms was produced, and the *mousse* of *jambon*, although it seemed "odd," was very light.

"Why didn't I have boiled mutton and rice pudding?" Margaret lamented in an aside to Gabriel when the *omelette au rhum* was most decisively declined. Cream cheese and gingerbread proved the last straw. Anne admitted it made her feel ill to see the others eat these in combination.

"I should like to get back to town as early as possible this afternoon," she said. "I am sure I don't know what has come over me, I felt well before I came. The place cannot agree with me. I hope you don't think me very rude, but if we can have a fly for the first train...."

Gabriel was full of consternation and remonstrated with her. Margaret whispered to him it was better so. Nothing was to be gained by detaining her against her will.

"We have next week...."

"All the weeks," he whispered back.

Margaret offered Stevens' services, but Anne said she preferred to pack for herself, then she knew just where everything was. The lovers had an hour to themselves whilst she was engaged in this congenial occupation. She reminded Gabriel that he too must put his things together, and he agreed. She thought this made matters safe.

"Stevens will do them for you," Margaret said softly. He did not care how they were jumbled in, or what left behind, so that he secured this precious hour.

"Something has upset her, it was not only the lunch," Margaret said sapiently. He did not wish to enlighten her.

"Has she worried you, beloved one?"

"Not very much, not as much as she ought to perhaps. I was selfish with her, left her too much alone. I shall know better another time. But at least we had yesterday afternoon, and this morning ... oh! and part of the evening, too. Did I frighten you very much?" she asked him.

"Before I had time to be frightened you smiled, something of your colour came back. Margaret, that reminds me. Do you mind if I suggest to you that if you were really seedy Dr. Kennedy is comparatively a young man...." She laughed.

"But look how devoted he is!"

"That is why." He spoke a little gravely, and she put her hand in his.

"Jealous!" Her voice was very soft.

"The whole world loves you."

"I don't love the whole world." And when she said this her voice was no longer only soft, it was tenderness itself.

"Thank God!" He kissed her hand.

But returned to his text as a man will. "No, I am not jealous. How could I be? You have honoured me, dowered me beyond all other men. But you are so precious, so supremely and unutterably precious. Margaret, my heart is suddenly shaken. Tell me again. You are not ill, not really ill? When this trying time is over, when I can be with you always...."

"How about those hours I want to myself?" she interrupted.

"When I can be within sound of you, taking care of you all the time, you will be well then?" Now she put a hand on his knee. "Your little fairy hand!" he exclaimed, capturing it.

"I want you to listen," she began. She did not know or believe herself that she was seriously ill, but remembered what Dr. Lansdowne had said and shivered over it a little.

"Suppose I am really ill, that it is heart disease with me as the German doctors and Lansdowne told me? Not only heart weakness as the others say, would you be afraid? Do you think I ought not to … to marry?"

"My darling, it is impossible, your beautiful vitality makes it impossible. But if it were true, incredibly true, then all the more reason that we should be married as quickly as possible. I must snatch you up, carry you away." There was an interlude. "You want petting…." He was a little awkward at it nevertheless, inexperienced.

"Isn't there some great man you could see, and who would reassure you, some specialist?"

"The Roopes?" She laughed, and her short fit of seriousness was over.

"I will find out who is the best man, the head of the profession. No one but the best is good enough for my Margaret. You will let me take you to him?"

"Perhaps. When I come back to London; if I am not well by then."

"You like this place, don't you?" he asked. "You don't think it is the place?"

"Pineland and Carbies? I am not sure. If I had not taken it for three months I believe I'd go back today or tomorrow. I ran away from you … and social guns. I'm armed now." He thanked her for that mutely. "Do you really love this ill-fixed house?"

"How should I not? But what does that matter? Leave it empty if it doesn't suit you. There is Queen Anne's Gate."

"I know, but we should never be alone."

"Nothing matters but that you should be well, happy. I'd take my vacation now, stay down, only I want at least six weeks in June. I could not do with less than six weeks." And this time the interlude was longer, more silent. Margaret recovered herself first.

"About Peter Kennedy. He really suits me better than any of the other doctors here. Lansdowne is a soft-soapy grinning pessimist, with an all-conquering air. He tells you how ill you are as if it doesn't matter since he has warned you, and will come constantly to remind you. There is a Dr. Lushington who, I believe, knows more than all of them put together, but he is a delicate man himself, overburdened with children, and cramped with small means. He gives me fresh heartache, I am so sorry for him all the time he is with me. Lansdowne and Lushington have each young partners or assistants, straight from London hospitals, smelling of iodoform, talking in abstruse medical or surgical terms, nosing for operations, as dogs for truffles. You don't want me to have any of these, do you?"

"I want you to do what you please, now and always."

"Even if it pleases me that Peter Kennedy should medicine and make love to me?"

"Even that. Does he make love to you?"

"What did he tell you?"

"That he adored you—that you treated him like a dog."

"He gives me amyl, bromide. He was only a country practitioner when I first knew him, with a gift for music, but not for diagnosis."

"And now?"

"He has done more reading, medical reading, since I have been here than in all his life before. Treatises on the heart; all that have ever been written. He is really studying, he intends to take a higher degree. In music too, I have given him an impetus."

Gabriel was obviously, nevertheless, not quite satisfied, started a tentative "but," and would perhaps have enquired whether ultimately it would be for Peter Kennedy's good that she had done so much for him. Anne, however, intervened, coming down dressed for the journey, very agitated at finding the two together. She gave him no opportunity for further conversation, monopolising the attention of the whole household, in searching for something she had mislaid, which it was eventually decided had possibly been left in Hampstead! Her conscience reproached her for her behaviour over lunch, and she found the cup of tea which Margaret pressed upon her before she left "delicious."

"I do so much like this Chinese tea, ever so much better than the Indian. You remember, Gabriel, don't you, that rough tea we used to have from Pounds? ..." And she told a wholly irrelevant anecdote of rival grocers and their wares.

She betrayed altogether in the last ten minutes an uneasy semi-consciousness that her visit had not been a great success and talked quickly in belated apology.

"You've been so kind to me. I am afraid I have not responded as I ought. My silly headache, which of course I never exactly had ... you know what I mean, don't you? And I did no credit to your beautiful lunch."

Margaret succeeded in assuring her that she had behaved exactly as a guest should, whilst Gabriel stood by silently.

"I hope you will come again," she said, and Anne replied nervously, noncommittal.

"That would be nice, wouldn't it? But I am always so busy, and now that I have my treatment it is so much more difficult to get away...."

A kiss was avoided. Margaret went to the hall door with them, but not to the station. Gabriel had asked her not to do so.

"You ought to rest after yesterday."

"Yes, of course she ought to rest," Anne chorussed. There was a certain awkwardness in the farewells, somewhat mitigated by the luggage that occupied, so to speak, the foreground of the picture. As they drove away Anne nodded her head, threw a kiss. But neither Margaret nor Gabriel was conscious of her condescension, only of how long it was from now until next Friday.

"I am glad that is over," Anne said complacently, as the carriage turned through the gates. "It was very trying, very trying indeed. In many ways she is quite a nice person. But not suited to us, in our quiet lives. Divorced too! I thought there was something last night. So ... so overdressed and peculiar. I am glad I came down before things had gone any further...."

"Further than what?" Gabriel asked her, waking up, if a little slowly, to the position. "Margaret and I are to be married in about a month's time. You shall stay on in the flat if you wish. I think I shall be able to arrange.... Have you thought about any one you would like to share it with you?"

"Any one I should like! Share it with me?"

She was very shrill and he hushed her, although there was no one to hear but the flyman, who flicked at the trotting horse and wheezed indifferently. They got to the station long before Anne had taken in the fact that Gabriel was telling her his intention, not asking her advice. In the train; after they got home; and for many weary days she showed her unreasoning and ineffective opposition. It was not worth recording, or would not be but for the sympathetic interest taken by the Roopes, when Anne, reluctantly and under pressure, gave her brother's approaching marriage as a reason for her own impaired health, and the failure of their ministrations. Anne felt it her duty to tell them this, and Mrs. Roope no less hers to make further enquiries; the results being more far-reaching than either of them could have anticipated. James Capel was a relation of the Roopes and it was natural they should be interested in the wife who had so flagrantly divorced him.

Ten days after Anne's unlucky visit to Carbies, Gabriel received a bewildering telegram. He had been down once in the interval, but had found it unnecessary to speak of Anne, her vagaries or vapours. He stayed at Carbies because once having done so it seemed absurd that his room should remain empty. The very contrast between this visit and the last accentuated its intimate charm. Anne was not there, and Peter Kennedy's services not being required, he had the good sense or taste to keep away. Margaret, closely questioned, admitted to having stayed a couple of days in bed, after the last week-end, admitted to weakness, but not illness.

"I have always been like that ever since I was a child. What is called, I believe, 'a little delicate.' I get very easily over-tired. Then if I don't pull up and recuperate with bed and Benger, I get an attack of pain...."

"Of pain! My poor darling!"

"Unbearable. I mean *I* can't bear it. Gabriel, don't you think you are doing a very foolish thing, taking this half-broken life of mine?"

"If only the time were here!"

"Sometimes I think it will never come," she sighed. "I am *clairvoyante* in a way. I don't see myself in harbour."

"Only three weeks more, then you shall be as *clairvoyante* as you like." He laughed happily, holding her to him.

On this visit she seemed glad of his love, to depend upon and need him. He always had that for which to be glad. In truth that weakness of which she spoke, and which was the cause, or perhaps the effect, of two unmistakable heart attacks, had left her in the mood for Gabriel Stanton, his serious tenderness, and deep, almost overwhelming devotion. She was a whimsical, strange little creature, genius as she called herself, and for the moment had ceased to act.

The weather changed, it rained almost continuously from Saturday night until Monday morning. They spent the time between the music room and the uncongenial dining-room where they had their meals. On the sofa, she lay practically in his arms, she sheltered there. She had been frightened by her own agitation and uncertainty; the attacks that followed. And now believed that all she needed was calm; happy certainty; Gabriel Stanton.

"Don't make me care for you too much," she said on one of these days. "I want you to rest me, not to get excited over you, to keep calm."

"I am here only for you to use. Think of me as refuge, sanctuary, what you will."

"A sort of cathedral?"

"You may laugh at me. I like you to laugh at me. Why not as a cathedral, cool and restful?"

"Cool and restful," she repeated. "Yes, you are like that. But suppose I want to wander outside, restless creature that I am; suppose nothing you do satisfies me?"

"I'll do more."

"And after that?"

"Always more."

There were no scenes between them; Gabriel was not the man for scenes, he was deeply happy, humbly happy, not knowing his own worth, much more careful of her than any woman could have been, and gentle beyond speech. Even in those days she wondered how it would be with her if she were well, robust, whether all these little cares would not irritate her, whether this was indeed the lover for her. There was something donnish and Oxonian about him.

"I'm not sure I look upon you as a cathedral, whether it isn't more as a college."

When he could not follow her he remained silent.

"Think of me any way you want so long as you do think of me," he said, after a pause.

"I thought you would say that."

"Was it what you wanted me to say?"

"I only want to hear you say you adore me. You say it so nicely too."

"Do I? I don't know what I have done to deserve you."

"Just loved me," she said dreamily.

"Any man would do that."

"Not in the same way."

"As long as my way pleases you I am the most fortunate of men."

"Even if I never wrote another line?"

"As if it mattered which way you express yourself, by writing or simply living."

"Such love is enervating. Are you not ambitious for me?"

"You've done enough."

"I am capable of doing much better work."

"You are capable of anything."

"Except of that book on Staffordshire Pottery."

"That was only to have been a stop-gap. You replaced that with me, darling that you are!"

"What will Sir George say when he knows?"

"He will say 'Lucky fellow' and envy me. Margaret, about how we shall live, and where?"

He told her again he was not rich. There was Anne, a certain portion of his income must be put aside for Anne.

"You are quite rich enough. For the matter of that I have still my marriage settlement. Father would give me more if we needed it. James had thousands from him."

Then they both coloured, she in shame that this ineffable James had ever called her wife. He, because the idea that any of her comforts or luxuries should emanate from her father or from any one but himself was repellent to him. He would have talked ways and means, considered the advantages of house or flat, spoken of furniture, but that at first she was wayward and said it was unlucky to "count chickens before they were boiled, or was it a watched pot?" She would only banter and say things that were without meaning or for which he could not find the meaning. Presumably, however, she allowed him to lead her back to the subject.

"I have in my mind sometimes a little old house in Westminster, built in the seventeenth or eighteenth century, with panelled walls and uneven floors. And hunting for furniture in old curiosity shops. It mustn't be earlier than the eighteenth century, by the way. Not too early in that; or my Staffordshire won't look well. In the living-room with the eighteenth-century chintz I see all little rosebuds and green leaves. A few colour prints on the walls."

Gabriel had spoken of his collection of old prints. He said he would set about looking for the house at once. He told her there were a few such still standing, they were snapped up so eagerly.

Soon, quite excitedly they were both planning, talking of old oak, James I. silver, William and Mary walnut. Of all their happy hours this I think was the happiest they ever spent. Their tastes were so congenial, Gabriel's knowledge so far beyond her own; the home they would build so essentially suited to them. There Margaret would write and play, hold something of a salon. He would see that all her surroundings were appropriate, dignified, congenial. She would be the centre of an ascending chorus of admiration. He would, as it were, conduct the band. With adoring eyes he would watch her effects, temper this or straighten that, setting the stage and noting the audience; all for her glorification.

When they parted on that Sunday night they could scarcely tear themselves asunder. Three weeks seemed so long, so desperately long. Margaret, woman of moods, suddenly launched at him that they would have no honeymoon at all. He was to look for the house at once, to find it without difficulty.

"Then I'll come up and confirm; set the painters to work, begin to look for things."

Gabriel pleaded for his honeymoon.

"But it will all be honeymoon."

"I want you all to myself; for at least a little time. I won't be selfish, but for a little while, just you and I…."

He must have pleaded well, for though she made him no promise in words he knew she had answered "yes" by her eyes downcast, and breath that came a little quicker, by the clinging hands, by finding her in his arms, her undenying lips.

CHAPTER XII

On Monday morning he went up to town without seeing her again. Tuesday he got that fateful telegram:

Stevens seen man hanging about house, shabby peering man. Questioned cook. Sick with fear. Send back all my letters at once by special messenger. In panic. On no account come down or near me but letters urgent.

Stevens had told her in the evening whilst putting her to bed. Stevens knew all about the case and was alert for possible complications. The shabby man had been under the observation of cook and housemaid.

"And much satisfaction he got out of what they told him. Askin' questions an' peerin' about! Cook told him off, said no one hadn't been stayin' here, an' if they had 'twas no business of his."

Margaret, pale and stricken, asked if the man looked like ... like a detective.

"Lawyer's clerk more like, but I thought I'd best let you know."

The news would have kept until the morning, but one could not expect a servant to take into consideration the effect her stories might have on Margaret's sensitiveness. She had no sleep at all. Sleepless and shaken she lay awake the whole night, conjuring up ghosts, chiefly the ghost or vision of James, coarse-mouthed, cruel, vindictive. The bare idea of the case being reopened made her shudder, she had been so tormented in court, her modesties outraged. She knew she could never, would never bear it again. If the dreadful choice were all that was left to her she would give up Gabriel. At the thought of giving up Gabriel it seemed there was nothing else for which she cared, nothing on earth.

She conjured up not only ghosts but absurdities. The shabby peering man would go to Hampstead, question Gabriel's silly sister, *be shown letters*. This was more than she could bear. On the last occasion letters of hers had been read in court; love letters to James! She cringed in her bed at the remembrance of them. And what had she written to Gabriel? Not one word came back to her of anything she had written. At first she knew they had been laboured letters, laboured or literary. But since she had been down here, and Peter Kennedy, by sheer force of contrast, had taught her how much she could care for a really good and clever man, she had written with entire unrestraint, freely.

She wrote that telegram to Gabriel Stanton at four o'clock in the morning, going down to the drawing-room for a telegram form in dressing-gown and slippers, her hair in two plaits, shivering with cold and apprehension. The house was full of eerie sounds; she heard pursuing feet. After she had secured the forms she rushed for the shelter of her room and the warmth of her bed; cowering under the clothes, not able for a long time to do the task she had set herself. When she became sufficiently rested she took more time and care over the wording of her telegram to Gabriel than she might have done over a sonnet. She wanted to say just enough, not too much, not to bring him down, yet to make the matter urgent. Stevens was rung for at six o'clock for tea and perhaps sympathy.

"Get me a cup of tea as quickly as you can, I've been awake the whole night. I want this telegram sent off as soon as the office opens, not later anyway than eight o'clock. Keep the house as quiet as you can. I shall try and sleep now."

She slept until Gabriel's telegram came back.

One of our own men coming with package by 3.15.

She met the train, looking pale and wretched. Stanton's man wore the familiar cap. She had been to the office two or three times about the pottery book, and he recognised her easily.

"You have a parcel for me?"

"Mr. Gabriel said I was to tell you there was a letter inside."

"A letter! But I thought ... oh, yes! Give it to me."

"And I was to ask if there was an answer."

"An answer, but I can't write here!"

"He didn't know you was meeting me. 'Go up to the house,' he said; 'give it to her in her own hands. Ask if there is any answer.'"

"Tell him ... tell him I'll write," she said vaguely.

But as yet she had not read. What would he say, what comfort send her? For all her wired definiteness she wished he had come himself, had a moment's disloyalty to him, thought he should have disregarded her wishes, rushed down, even if they had met only at the station. He need not have been so punctilious!

She could not let the man go back until she had read and answered Gabriel's letter. She made him drive back with her to Carbies, seated on the box beside the driver. She held the precious package tight, but did not open it. For that she must be alone.

Stanton's man was handed over to the household's care for lunch or tea. He was to go back by the 5.5. "Mr. Gabriel" had given him his instructions.

Now she was at her writing-table and alone. The packet was sealed with sealing-wax. Inside there were all her own letters, and a closed envelope superscribed in the dear familiar handwriting. She tore it open. After she had read her lover's letter she had no more reproaches for him, vague or otherwise.

My Own, my Beloved:—

Here are the letters. I could refuse you nothing, but to part from these has overwhelmed me, weakened me. I have turned coward. For it is all so unknown. I am in the dark, bewildered. Your wire was an awful shock. I am haunted with terror, the harder to bear because it came in the midst of all the sweet sacred thoughts and remembrances of a wonderful week-end, of the things you said or allowed me to say which filled me with high hopes, promise of joy and happiness I dared hardly dwell upon. I don't know what has happened. I only know you must not be alone and have forbidden me to come to you. Rescind your decision, I implore you. As I think and think with restless brain and heart my great ache and anxiety are that you are in trouble and that I am away and useless, just when I would give my soul for the chance of standing by you and with you in any need and for always. By all the remembrance of our happy hours, by all the new and sweet happiness you have given me, by all I yearn for in the future give me this chance. Let me come to you. To think of you suffering alone is maddening. Trust me, give me your trust, solemnly I swear not to fail you whatever may happen. It is of you only I am thinking. I can be strong for *you*, wise for *you*, and should thank God, both in pride and humbleness, for the chance to serve you; to serve you with reverence and love. *Send for me.* Tell me—let me share all and always.

Devotedly yours,

       G. S.

She sat a long time with the letter in her hand, read it again and yet again. She forgot the night terrors, began to question herself. Of what had she been so frightened? What had Stevens told her? Only that a shabby man had questioned cook about their visitors. Now she wanted to analyse and sift the trouble, get to bedrock with it. She rang the bell and sent for the maids. They had singularly little to tell her; summarised it came to this: A shabby man had hung about Carbies all Monday; cook had called him up to the back door and asked him what he was after—"No good, I'll be bound," she told him. He had paid her a compliment and said that "with her in the kitchen it was no wonder men 'ung about." And after that they seemed to have had something of a colloquy and cook had been asked if she walked out with anybody. "Like his nasty impidence," she commented, when telling the story to her mistress. "I up and told him whether I walked out with anybody or not I wasn't for the likes of him."

It was not without question and cross-question Margaret elicited that this final snub was not given until after tea. Cook defended the invitation.

"It's 'ard if in an establishment like this you can't offer a young man a cup of tea." She complained, not without waking a sympathetic echo in Margaret's own heart, that Pineland was that dull, not a bit o' life in it. Married men came round with the carts and a girl delivered the milk.

"'E was pleasant company enough till 'e started arskin' questions."

Then it appeared it was Stevens who "gave him as good as he gave," asking him what it was he did want to know, and being satirical with him. The housemaid had chimed in with Stevens; there may have been some little feminine jealousy at the back of it. Cook was young and frivolous, the two others more sedate. Stevens and the housemaid must have set upon cook and her presumed admirer. In any case the young man was given his congé immediately after tea, before he had established a footing. Stevens' report had been exaggerated, Margaret's terror excessive and unreasonable. She dismissed the erring cook now with the mildest of rebukes, then set herself to write to Gabriel. The time was limited, since the man was returning by the 5.5. She heard later, by the way, that he quite replaced the stranger in the cook's facile affections. Stevens again was responsible for the statement that cook was "that light and talked away to any man." Contrasting with herself, Stevens, who "didn't 'old with making herself cheap."

Margaret wrote slowly, even if it were only a letter. She had to recall her mood, to analyse the panic. She was quite calm now. *His* letter seemed exaggerated beyond what the occasion or the telegram demanded.

Dearest:—

How good you are, and safe. Your letter calmed and comforted me. Panic! no other word describes my condition at four o'clock this morning after a sleepless night. Servants' gossip was at the bottom of it. I have always wished for a dumb maid, but Stevens' tongue is hung on vibrating wires, never still. There *was* a man, it seems now he was a suitor of cook's! He *did* ask questions, but chiefly as to her hours off duty, whether she was already "walking out," an expression for an engagement on probation, I understand. He was an aspirant. I cannot write you a proper letter, my bad night has turned me into a wreck, a "beautiful ruin" as you would say. No, you wouldn't, you are too polite. You must take it then that all is well; except that your choice has fallen upon a woman easily unnerved. Was I so foolish after all? James is capable of any blackguardism, he would hate that I should be happy with you. He can no longer excuse his conduct to me, or my resentment of it on the plea that I am unlike other women. I know his mind so well! "Women of genius have no sex," he said among other things to account for the failure of our married life. He can say so no longer. "Women of genius have no sex!" *It isn't true.* Do you see me reddening as I write it? What about that little house in Westminster? Have you written to all the agents? Are you searching? Sunday night I was so happy. One large room there must be. Colour prints on the walls and chintz on the big sofas, my Staffordshire everywhere, a shrine somewhere, central place for the musicians; cushions of all shades of roses, some a pale green. I can't *see* the carpets or curtains yet. I incline to dark green for both. No, I am not frivolous, only emotional. I think I shall alter when we are together, begin to develop and grow uniform in the hothouse of your love, under the forcing glass of your great regard. It is into that house, under that glass I want to creep, to be warmed through, to blossom.

Picture me then as no longer unhappy or distressed, although all day I have neither worked nor played.

Your letter healed me; take thanks for it therefore and come down Saturday as usual, with a plan of the house that is to be. (By the way, I *must* have dog stoves.) In a few days now I, or you, will tell my father and stepmother. The days crawl, each one emptier than the other, until the one that brings you. *Arrivederci.*

She sent it, but not the old ones back. She wanted to read them again, it would be an occupation for the evening. She would place them in order, together with his answers. She saw a story there. "The Love Tale of a Woman of Genius." After all, both she and Gabriel were of sufficient interest for the world to wish to read about them. (It was not until a few days later, by the way, that the title was altered, others tried, that the disingenuous diary began, the MS. started.)

She slept well that night and wrote him again in the morning, the most passionate love-letter of any of the series. Then she sent for Peter Kennedy. Wednesday, Thursday, and Friday had to be got through. And then another week, and one other. And Safety, safety with Gabriel!

Peter came hot-foot like a starving animal. It was five days since he had seen her, and he looked worn and cadaverous. She gave him an intermittent pulse to count, told him she had had a sleepless night, found herself restless, unnerved, told him no more. He was purely professional at first, brusquely uneasy about her, blaming her for all she had done and left undone, the tonic she had missed, the unrest to which she admitted. After that they found little more to say to each other, though Peter could not tear himself away.

She talked best to Peter through the piano, as he to her. Even in these few weeks his playing had enormously improved. The whole man had altered. She had had more and different effect upon him than would have seemed possible at first. He had never been in love before, only known vulgar intrigue, how to repel the glad-eye attentions of provincial maidens to whom his size was an attraction, and his stupidity no deterrent. This was something altogether different, and in a measure he had grown to meet it, become more ambitious and less demonstrative, perceptibly humbler. She knew he loved her but made light of it. He filled up the hours until Gabriel would come again. That was all. But less amusingly now that she had less difficulty in managing him. This mutual attraction of music slurred over many weak places in their intercourse.

Wednesday he sat through the afternoon, stayed on to dinner playing to her and listening. Thursday he paid her a professional visit in the morning, would have sounded her heart but that his stethoscope was unsteady, and he heard his own heartbeats louder and more definitely than hers. Thursday evening he ran up on his bicycle to see if she was all right. There was more music, and for all his newly found self-restraint a scene at parting, a scene that troubled her because she could not hold herself guiltless in bringing it about, and Gabriel was in her mind now to the exclusion of any other man. Gabriel had won solidly that which at first was little more than an incitement, an inclination.

Gabriel Stanton would not have made love to another man's fiancée. His standard was higher than her own, just as his scholarship was deeper and more profound. She was proud that he loved her, simpler and more sincere than she had ever been before.

Tonight, when Peter Kennedy broke down, and cried at her feet and told her that his days were hell and all his nights sleepless, she was ashamed and distressed, much more repelled than attracted. She told him she would refuse to see him, that she would not have him at the house at all if he could not learn to behave himself.

"You are a disgrace to your profession," she said crossly, knowing she was not blameless.

"You do not really think so, do you?" he asked. "I can't help being in love with you."

"Yes, I do. You have given me a pain."

When she said that and pressed both hands over her heart his whole attitude changed. It was true that under the influence of his love his skill had developed. Her lips grew pale and her eyes frightened. He made her lie down, loosened her dress, gave her restoratives. The pain had been but slight, and she recovered rapidly.

"It was entirely your fault," she said when she was able to speak. "You know I can't bear any agitation or excitement."

"The last you'll have through me, I swear it. You can trust me."

"Until the first time the spirit moves you." She never had considered his feelings and did not pause to do so now. "You've no self-control. You dump your ungainly love upon me...."

"And you throw it back in my face with both hands, as if it were mud. But you'll never have another chance, never...."

She was a little sorry for him, and to show it reproached him more.

"Why do you do it, then? You know that, as far as I can be, I am engaged to Gabriel Stanton, that the moment the decree is made absolute we shall be married. Perhaps I ought not to have let you come so often...."

"I fell in love with you the very first moment I saw you. If I'd never seen you again it would have been the same thing. And you've nothing to reproach yourself with. You've made a different man of me. I play better."

"And your taste in music has improved." He looked so forlorn standing up and saying he played the piano better since he had known her, that she regretted the cruelty of her words. He had relieved her pain not once but many times. Instead of sending him away, as she had intended, she kept him with her until quite late. She let him tell her about himself; and what a change his love for her had brought into his life, and there was nothing he would not do, nor sacrifice for her. He said, humbly enough, that he knew she could never, never have cared for such a man as himself.

"Stanton has been to a public school and university, is no end of a swell at classics. I got what little education I have at St. Paul's and the London University, walked the hospitals and thought well of myself for doing it, that I was coming up in the world. My father was a country dentist. I've studied more, learnt more since you've been here than in all my student days. You've opened a new world to me. I didn't know there were women like you. After the girls I've met! You were such a ... lady, and all that. You are so clever too, and satirical, I don't mind you being down on me. It isn't as if you were strong."

She smiled and asked him whether her delicacy was an additional charm.

"Well, yes, in a way it is. I can always bring you round. I want you to go on letting me be your doctor. You hardly had that pain a minute tonight. It is angina, you know, genuine *angina pectoris*, and I can do no end of things for it."

"You don't mean I must always have these pains, that they will grow worse?" She grew pale and he saw he had made a mistake, hastening to reassure her.

"You've only got to live quietly, take things easily."

"Oh, that will be all right. When I am married everything will be easy," she said almost complacently. And then in plaintive explanation or apology added, "I bear pain so badly."

"And I may go on doctoring you?"

"I don't suppose I shall send to Pineland if I should feel not quite well," she answered seriously. "We are going to live in London."

"I'll come up to London. There is no difficulty about that. I've started reading for my M.D. I can get back to my old hospital." She rallied him a little and then sent him away.

"I shall expect to hear you are house physician when I return from my honeymoon!"

"May I come up in the morning? I want to hear that attack has not recurred."

"The morning is a long way off, the night has to be got through first." Suddenly she remembered her panic and had a faint recrudescence of fear. "I've so many things on my mind. I wish you could ensure me a good night."

"But I can," he said eagerly. "I can easily."

"And without after-effects?"

"Without any bad after-effects."

"The bromide! but it always makes me feel dull and stupid."

"Veronal?"

"I am frightened of veronal."

"Adolin, paraldehyde, trional, a small injection of morphia?"

"But it is so late. You would have to get anything from a chemist."

"No, I shouldn't. I've got my case."

"Your case!"

"Yes." He showed it to her, full of strange little bottles and unknown drugs. She showed interest, asking what was this or the other, then changing her mind suddenly:

"No, I won't try any experiments. I'll sleep, or I'll stay awake."

"You don't trust me?"

"Indeed I do, but I distrust drugs. Unless I am in pain, then I would take anything. Tell me, can you really always help me if I get into pain? Would you? At any risk?"

"At any risk to myself, not at any risk to you. But we won't talk of pain, it mustn't happen."

"But if it did?" she persisted.

"Don't fear, I couldn't see you in pain."

"Yet I've always heard and sometimes seen how callous doctors are."

"But I'm not only a doctor...."

"Hush! I thought we had agreed you were. My very good and concerned doctor. Now you really must go. Yes, you can come up in the morning."

"You will take your bromide?"

"If I need it. Good-night!"

Margaret slept well. But she heard from Stevens again next morning over her toilette that cook was not to be trusted, should be got rid of, that she was deceitful, had been seen, after all, with the shabby man from London.

"She took her oath that she'd never mentioned you to him, you nor your visitors, only Dr. Kennedy who attends you. But I'd not believe her oath. A hat with feathers she had on, and a ring on her finger when she went out with him. Such goings-on are not fit for a respectable Christian house, and so I told her."

Margaret listened inattentively, and irritably. She did not want ever to think again of that shabby man or her own unreasoned fears. She bade the maid be silent, attend to her duties. Stevens sniffed and grumbled under her breath. Afterwards she asked if the doctor were coming up again this morning.

"Why?"

"He might want to sound you. You'd best have your Valenciennes slip."

"Don't be so absurd."

Nevertheless the query set her thinking of Peter Kennedy and his love for her. Desultory thinking connects itself naturally with a leisurely toilette. She was sorry for Peter and composed phrases for him, comforting noncommittal phrases. She thought it would do him good to get to London, his ideas wanted expanding, his provincialisms brushed off. She was under the impression she would do great things for Peter one day, let him into her circle; that salon she and Gabriel would hold. Her father should consult him, she would help him to build up a practice.

When he came up, later on, she told him something of her good intentions. They did not interest him very much, it was not service he wanted from her. He heard her night had been good, that she felt rested and better this morning. He had not been told what had disturbed the last one. They were sitting together in the drawing-room, doctor and patient, when the parlourmaid came in with a card. Margaret looked at it and laughed, passed it over to him.

"That's Anne," she said. "Anne evidently thinks I am a hopeful subject."

The card bore the name of "Mrs. Roope, Christian Healer."

"Stay and see her with me," she said to Peter. "It will be almost like a consultation, won't it?... Yes," she told the parlourmaid, "I will see the lady. Let her come up. Now, Peter Kennedy, is opportunity to show your quality, your tact. I expect to be amused, I want to be amused."

Peter was not loath to stay, whatever the excuse.

Mrs. Roope, tall, and dressed something like a hospital nurse, in long flowing cloak and bonnet with veil, was ushered in, but delayed a little in her greeting, because that hysterical affection of the throat of which Anne had spoken, caught and held her, and at first she could only make uncanny noises, something between a hiccough and a bad stammer.

"I've come to see you," she said not once but several times without getting any further.

"Sit down," Margaret said good-naturedly. "This is my doctor. I would suggest you ask him to cure your affliction, only I understand you prefer your own methods."

"There is nothing the matter with me," said the Christian Scientist with an unavoidable contortion.

"So I see," said Margaret, her eyes sparkling with humour.

"I would prefer that this interview should take place without witnesses."

Margaret found that a little surprising, but even then she was not disturbed. There was no connection in her mind between Anne Stanton's healer and the shabby man who had wooed her cook.

"I have no secrets from this gentleman," she answered, her eyes still laughing. "He has no prejudice against you irregular practitioners. You can decide together what is to be done for me. He is my present physician."

"I had thought he was"—bupp, bupp, explosion—"your co-respondent."

When she said that Peter Kennedy looked up. He tingled all over and his forehead flushed. He made a step forward and then stood still. His instinct told him here was an enemy, an enemy of Margaret's. He looked, too, at Margaret.

"Your name is Gabriel Stanton."

"My name is Peter Kennedy."

Margaret's quick mind leapt to the truth, saw, and foresaw what was coming. She turned very pale, as if she had been struck. Peter Kennedy moved nearer to her.

"Shall I turn her out?" he asked.

Mrs. Roope fanned herself with her bonnet strings as if she had said nothing unusual.

"You had better see me alone," she said, not menacingly but as if she had established her point. To save repetition the rest of her conversation can be recorded without the affliction that retarded it.

"No," Margaret answered, her courage at low ebb. "Stay where you are," she said to Peter Kennedy.

"You don't suppose I am going, do you?" he asked. Mrs. Roope, after a glance, ignored him.

"Perhaps you are not aware that you have been under observation for some time. My call on you is one of kindness, of kindness only. James Capel is my husband's cousin."

At the name of James Capel Margaret gave a little low cry and Peter Kennedy sat down by her side, abruptly.

"We heard you were being visited by Gabriel Stanton and a watch was set upon you. Your decree is not yet made absolute. It never will be now, if the King's Proctor is informed. James, I know, does not wish for a divorce from you."

Margaret sat very still and speechless,—any movement, she knew, might bring on that sickening pain. Peter too realised the position, although he had so little to guide him.

"Answer her. Don't let her think you are afraid. It's blackmail she's after. I am sure of it," he whispered to his patient. Thus strengthened Margaret made an effort for self-control. Peter saw then that the fear was not as new to her as it was to him.

"So it is you who have been having this house watched? Is it perhaps your husband who has been making love to my cook?" Since Peter Kennedy was here she would not show the cold fear at her heart. Mrs. Roope was not offended. She had been kicked out of too many houses by irate fathers, brothers, and husbands to be sensitive.

"No, that is not my husband. The gentleman who has been here is my nephew. As for making love to your cook, I will not admit it. I suggested your maid."

"If she had only sent her husband instead of coming herself. One can talk to a man."

Peter might have been talking to himself. He had risen and now was walking about the room on soft-balled feet like a captive panther.

"You don't know our religion, our creed. We have the true Christian spirit and desire to help others. The sensual cannot be made the mouthpiece of the spiritual. Sensuality palsies the right hand and causes the left to let go its divine grasp. That is why I interfere, for your own good as we are enjoined. Uncleanliness must lead to the body's hurt, in so far as it can be hurt. But mind and matter being one, what hurts the one will hurt the other."

"You can cut the cackle and come to the horses," Peter interrupted rudely. He had summed up the situation and thought he might control it. To him it was obvious the woman was a common blackmailer, although she had formulated no terms. "You are making a great deal of the fact that Mr. Stanton has been down here two or three times. I suppose you know he is Mrs. Capel's publisher."

"Do not interfere, young man. You are a member of a mendacious profession. I am not here to speak to you. I know Gabriel Stanton slept in the house," she said to Margaret.

"What then? Show us your foul mind, if you dare."

"There is no mind...."

"Oh! damn your jargon. What have you come here for? What do you want?" He stopped opposite to her in his restless walking. There shot a gleam of avarice into her dull eye.

"Is he your mouthpiece?" she asked Margaret, who nodded her assent. "I want nothing for myself."

"For whom, then?"

"The labourer is worthy of his hire.... Our Church...."

"You call it a church, do you? And you are short of cash. There are not enough silly women, half-witted men. You want money...."

"For the promulgation of our tenets." She interrupted. "Yes, we need money for that, for the regeneration of the world."

"And to keep your own house going."

"Your insults do not touch me. I am uplifted from them. Nothing touches the true believer."

Margaret called him over to her and whispered:

"Find out whether James knows anything of this or whether she is acting on her own; what she really wants. I can't talk to her."

Mrs. Roope went on talking and spluttering out texts.

"Cannot you see that Mrs. Capel is ill?" he said angrily.

The Christian Healer was quick to take the opening he gave her.

"Sickness is a growth of error, springing from man's ignorance of Christian Science."

"Oh! more rot—rot—rot, *rot*! Shut it! What we want to know is if there is any one in this but yourself. We don't admit a word of truth in your allegations.

They are lies, and we have no doubt you know they are lies."

"Mrs. Capel will make her own deductions. What have you to do with it, young man?"

"I'll tell you what I have to do with it. I am here to protect this lady."

"Mr. Capel and his lawyer will understand."

"That isn't what you came down here to say."

"I knew that I should be guided. I prayed about it with my husband."

"A pretty sight! 'The Blackmailers' Prayer!' How it must have stank to Heaven! And this fellow here?"

"My nephew. An honourable young man, one of the believers."

"He would be. What's the proverb? *Bon sang ne peut pas mentir.* Well, for the whole lot of you, your prayerful husband, your honourable nephew, and yourself?"

"What is it you are asking me?"

"As you are here and not with James Capel it is fair to presume you've got your price. Mrs. Capel does not wish to argue or defend herself, she wants to be left alone. You don't know anything because there is nothing to know. But I daresay you could make mischief. What are you asking to keep your venomous mouth shut? There is no good beating about the bush or talking Christian Science. Come to the point. How much?"

"A thousand pounds!" They were both startled, but Peter spoke first.

"That be damned for a tale." A most unedifying dialogue ensued. Then Peter said, after a short whispered colloquy with Margaret:

"She will give you a hundred pounds, no more and no less. Come, close, or leave it alone. A hundred pounds! Take it or leave it."

Margaret would have interrupted. "I said double," she whispered. He translated it quickly:

"Not a farthing more, she says. She has made up her mind. Either that or clear out and do your damnedest."

Sarah Roope stood out for her price until she nearly exhausted his patience, would have exhausted it but that Margaret, terrified, kept urging and soothing him. Before the end Mrs. Roope said a word that justified him—and he put his two hands on her shoulders. He made no point now of her being a woman. There are times when a man's brutality stands him in good stead, and this was one of such occasions.

"Get out of that chair," he jerked it away from her. "Out of her presence. You'll deal with me, or not at all."

He slid his hands from her shoulders to under her elbows: the noises she made in her throat were indescribable, but her actual resistance was small.

"You are not to sit down in her presence."

"I prefer to stand."

"Nor stand either. Outside...." he bundled her towards the door, she tried to hold her ground, but he forced her along. "We've had nearly enough of you, very nearly enough. You wait outside that door. I'll have a word with Mrs. Capel and give you your last chance." She bup—ped out her remonstrance.

"I came here to do her a service. As Mrs. Eddy writes: 'Light and darkness cannot mingle.' I must do as I am guided, and I said from the first we should go to James Capel. Husband and wife should never separate if there is no Christian demand for it."

"Oh! go to hell!"

He shut the door in her face and came back to Margaret.

"You'd better let me get rid of her for you. I shouldn't pay her a brass farthing."

"I'd pay her anything, anything, rather than go through again what I went through before." She burst into tears.

"Oh! if that's the case ..." he said indecisively.

"Pay her what she wants."

"I can get her down a good bit." He had no definite idea but to stop her tears, carry out her wishes. In a measure he acted cleverly, going backward and forward between dining and drawing-room negotiating terms. Mrs. Roope said she had no wish to expose Mrs. Capel, and repeated, "I came here to do her a kindness."

In the end two hundred and fifty pounds was agreed upon, a hundred down and a hundred and fifty when the decree was made absolute, this latter represented by a post-dated cheque. Peter had to write the cheques himself, it was as much as Margaret could do to sign them. Her hands were shaking and her eyelids red, the sight swept away all his conventions.

"You've got to go to bed and stay there," he told her when he came back to her finally. He forgot everything but that she looked terribly ill and exhausted, and that he was her physician. "You need not have a minute's more anxiety. I know the type. She has gone. She won't bother you again. She's taken her hundred pounds. That's a lot to the woman who makes her money by shillings. That absent treatment business is a pound a week at the outside. There's a limited number of fools who pay for isolated visits. Did you see her boots? They didn't look like affluence! and her cotton gloves! She will have another hundred and fifty if nothing comes out, if she keeps her mouth shut until the 30th of May. You are quite safe. Don't look so woebegone. I ... I can't bear it."

He turned his back to her.

"What will Gabriel say?"

"The most priggish thing he can think of," he answered roughly.

"He doesn't look at things in the same way you do."

"Do you think I don't know his superiority?"

"Now you are angry, offended."

"You've done the right thing. You are not in the health for any big annoyance."

She was holding her side with both hands.

"I believe the pain is coming on again."

"Oh; no, it isn't." But he moved nearer to her. No contradiction or denial warded off the attack. She bore it badly too, pulse and colour evidencing her collapse. Hurriedly and perhaps without sufficient thought he rang for Stevens, called for hot water, gave her her first injection of morphia.

Stevens knew or guessed what had been going on, and took a gloomy view. Every one in the house knew of Mrs. Roope's visit.

"It will be the death of her."

"No, it won't," he said savagely. "You do what you are told."

"I 'ope I know my duty," she replied primly.

"I'm sure you do, but not the effect of a morphia injection," he retorted.

He said Stevens knew nothing of the effect of a morphia injection, but he was not quite sure of it himself in those days and with such a patient. The immediate effect was instantaneous. Margaret grew easier, she smiled at him with her pale lips:

"How wonderful," she said. He made her stay as she was for half an hour, then helped to carry her to bed. Stevens said she required no help in undressing her.

"You are not to let her do a thing for herself, not to let her move. Give her iced milk, or milk and soda...."

The afternoon was not so satisfactory, there were disquieting symptoms, and not the sleep for which he hoped. He suggested Dr. Lansdowne, but she would not hear of him being sent for. When night fell he found it impossible to leave her.

He walked up and down outside the house for a long time, only desisting when Margaret herself sent down a message that she heard his footsteps on the gravel and they disturbed her. The rest of the night he spent on the drawing-room sofa, running upstairs to listen outside her bedroom door, now and then, to reassure himself. Tomorrow he knew Gabriel would be there and he would not be needed. But tonight she had no one but himself. Wild thoughts came to him in the dawn. What if Gabriel Stanton were not such a good fellow after all? What if he were put off by the thought of a scandal and figuring as a co-respondent? He, Peter, would stick to her through thick and thin. She might turn to him, get to care.

But he had not an ounce of real hope. He was as humble as Gabriel by now, and the nearer to being a true lover.

CHAPTER XIII

Margaret was not a very good subject for morphia. True it relieved her pain, set her mind at rest, or deadened her nerve centres for the time. But when the immediate effect wore off she was intolerably restless, and although the bromide tided her over the night, she drowsed through an exhausted morning and woke to sickness and misery, to depression and a tendency towards tears. She was utterly unable to see her lover, she felt she could not face him, meet him, conceal or reveal what had happened. Dr. Kennedy came up and she told him exactly how she felt. She told him also that he must go to the station in her stead. She said she was too broken, too ill.

This unnerved and weakened Margaret distracted Peter, and he thought of every drug in the pharmacopœia in the way of a pick-me-up. He said that of course he would go to the station, go anywhere, do anything she asked him. But, he added gloomily, that he would probably blunder and make things worse.

"He would ever so much rather hear it from you if it must be told him," he urged. "He'll guess you are ill when you are not at the station. He'll rush up here and see you and everything will be all right. He has only got to see you."

Dr. Kennedy then begged her to go back to bed, but without effect. Fortunately the only drug to which he could ultimately persuade her was carbonate of soda! That and a strong cup of coffee helped to revive her. Stevens had the qualities of her defects and insisted later upon beef tea. Margaret, although still looking ill, was really almost normal when four o'clock came bringing Gabriel. Her plan of Peter Kennedy meeting him miscarried, and she need not have feared his anxiety when she was not at the station. Gabriel had caught an earlier train than usual. Ever since Tuesday his anxiety had been growing, notwithstanding her letters and reassurances.

He was dismayed at seeing Dr. Kennedy's hat in the hall. Little more so than Margaret was when she heard the wheels of the car on the gravel and learnt from Peter, at the window, that Gabriel was in it. They were unprepared for each other when he walked in. Yet if Peter had not been there all might still have been well. It was Dr. Kennedy's instinct to stand between her and trouble, and his misfortune to stand between her and Gabriel Stanton.

"You are ill?" and

"You are early?" came from each of them simultaneously. If the doctor had slipped out of the room they would perhaps have found more to say. But he stayed and joined in that short dialogue, thinking he was meeting her wishes.

"She has had an attack of angina, a pretty hot one at that. I gave her a morphia injection and it did not suit her. She is simply not fit for any emotion or excitement. As a matter of fact she ought not to be out of bed today."

"Has my coming by an earlier train distressed you?" Gabriel asked Margaret, perhaps a little coldly. Certainly not as he would have asked her had they been alone. Nor were matters improved when she answered faintly:

"Tell him, Peter."

Her lover wanted to hear nothing that Peter Kennedy might tell him. He was startled when she used his Christian name. He had a distaste at hearing his fiancée's health discussed, a sensitiveness not unnatural. From an older or more impersonal physician he might have minded it less; or from one who had not admitted to him, and gloried in the admission, that he was in love with his patient.

"I don't want to hear anything that Dr. Kennedy can tell me," was what he said, but it misrepresented his mind. It sounded sullen or ill-tempered, but was neither, only an inarticulate evidence of distress of mind.

"Surely, Margaret, your news can wait...." This was added in a lower tone. But Margaret was beyond, and Peter Kennedy impervious to hint. The only thing that softened the situation to Gabriel was that she made room for him on the sofa, by a gesture inviting him to seat himself there. Almost he pretended not to see it, he felt rigid and uncompromising. Nevertheless, after a moment's hesitation, he found himself beside her, listening to Dr. Kennedy's unwelcome voice.

"You knew, didn't you, that there had been a man hanging about the place, trying to get information from the servants? Margaret first heard of this last Tuesday...." Gabriel missed the next sentence. That the fellow should speak of her as "Margaret" made him see red. When his vision cleared Peter was still talking. There had been some allusion to or description of cook's weakness, and the discursiveness was a fresh offence.

"What she told him in her amorous moments we have no means of knowing, but that it included the information that you had stayed in the house there is not much reason to doubt. And down came this woman like a ton of bricks on

Wednesday morning and flung a bomb on us in the shape of a demand for a thousand pounds."

"What woman?"

"The man's employer. She had set him on to it."

"Who?"

"This blackmailing person."

The "us" tightened Gabriel's thin lips and hardened his deep-set eyes. Had they been alone he might have remembered what Margaret must have suffered, what a dreadful thing this visit must have been to her. As it was, and for the moment, he thought of nothing but of Peter Kennedy's intervention, interference.

"Why did you see her?" he asked Margaret.

"I thought she came from Anne," she faltered.

"From Anne!"

"She is the Christian Science woman," Peter explained.

And now indeed the full force of the blow struck him.

"Mrs. Roope?" he got out.

"No other," Peter answered. "Crammed choke-full of extracts from Mrs. Eddy. James Capel is her husband's cousin. At least so she says. And that he never wanted to be divorced from his wife, and would welcome a chance of stopping the decree from being made absolute. She said the higher morality bade her go to him. 'Husband and wife should never separate if there is no Christian demand for it,' she quoted. But help toward the Christian Science Church, or movement, she would construe as 'a Christian demand.' She asked for a thousand pounds! Mrs. Capel," this time for some unknown reason he said "Mrs. Capel" and Gabriel heard better, "was quite overwhelmed, knocked to pieces by her impudence. That's when I came on the scene. I told the woman what I thought of her; you may bet I didn't mince matters. And then I offered her a hundred...."

Gabriel got up suddenly, abruptly, his face flushed.

"You ... you offered her a hundred pounds?"

"Well! there was not a bit of good trying for less. It was a round sum."

"You allowed Mrs. Capel to be blackmailed!"

"What would you have done? Of course I did."

"It was disgraceful, indefensible."

"Gabriel." She called him by his name, she wanted him to sit down by her, but he remained standing. "There was no time to send for any one, ask for advice...."

"It was a case of 'your money or your life.' The woman put a pistol to our heads. 'Pay up or I'll take my tale to James Capel' was the beginning and end of what she said. I got her down finally to £250."

"You gave the woman, this infamous, blackmailing person, £250?"

"And cheap enough too. Wait a bit. I can guess what you are thinking. I'm not such a fool as you take me for. She only had a hundred in cash, the other is a post-dated cheque, not due until the decree is made absolute. Then I ran her out of the house."

"Who wrote those cheques?" The flush deepened, Gabriel could hardly control his voice.

"I wrote them and Mrs. Capel signed them. She was absolutely bowled over, it was as much as she could do to sign her name."

Gabriel was beside himself or he would not have spoken as he did.

"You did an infamous thing, sir, an infamous thing. You should have guarded this lady, since I was not here, sheltered her innocence. To allow oneself to be blackmailed is an admission of guilt. The way you sheltered her innocence was to advise her practically to admit guilt." He was choked with anger.

"Gabriel," she pleaded.

"My dear," never had he spoken to her in such a way, he seemed hardly to remember she was there, "I acquit you entirely. You did not know what you were doing, could not be expected to know. But *this* fellow, this blackguard...." He actually advanced a step or two toward him, threateningly. "Her good name was at stake, mine as well as hers, was and is at stake."

"And I saved it for you, for both of you. I've shut Mrs. Roope's mouth. You'll never hear a word more...."

"Not hear more?" Gabriel was deeply contemptuous. "Did you ever know a blackmailer who was satisfied with the first blood? You have opened the door wide to her exactions...."

"You are taking an entirely wrong view, you are prejudiced. Because you don't like me you blame me whether I am right or wrong."

"You don't know the difference between right and wrong."

"I wasn't going to have my patient upset," he said obstinately.

"Gabriel, listen to me, hear me. Don't be so angry with Peter. *I* wanted the woman paid to keep quiet. I insisted upon her being paid." And then under her breath she said, "There is such a little time more."

"There is all our lives," Gabriel answered in that deep outraged voice. "All our lives it will be a stain that money was paid. As if we had something to conceal."

His point of view was not theirs, neither Peter's nor Margaret's. They argued and protested, justifying themselves and each other. But it seemed to Gabriel there was no argument. When Margaret pleaded he had to listen, to hold himself in hand, to say as little as possible. Toward Peter Kennedy he was irreconcilable. "A man *ought* to have known," he said doggedly.

"He wanted to ward off an attack."

Dr. Kennedy went away ultimately, he had that amount of sense. By this time he was at least as antagonistic to Gabriel Stanton as Gabriel to him.

"Stiff-necked blighter! He'd talk ethics if she were dying. What does it matter whether it was right or wrong? Anyway, I got rid of the woman for her, set her mind at rest. I bet my way was as good as any *he'd* have found! Now I suppose he'll argue her round until she looks upon me as the villain of the play." In which, as the sequel shows, he wronged his lady love. "Insufferable prig!" And with that and a few more muttered epithets he went off to endure a hideous few days, fearing for her all the time, in the hands of such a man as Gabriel Stanton, whom he deemed hard and self-righteous.

But he need not have feared. The two men were poles apart in temperament, education, and environment. Circumstances aided in making them intolerant of each other. Their judgment was biased. Margaret saw them both more clearly than they saw each other. Her lover was the stronger, finer man, had the higher standard. And he was right, right this time, as always. Yet she thought sympathetically of the other and the weakness that led him to compromise. The Christian Scientist should not have been paid, she should have been prosecuted. Margaret saw it now,—she, too, had not seen it at the moment. She confessed herself a coward.

"But our happiness was at stake, our whole happiness. In less than three weeks now...."

Now that they were alone Gabriel could show his quality. The thing she had done was indefensible. And he had hardly a hope that it would achieve its object. He, himself, would not have done evil that good might come of it, submitted, admitted ... the blood rushed to his face and he could not trust himself even to think of what had practically been admitted. But she had done it for love of him to secure their happiness together. What man but would be moved by such an admission, what lover? He could not hold out against her, nor continue to express his doubts.

"Must we talk any more about it? I can't bear your reproaches. Gabriel, don't reproach me any more." She was nestling in the shelter of his arms. "You know why I did it. I wish you would be glad."

"My darling, I wish I could be. It was not your fault. I ought to have come down. You ought not to have been left alone, or with an unscrupulous person like this doctor."

"Peter acted according to his lights. He did it for the best, he thought only of me."

"His lights are darkness, his best outrageous. Never mind, I will not say another word, only you must promise me faithfully, swear to me that if you do hear any more of this woman, or of the circumstance, from this or any other quarter, you will do nothing without consulting me, you will send for me at once...."

Margaret promised, Margaret swore.

"I want to lean upon your strength. I have so altered I don't know myself. Love has loosened, weakened me. I am no longer as I was, proud, self-reliant. Gabriel, don't let me be sorry that I love you. I am startled by myself, by this new self. What have you done to me? Is this what love means—weakness?"

When she said she needed to lean upon his strength his heart ran like water to her. When she pleaded to him for forgiveness because she had allowed herself to be blackmailed rather than delay their happiness together, his tenderness overflowed and flooded the rock of his logic, of his clear judgment. His arms tightened about her.

"I ought to have come to you whether you said yes or no. I knew you were in trouble."

"Not any longer." She nestled to him.

"God knows...."

He thrust aside his misgivings later and gave himself up to soothing and nursing her. Peter Kennedy need have had no fear, but then of course this was a Gabriel Stanton he did not know.

Gabriel would not hear of Margaret coming down to dinner nor into the drawing-room. She was to stay on the sofa in the music room, to have her dinner served to her there. He said he would carve for her, not be ten minutes away.

"All this trouble has made me forget that I have something to tell you. No, no! Not now, not until you have rested."

"I can't wait, I can't wait. Tell me now, at once. But I know. I know by your face. It is about our little house. You have seen a house—our house!"

"Not until after dinner. I must not tell you anything until you have rested, had something to eat. You have been too agitated. Dear love, you have been through so much. Yes, I have seen the house that seems to have been built for us. Don't urge me to tell you now. This has been the first cloud that has come between us. It will never happen again. You will keep nothing from me."

"Haven't I promised? Sworn?"

"Sweetheart!" And as he held her she whispered:

"You will never be angry with me again?"

"I was not angry with you. How could I be?"

She smiled. She was quite happy again now, and content.

"It looked like anger."

"You focussed it wrongly," he answered.

After they had dined; she on her sofa from a tray he supervised and sent up to her, he in solitary state in the dining-room, hurrying through the food that had no flavour to him in her absence: he told her about the little house in Westminster that he had seen, and that seemed to fit all their requirements. It was very early eighteenth-century, every brick of it had been laid before Robert Adam and his brother went to Portland Place, the walls were panelled and the mantelpieces untouched. They were of carved wood in the drawing-room, painted alabaster in the library and bedrooms, marble in the dining-room only. It was almost within the precincts of the Abbey and there was a tiny courtyard or garden. Margaret immediately envisaged it tiled and Dutch. Gabriel left it stone and defended his opinion. There was a lead figure with the pretence of a fountain.

"I could hardly believe my good luck when first I saw the place. I saw you there at once. It was just as you had described, as we had hoped for, unique and perfect in its way, a real home. It needs very careful furnishing, nothing must be large, nor handsome, nor on an elaborate scale. I shall find out the history, when it was built and for whom. A clergy house, I think."

She was full of enthusiasm and pressed for detail. Gabriel had to admit he did not know how it was lit, nor if electric light had been installed. He fancied not. Then there was the question of bathroom. Here too there was a lapse in his memory. But that there was space for one he was sure. There was a powder room off the drawing-room.

"In a clergy house?"

"I am not sure it was a clergy house."

"Or that there *is* a powder room!"

"It may have been meant for books. Anyway, there is one like it on the next floor."

"Where a bath could be put?"

"Yes, I think so. I am not sure. You will have to see it yourself. Nurse yourself for a few days and then come up."

"For a few days! That is good. Why, I am all right now, tonight. There, feel my pulse." She put her hand in his and he held it; her hand, not her pulse.

"Isn't it quite calm?"

"I don't know ... *I* am not."

"I shall go up with you on Monday morning, or by the next train."

He argued with her, tried to dissuade her, said she was still pale, fatigued. But the words had no effect. She said that he was too careful of her, and he replied that it was impossible.

"When a man has been given a treasure into his keeping ..." She hushed him.

They were very happy tonight. Gabriel may still have had a misgiving. He knew money ought never to have been paid as blackmail. That the trouble should have come through Anne, Anne and her mad religion, was more than painful to him. But true to promise he said no further word. He had Margaret's promise that if anything more was heard he would be advised, sent for.

When he went back to the hotel that night he comforted himself with that, tried to think that nothing further would be heard. Peter Kennedy's name had not been mentioned again between them. He meant to persuade her, use all his influence that she should select another doctor. That would be for another time. Tonight she needed only care.

He had taken no real alarm at her delicate looks, he had lived all his life with an invalid. As for Margaret, there were times when she was quite well, in exuberant health and spirits. She was under the spell of her nerves, excitable, she had the artistic temperament *in excelsis*. So he thought, and although he felt no uneasiness he was full of consideration. Before he had left her tonight, at ten o'clock for instance, and notwithstanding she wished him to stay, he begged her to rest late in the morning, said he would be quite content to sit downstairs and await her coming, to read or only sit still and think of her. She urged the completeness of her recovery, but he persisted in treating her as an invalid.

"You are an invalid tonight, my poor little invalid, you must go to bed early. Tomorrow you are to be convalescent, and we will go down to the sea, walk, or drive. I will wrap you up and take care of you. Monday …"

"Monday I have quite decided to go up to town."

"We shall see how you are. I am not going to allow you to take any risks."

Such a different Gabriel Stanton from the one Peter Kennedy knew! One would have thought there was not a hard spot in him. Margaret was sure of it … almost sure.

The morphia that had failed her last night put out its latent power and helped her through this one. The dreams that came to her were all pleasant, tinged with romance, filled with brocade and patches, with fair women and gallant men in powder and knee-breeches. No man was more gallant than hers. She saw Gabriel that night idealised, as King's man and soldier, poet, lover, on the stairs of that house of romance.

The next day was superb, spring merging into summer, a soft breeze, blue sky flecked with white, sea that fell on the shore with convoluted waves, foam-edged, but without force. Everything in Nature was fresh and renewed, not calm, but with a bursting undergrowth, and one would have thought Margaret had never been ill. She laughed and even lilted into light song when Gabriel feared the piano for her. Her eyes were filled with love and laughter, and her skin seemed to have upon it a new and childish bloom, lightly tinged with rose, clear pale and exquisite. Today one would have said she was more child than woman, and that life had hardly touched her. Not touched to soil. Yet beneath her lightness now and again Gabriel glimpsed a shadow, or a silence, rare and quickly passing. This he placed to his own failure of temper yesterday, and set himself to assuage it. He felt deeply that he was responsible for her happiness. As she said, she had altered greatly since they first met. In a way she had grown younger. This was not her first passion, but it was her first surrender. That there was an unknown in him, an uncompromising rectitude, had as it were buttressed her love. She had pride in him now and pride in her love for him. For the first and only time in her life self was in the background. He was her lover and was soon to be her husband. Today they hardly held each other's hand, or kissed. Margaret held herself lightly aloof from him and his delicacy understood and responded. Their hour was so near. There had been different vibrations and uneasy moments between them, but now they had grown steady in love.

Margaret went up to town with Gabriel on Monday. She forgot all about Peter Kennedy eating his heart out and wondering just how harsh and dogmatic Gabriel Stanton was being with her. They were going first to see the house.

"I must show it you myself."

"We must see it together first."

They were agreed about that. Afterwards Margaret had decided to go alone to Queen Anne's Gate and make full confession. She had wired, announcing herself for lunch, asking that they should be alone. Then, later on in the day, Gabriel was to see her father. In a fortnight they could be married. Neither of them contemplated delay. The marriage was to be of the quietest possible description. She no longer insisted upon the yacht. Gabriel should arrange their honeymoon. They were not to go abroad at all, there were places in England, historic, quite unknown to her where he meant to take her. The main point was that they would be together ... alone.

The first part of the programme was carried out. The house more than fulfilled expectations. They found in it a thousand new and unexpected beauties; leaded windows and eaves with gargoyles, a flagged path to the kitchen with grass growing between the flags, a green patine on the Pan, which Margaret declared was the central figure in her group of musicians. Enlarged and piping solitary, but the same figure; an almost miraculous coincidence. A momentary fright she had lest it was all too good to be true, lest some one had forestalled them, would forestall them even as they stood here talking, mentally placing print and pottery, carpeting the irregular steps and slanting floors. That was Gabriel's moment of triumph. He had been so sure, he felt he knew her taste sufficiently that he need not hesitate. The day he had seen the house he had secured it. Nothing but formalities remained to be concluded. She praised him for his promptitude and he wore her praise proudly, as if it had been the Victoria Cross. A spasm of doubt may have crossed her mind as to whether her father and stepmother would view it with the same eyes, or would point out the lack of later-day luxuries or necessities; light, baths, sanitation. Gabriel said everything could be added, they had but to be careful not to interfere with the main features of the little place, not to disturb its amenities. Margaret was insistent that nothing at all should be done.

"We don't want glaring electric light. We shall use wax candles...." He put her into a cab before the important matter was decided. Privately he thought one bath at least was desirable, but he found himself unable to argue with her. Not just now, not at this minute when they came out of the home they would make together. Such a home as it would mean!

Mrs. Rysam was less reticent and Margaret persuadable, but that came later. Her father and stepmother were alone to lunch as she had asked them. And she broke her news without delay. She was going to marry Gabriel Stanton. There followed exclamation and surprise, but in the end a real satisfaction. The house of Stanton was a great one. More than a hundred years had gone to its upbuilding. Sir George was the doyen of the profession of publisher. He was the fifth of his line. Gabriel, although a cousin, was his partner and would be his successor. And he himself was a man of mark. He had edited, or was editing the Union Classics, and had contributed valuable matter to the Compendium on which the whole strength of the house had been employed for the last fifteen years, and which had already Royal recognition in the shape of the baronetcy conferred on the head of the firm.

"Of course it should have been given to Gabriel," Margaret said when she had explained or reminded them of his position. Naturally she thought this. They consoled her by predicting a similar honour for him in the future. Margaret said she did not care one way or the other. She did not unbare her heart, but she gave them more than a glimpse of it. That this time she was marrying wisely and that happiness awaited her was sufficient for them. Edgar B. looked forward to seeing Gabriel and telling him so. He promised himself that he would find a way of forwarding that happiness he foresaw for her. Giving was his self-expression. Already before lunch was over he was thinking of settlements. Mrs. Rysam, a little disappointed about the wedding, which Margaret insisted was to be of the quietest description, was compensated by talk about the house. Margaret might arrange, but her stepmother made up her mind that she would superintend the improvements. Then there were clothes. However quiet the wedding might be a trousseau was essential. From the time the divorce had been decided upon until now Margaret had had no heart for clothes. Her wardrobe was at the lowest possible ebb. Father and stepmother agreed she was to grudge herself nothing. And there was no time to lose, this very afternoon they must start purchasing, also installing workmen in The Close, for so the little house was named. A tremendous programme. Margaret of course must not go back to Pineland, but must stay at Queen Anne's Gate for the fortnight that was to elapse before the wedding. Margaret demurred at this, but thought it best to avoid argument. It was not that she had grown fond of Pineland, or that Carbies suited her any better than it did. But the atmosphere of Queen Anne's Gate was not a romantic one, and her mood was attuned to romance. Father and stepmother were material. Mr. Rysam gave her a cheque for five hundred pounds and told her to fit herself out properly. Mrs. Rysam promised house linen. Margaret could not but be grateful although the one spoke too much and shrilly, and the other too little and to the point.

"What is his income?" Edgar B. asked.

"That's what I've got to learn and see what's to be added to it to make you really comfortable."

"We shall want so little, Gabriel doesn't care a bit about money," Margaret put in hastily.

"I daresay not."

"And neither do I," she was quick to add. Edgar B. with a twinkle in his eye suggested she might not care for money but she liked what money could buy. He was less original than most Americans in his expressions, but unvaryingly true to type in his outlook.

What an afternoon they had, Margaret and her stepmother! The big car took them to Westminster and the West End and back again. They were making appointments, purchasing wildly, discussing endlessly. Or so it seemed to Margaret, who, exhilarated at first, became conscious towards the end of the day of nothing but an overmastering fatigue. She had ordered several dozens of underwear, teagowns, dressing-gowns, whitewash, a china bath, and electric lights! They appeared and disappeared incongruously in her bewildered brain. She had protected her panels, yet yielded to the necessity for drains. Her head was in a whirl and Gabriel himself temporarily eclipsed. Her stepmother was indefatigable, the greater the rush the greater her enjoyment. She would even have started furnishing but that Margaret was firm in refusing to visit either of the emporiums she suggested.

"Gabriel and I have our own ideas, we know exactly what we want. The glib fluency of the shopmen takes my breath away."

Mrs. Rysam urged their expert knowledge. Whatever her private opinion of the house, its size or position, she fell in easily with Margaret's enthusiasm.

"You must not risk making any mistake. Messrs. Rye & Gilgat or Maturin's, that place in Albemarle Street, they all have experts who have the periods at their fingers' ends. You've only got to tell them the year, and they'll set to work and get you chintzes and brocades and everything suitable from a coal scuttle to a cabinet...."

Margaret, however, although over-tired, was not to be persuaded to put herself and her little house unreservedly into any one's hands. She was not capable of effort, only of resistance. Tea at Rumpelmayer's was an interregnum and not a rest. More clothes became a nightmare, she begged to be taken home, was alarmed when Mrs. Rysam offered to go on alone, and begged her to desist. When the car took them back to Queen Anne's Gate, Gabriel had already left after a most satisfactory interview with her father. Edgar B., seeing his daughter's exhaustion and pallor, had the grace not to insist on explaining the word "satisfactory." He insisted instead that she should rest, sleep till dinnertime. The inexhaustible stepmother heard that Gabriel had been pleased with everything Margaret's father had suggested. He would settle house and furniture, make provision for the future. Whatever was done for Margaret or her children was to be done for her alone, he wanted nothing but the dear privilege of caring for her. Edgar appreciated his attitude and it did not make him feel less liberal.

"And the house? How about this house they've seen in Westminster? Is it good enough? big enough? He said it was a little house, but why so small?"

"They are just dead set on it. Small or large you won't get them to look at another. It's just something out of the way and quaint, such as Margaret would go crazy on. No bathroom, no drains, but a paved courtyard and a lead figure...."

"Well, well! each man to his taste, and woman too. She knows what she wants, that's one thing. She made a mistake last time and it has cost her eight years' suffering. She's made none this time and everything has come right. He's a fine fellow, this Gabriel Stanton, a white man all through. One might have wished him a few years younger, he said that himself. He's going on for forty."

"What's forty! Margaret is twenty-eight, herself."

"Well! bless her, there's a lifetime of happiness before her and I'll gild it."

"The drawing-room will take a grand piano."

"That's good."

"And I've settled to give her the house linen myself."

"No place for a car, I suppose. In an out-of-the-way place like that she'll need a car."

So they planned for her; having suffered in her suffering and eclipse, and eager now to make up to her for them, as indeed they had always been. Only in the bitter past it proved difficult because her sensitiveness had baffled them. It was that which had kept her bound so long. All that could be done had been done, to arrange a divorce *via* lawyers through Edgar B.'s cheque-book. But James Capel, when it came to the end, proved that he cared less for money than for limelight, and had defended the suit recklessly with the help of an unscrupulous attorney. The nightmare of the case was soon over, but the shadow of it had darkened many of their days. This wedding was really the end and would put the coping stone on their content.

Neither Edgar B. nor his wife heard anything of the attempt at blackmail. Gabriel, of course, did not tell them. Margaret, strange as it may sound, had forgotten all about it! Something had given an impetus to her feeling for Gabriel: and now it was at its flood tide. She had written once, "Men do not love good women, they have a high opinion of them." She would not have written it now, she herself had found goodness lovable. Gabriel Stanton was a better man than she had ever met. He was totally unlike an American, and had scruples even about making money.

Her father and he, discoursing one evening upon commercial morality, she found that they spoke different languages, and could arrive at no understanding. But she discovered in herself a linguistic gift and so saw through her father's subtlety into Gabriel's simplicity. She knew then that the man who enthralled her was the type of which she had read with interest, and written with enthusiasm, but never before encountered. An English gentleman! With this in her consciousness she could permit herself to revel in all his other attractions, his lean vigour and easy movements, shapely hands and deep-set eyes under the thin straight brows. His mouth was an inflexible line when his face was in repose. When he smiled at her the asceticism vanished. He smiled at her very often in these strange full days. The days hurried past, there was little time for private conversation, an orgy of buying held them.

Margaret, yielding to pressure and inclination, stayed on and on until the week passed and the next one was broken in upon. Now it was Tuesday and there was only one more week. One more week! Sometimes it seemed incredible. Always it seemed as if the sun was shining and the light growing more intense, blinding. She moved toward it unsteadily. This semi-American atmosphere into which she and her lover had become absorbed was an atmosphere of hustle, kaleidoscopic, shifting.

"If they had only given me time to think I should have known that the clothes and the house-linen, the carpets and curtains, the piano and the choice of a car, could all wait until we came back, could wait even after that. But they tear along and carry us after them in a whirlwind of tempestuous good-nature," Margaret said ruefully in the five minutes they secured together before dinner that Tuesday evening.

"You are doing too much, exhausting your energy, using up your strength.

And we have not found time for even one prowl after old furniture in our own way, that we spoke of at Carbies."

"They are spoiling the house with the talk of preserving it. Today Father told me it was absolutely necessary the floors should be levelled...."

"I know. And he wants the kitchen concreted. Some wretched person with the lips of a day-labourer and the soul of an iconoclast told him the place was swarming with rats...."

"We wanted to hear mysterious noises behind the wainscot."

They were half-laughing, but there was an undercurrent of seriousness in their complaining. They and their house were caught in the torpedo-netting of the parental Rysams' strong common sense. Confronted and caught they had to admit there was little glamour in rats and none at all in black beetles. Still ... concrete! To yield to it was weakness, to deny it, folly.

"I have lost sight of logic and forgotten how to argue. There is nothing for it but to run away again. Gabriel, I have quite made up my mind. Tomorrow, I am going back to Carbies. There are things to settle up there, arrange. Stevens is coming back with me, and we are going before anybody is up. Every day I have said that I must go, and each time Father and Mother have answered breathlessly that it was impossible, interposed the most cogent arguments. Now I am going without telling them."

"I am sure there is nothing else to be done. And stay until next week. Let me come down Saturday. We need quiet. I feel as if I had been in a machine room the last few days."

"'All day the wheels keep turning,'" she quoted.

"Yes, that expresses it perfectly. Run away and let me run after you. Saturday afternoon and Sunday we will be on the beach, listen to the sea, and forget the use of speech."

"The use and abuse of speech. I'll wear my oldest clothes. No! I won't. You shall have a treat. I really have some most exquisite things. I'll take them all down; change every hour or two, give you a private view...."

"You are lovely in everything you wear. You need never trouble to change. Think what a fatigue it will be. I want you to rest."

"How serious you are! I was not in earnest, not quite in earnest. But I can't wait to show you a teagown, all lacy and transparent, made of chiffon and mist...."

"Grey mist?"

"Yes."

"I love you in grey."

She laughed:

"You have had no opportunity of loving me in any other colour. Not indoors at least. But you will. I could not have a one-coloured trousseau. I've a wonderful beige walking-dress; one in blue serge, lined with chiffon...."

"Tell me of your wedding-dress. Only a week today...." Before she had told him her stepmother bustled in, her arms full of parcels that Margaret must unpack, investigate, try on immediately after dinner, or before. Dinner could wait. Margaret had already been tried on and tried on until her head swam. She yielded again and Gabriel and her father waited for dinner.

Nothing was as they had planned it. So, although they were too happy to complain, and too grateful to resent what was being done for them, the scheme that Margaret should return to Carbies without again announcing her intention was hurriedly confirmed between them and carried out.

This time Margaret did not complain that the place was remote, the garden desolate, the furniture ill-sorted and ill-suited. She was glad to find herself anchored as it were in a quiet back-water, out of the hurly-burly, able to hear herself breathe. Wednesday she spent in resting, dreaming. She went to bed early.

Thursday found her at her writing-desk, sorting, re-sorting, reading those early letters of hers, and of his; recapturing a mood. She recognised that in those early days she had not been quite genuine, that her letters did not ring as true as his. She saw there was a literary quality in them that detracted from their value. Yet, taking herself seriously, as always, and remembering the Brownings, she put them all in orderly sequence, made attempts at a title, in the event of their ever being published, wrote up her disingenuous diary. All that day, all Thursday and part of Friday, she rediscovered her fine style, her gift of phrase. The thing that held her was her own wonderful and beautiful love story. And it was of that she wrote. She knew she would make her mark upon the literature of the nineteenth century, had no doubt of it at all. She had done much already. She rated highly her three or four novels, her two plays. Unhappiness had dulled her gift, but today she felt how wondrously it would be revived. There are epigrams among her MS. notes.

"All his life he had kept his emotions soldered up in tin boxes, now he was surprised that they were like little fish, compressed and without life." This was tried in half a dozen ways but never seemed to please her.

"Happiness, true happiness, holds the senses in solution, it requires matrimony to diffuse them."

It seemed extraordinary now that she should have found content in these futilities. But it was nevertheless true. She came down to Carbies on Wednesday and it was Friday before she even remembered Peter Kennedy's existence, and that it would be only polite to let him know she was here, greatly improved in health, on the eve of marriage. Friday morning she telephoned for him. When he came she was sitting at her writing-table, with that inner radiance about her of which he spoke so often, her soft lips in smiling curves, her eyes agleam.

Peter had known she was there, known it since the hour she came. He had bad news for her and would not hurry to tell her, not now, when she had sent for him. In the presence of that radiance he found it difficult to speak. He could not bear to think it would be blurred or obscured. If the cruellest of necessities had not impelled him he would have kept silence for always.

CHAPTER XIV

"Are you glad to see me?"

"I am not sure," was an answer she understood.

"Surprised?"

"I know you have been down here since Wednesday."

"You knew it! Then why didn't you come and see me? You are very inattentive."

"I knew you would send if you wanted me." Now he looked at her with surprised, almost grudging admiration. "Your change has agreed with you; you look thundering well."

"Thundering! What an absurdly incongruous word. Never mind, I always knew you were no stylist. Yes, I am quite well, although from morning till night I did almost everything you told me not to do. I was in a whirl of excitement, tiring and overtiring myself all the time."

"I suppose I was wrong then. It seems you need excitement." He spoke with less interest than he usually gave to her, almost perfunctorily, but she noticed no difference and went on:

"The fact is I have found the elixir of life. There *is* such a thing, the old necromancers knew more than we. The elixir is happiness."

"You have been so happy?"

She leaned back in her chair, her eyes sought not him but the horizon. The window was open and the air was scented with the coming summer, with the fecund beauty of growing things.

"So happy," she repeated. "Incredibly happy. And only on the threshold...." Then she looked away from the sky and toward him, smiled.

"Peter, Peter Kennedy, you are not to be sour nor gloomy, you are to be happy too, to rejoice with me. You say you love me." He drew a long breath.

"You will never know how much."

"Then be glad with me. My health has revived, my youth has come back, my wasted devastated youth. I am a girl again with this added glory of womanhood. Am I hurting you? I don't want to hurt you, I only want you to understand, I can speak freely, for you always knew I was not for you. Would you like me to be uncertain, delicate, despondent? Surely not."

"I want you to be happy," he said unevenly.

"Add to it a little." She held out her hand to him. "Stay and have tea with me. Afterwards we will go up to the music room, I will give you a last lesson. Have you been practising? Peter, are you glad or sorry that we ever met? I don't think I have harmed you. You admit I roused your ambition, and surely your music has improved, not only in execution, but your musical taste. Do you remember the first time you played and sang to me? 'Put Me Among the Girls!' was the name of the masterpiece you rolled out. I put my fingers to my ears, but afterwards you played without singing, and you listened to me without fidgeting. Peter, you won't play 'Put Me Among the Girls' this afternoon, will you? What will you play to me when tea is over and we go upstairs?"

Peter Kennedy, with that strange uneasiness or lambent agony in his eyes, eyes that all the time avoided hers, answered:

"I shall play you Beethoven's 'Adieu.'"

"Poor Peter!" she said softly.

She thought he was unhappy because he loved and was losing her, because she was going to be married next week and could not disguise that the crown of life was coming to her. She was very sweet to him all that afternoon, and sorry for him, fed him with little cress sandwiches and pretty speeches, spoke to him of his talents and pressed him to practise assiduously, make himself master of the classical musicians. She really thought she was elevating him and was conscious of how well she talked.

"Then as to your profession, I am sure you have a gift. No one who has ever attended me has done me more good. I want you to take your profession very, very seriously. If it is true that you have the gift of healing and the gift of music, and I think it is, you will not be unhappy, nor lonely long."

And the poor fellow, who was really thinking all that time of the bad news and how to break it, listened to her, hearing only half she said. He did not know how to break his news, that was the truth, yet dared not leave it unbroken.

"When is Mr. Stanton coming down?" he asked her.

"Why do you dwell upon it? You have this afternoon, make the best of the time. I should like to think you were glad, not sorry we met."

He broke into crude and confused speech then and told her all she had meant to him, what new views of life she had given to him.

"You have been a perfect revelation to me. I had not dreamed a woman could be so sweet...." And then, stammeringly, he thanked her for everything. He was a little overcome because he was not sure this happiness of hers was going to last, that it would not be almost immediately eclipsed. He really did love her and in the best way, would have secured her happiness at the expense of his own, would have sacrificed everything he held dear to save her from what he feared was inevitable. He was miserably undecided, and could not throw off his depression. Not, as Margaret thought, because of his jealousy of Gabriel and ungratified love, but because he feared the wedding might never take place. He eat a great many hot cakes and sandwiches, drank two cups of tea. Afterwards in the music room he played Beethoven, and listened when she replied with Chopin. Or if he did not listen the pretence he made was good enough to satisfy her. She was secretly flattered, elated, at the effect she had produced, a little sorry for him, a little sentimental. "Why should a heart have been there in the way of a fair woman's foot?" she quoted to herself.

She sent him away before dinner. She had promised Gabriel she would keep early hours, rest, and rest, and rest until he came down on Saturday, and she meant to keep her promise. She gave Dr. Kennedy both her hands in farewell.

"I wish you did not look so woebegone. Say you are glad I am happy."

"Oh, my God!" he lost himself then, kissing the hands she gave him, speaking wildly. "If the fellow were not such a prig, if only your happiness would last...."

She drew her hands away, angry or offended.

"Last! of course it will last. Hush! don't say anything unworthy of you. Don't make me disappointed. I don't want to think I have made a mistake."

With something very like a groan he made a precipitate retreat. He could not tell her what he had come here to say, to consult her about, he would have to write, or wait until Stanton was there. He wanted her to have one more good night. He loved her radiance. She wronged him if she thought he was jealous of her happiness, or of Gabriel Stanton, although he wished so desperately and so ignorantly that her lover had been other than he was.

Margaret had her uninterrupted night, her last happy night. Peter Kennedy turned and tossed, and tossed and turned on his narrow bed, the sheets grew hot and crumpled and the pillow iron-hard, making his head ache. Towards morning he left his bed, abandoning his pursuit of the sleep that had played him false, and went for a long tramp. At six o'clock, the sun barely risen and the sea cold in a retreating tide, he tried a swim. At eight o'clock he was nevertheless no better, and no worse than he had been the day before, and the day before that. He breakfasted on husks; the bacon and eggs tasted little better. Then he read Mrs. Roope's letter for about the twentieth time and wished he had the doctoring of her!

Dear Dr. Kennedy:—

I am sorry to say that since I last saw you additional facts have come to my knowledge which in fairness to the purity which is part of the higher life I cannot ignore. That Mr. Gabriel Stanton had been visiting my cousin's wife during the six months in which she should have been penitently contemplating the errors and misdemeanours of her past, her failure in true wifeliness, I knew. That you had been passing many hours daily with her, and at unseemly hours, have also slept in her house, has only now come to my knowledge. I am nauseated by this looseness. Marriage should improve the human species, becoming a barrier against vice. This has not been so with the wife of my husband's cousin. As Mrs. Eddy so truly says "the joy of intercourse becomes the jest of sin." I return you the cheque you gave me and which becomes due next Wednesday. If neither you nor Mrs. Capel has any argument to advance that would cause me to alter my opinion I am constrained to lay the facts in my possession before the King's Proctor. Two co-respondents make the case more complicated, but my duty more simple.

Yours without any spiritual arrogance but conscious of rectitude,

SARAH ROOPE.

"Damn her!" He had said it often, but it never forwarded matters. Time pressed, and he had done nothing, or almost nothing. He had received the letter Wednesday. On Friday before going up to Carbies he had wired, "Am consulting Mrs. C. wait result."

The early morning post came late to Pineland. Dr. Kennedy had to wait until nine o'clock for his letters. As he anticipated on Saturday morning there was another letter from the follower of Mrs. Eddy:

Dear Dr. Kennedy:—

It is my duty to let you know that I have an appointment with James Capel's lawyer for Monday the 29th inst.

In desperation he wired back, "Name terms, Kennedy," and paid reply. There were a few patients he was bound to see. The time had to be got through somehow. But at twelve o'clock he started for Carbies. Margaret had not expected to see him again. She had said good-bye to him, to the whole incident. Her "consciousness of rectitude," as far as Peter Kennedy was concerned, was as complete as Mrs. Roope's. She had found him little better than a country yokel, and now saw him with a future before him, a future she still vaguely meant to forward—only vaguely. Definitely all her thoughts were with Gabriel and the hours they would pass together. She was meeting him at the station at three o'clock. She remembered the first time she had met him at Pineland station, and smiled at the remembrance. He might cut himself shaving with impunity now, and the shape of his hat or his coat mattered not one jot.

Not expecting Peter Kennedy, but Gabriel Stanton, she was already arrayed in one of her trousseau dresses, a simple walking-costume of blue serge, a shirt of fine cambric, and was spending a happy hour trying on hat after hat to decide not only which was most suitable but which was the most becoming. Hearing wheels on the gravel she looked out of the window. Seeing Peter she almost made up her mind not to go down. She had just decided on a toque of pansies ... she might try the effect on Peter. She was a little disingenuous with herself, vanity was the real motive, although she sought for another as she went downstairs.

Peter was in the drawing-room, staring vacantly out of the window. He never noticed her new clothes. She saw that in his eyes, and it quenched any welcome there might have been in hers. It was her expression he answered with his impulsive:

"I had to come!"

"Had you?"

"You mustn't be satirical," he said desperately. "Or be what you like, what does it matter? I'd rather have shot myself than come to you with such news...." Her sudden pallor shook him. "You can guess of course."

"No, I can't."

"That blasted woman!"

"Go on."

"She has written again. Sit down." She sank into the easy-chair. All her radiance was quenched, she looked piteous, pitiable. He could not look at her.

"I came up here yesterday afternoon, meaning to tell you. You were so damned happy I couldn't get it out."

"So damned happy!" she repeated after him, and the words were strange on her white lips, her laugh was stranger still and made him feel cold.

"You haven't got to take it like that; we'll find a way out. I suppose, after all, it's only a question of money...."

"I cannot give her more money."

"I've got some. I can get more. You know I haven't a thing in the world you are not welcome to, you've made a man of me."

"It is not because I haven't the money to give her." She spoke in a strange voice, it seemed to have shrunk somehow, there was no volume in it, it was small and colourless.

"I don't know how much she wants. I have wired her and paid a reply. I daresay her answer is there by now. I'll phone and ask if you like."

"What's the use?"

"Well, we'd better know."

"He said that is what would happen. That she would come again and yet again." She was taking things even worse than he expected. "He will never give in to her, never...." She collapsed fitfully, like an electric lamp with a broken wire. "Everything is over, everything."

"I don't see that."

She went on in that small colourless voice:

"I know. We don't see things the way Gabriel does. I promised to tell him, to consult him if she came again."

He hesitated, even stammered a little before he answered:

"He ... he had better not be told of this."

She laughed again, that little incongruous hopeless laugh.

"I haven't any choice, I promised him."

"Promised him what?"

"To let him know if she came back again, if I heard anything more about it."

"This isn't exactly 'it.' This is a fresh start altogether. I suppose you know how I hate what I am saying. The position can't be faced, it's got to be dodged. It's not only Gabriel Stanton she's got hold of...."

He did not want to go on, and she found some strange groundless hope in his hesitation.

"Not Gabriel Stanton?" she asked, and there seemed more tone in her voice, more interest. She leaned forward.

"Perhaps you'd like to see her letter." He gave it to her, then without a word went over to the other window, turned his face away from her. There was a long silence. Margaret's face was aflame, but her heart felt like ice. Peter Kennedy to be dragged in, to have to defend herself from such a charge! And Gabriel yet to be told! She covered her eyes, but was conscious presently that the man was standing beside her, speaking.

"Margaret!" His voice was as unhappy as hers, his face ravaged. "It is not my fault. I'd give my life it hadn't happened. That night you had the heart attack I did stay for hours, prowled about … then slept on the drawing-room sofa. Margaret...."

"Oh! hush! hush!"

"You must listen, we must think what is best to be done," he said desperately. "Let me go up to London and see her. I'm sure I can manage something. It's not ... it's not as if there were anything in it." His tactlessness was innate, he meant so well but blundered hopelessly, even putting a hand on her knee in the intensity of his sympathy. She shook it off as if he had been the most obnoxious of insects. "Let me go up and see her," he pleaded. "Authorise me to act. May I see if there is an answer to my telegram? I sent it a little before nine. May I telephone?"

"Do what you like."

"You loathe me."

"I wish you had never been born."

He was gone ten minutes … a quarter of an hour perhaps. When he came back she had slipped on to the couch, was lying in a huddled-up position. For a moment, one awful moment, he thought she was dead, but when he lifted her he saw she had only fainted. He laid her very gently on the sofa and rang for help, glad of her momentary unconsciousness. He knew what he intended to do now, and to what he must try to persuade her. Stevens came and said, unsympathetically enough:

"She's drored her stays too tight. I told her so this morning." But she worked about her effectively and presently she struggled back, seeming to have forgotten for the moment what had stricken her.

"Have I had another heart attack?" she asked feebly.

"No."

"I told you you were lacing too tight. I knew what would happen with these new stays and things." She actually smiled at Stevens, a wan little smile.

"I feel rather seedy still."

Peter took the cushion from her, made her lie flat. Then she said in a puzzled way, her mind working slowly:

"Something happened?"

There was little time to be lost and he answered awkwardly, abruptly:

"I brought you bad news."

She shut her eyes and lay still thinking that over. She opened them and saw his working face and anxious eyes.

"About Mrs. Roope," he reminded her. They were alone, the impeccable Stevens had gone for a hot-water bottle.

"What is it exactly? Tell me all over again. I am feeling rather stupid. I thought we had settled and finished with her?"

"She has reopened the matter, dragged me in." She remembered now, and the flush in his face was reflected in hers. "But it is only a question of money. I've got her terms."

"We must not give her money. Gabriel says...."

He would not let her speak, interrupting her hurriedly, continuing to speak without pause.

"The sum isn't impossible. As a matter of fact I can find it myself, or almost the whole amount. Then there's Lansdowne, he's really not half a bad fellow when you know him. And he's as rich as Crœsus, he would gladly lend it to me."

"No. Nonsense! Don't be absurd." She was thinking, he could see that she was thinking whilst she spoke.

"It's my affair as much as yours," he pleaded. "There is my practice to consider."

She almost smiled:

"Then you actually have a practice?"

"I'm going to have. Quite a big one too. Haven't you told me so?" He was glad to get the talk down for one moment to another level. "It would be awfully bad for me if anything came out. I am only thinking of myself. I want to settle with her once for all."

Her faint had weakened her, she was just recovering from it. Physically she was more comfortable, mentally less alert, and satisfied it should be so.

"Perhaps I took it too tragically?" she said slowly. "Perhaps as you say, in a way, it *is* your affair."

He answered her eagerly.

"That's right. My affair, and nothing to do with your promise to him. Then you'll leave it in my hands...."

"You go so fast," she complained.

"The time is so short; she can't have anything else up her sleeve. I funked telling you, I've left it so late." He showed more delicacy than one would have given him credit for and stumbled over the next sentences. "He would hate to think of me in this connection. You'd hate to tell him. Just give me leave to settle with her. I'll dash up to town."

"How much does she want?"

"Five hundred. I can find the money."

"Nonsense; it isn't the money. I wish I knew what I ought to do," she said indecisively. "If only I hadn't promised...."

"This is nothing to do with what you promised ... this is a different thing altogether."

He was sophistical and insistent and she was weak, allowed herself to be persuaded. The money of course must be her affair, she could not allow him to be out of pocket.

They disputed about this and he had more arguments to bring forward. These she brushed aside impatiently. If the money was to be paid she would pay it, could afford it better than he.

"I'm sure I am doing wrong," she repeated when she wrote out the cheque, blotted and gave it to him.

"He'll never know. No one will ever know."

Peter Kennedy was only glad she had yielded. He had, of course, no thought of himself in the matter. Why should he? In losing her he lost everything that mattered, that really mattered. And he had never had a chance, not an earthly chance. He believed her happiness was only to be secured by this marriage, and he dreaded the effect upon her health of any disappointment or prolonged anxiety. "Once you are married it doesn't matter a hang what she says or does," he said gloomily or consolingly when she had given him the cheque.

"Suppose ... suppose ... Gabriel *were* to get to know?" she asked with distended eyes. Some reassurance she found for herself after Peter Kennedy had gone, taking with him the cheque that was the price of her deliverance.

Would Gabriel be so inflexible, seeing what was at stake? The last fortnight in a way had drawn them so much closer to each other. They must live together in that house within the Sanctuary at Westminster. *Must.* Oh! if only life would stand still until next Wednesday! The next hour or two crushed heavily over her. She knew she had done wrong, that she had promised and broken her promise. No sophistry really helped her. But, whatever happened, she must have this afternoon and a long Sunday, alone with him, growing more necessary to him. Finally she succeeded in convincing herself that he would never know, or that he would forgive her when he did know, at the right time, when the time came to tell him.

She forced herself to a pretence at lunch. Then went slowly upstairs to complete her interrupted toilette. Looking in the glass now she saw a pale and distraught face that ill-fitted the pansy toque. She changed into something darker, more suitable, with a cock's feather. All her desire was that Gabriel should be pleased with her appearance, to give Gabriel pleasure.

"I haven't any rouge, have I, Stevens?"

"I should 'ope not."

"I don't want Mr. Stanton to find me looking ill."

"You look well enough, considering. He won't notice nothing. The carriage is here." Stevens gave her gloves and a handkerchief.

Now she was bowling along the quiet country road, on the way to meet him. The sky was as blue, the air as sweet as she had anticipated. On the surface she was all throbbing expectation. She was going to meet her lover, nothing had come between them, could come between them.

But in her subconsciousness she was suffering acutely. It seemed she must faint again when the train drew in and she saw him on the platform, but the feeling passed. Never had she seen him look so completely happy. There was no hint or suggestion of austerity about him, or asceticism. The porter swung his bag to the coachman. Gabriel took his place beside her in the carriage. A greeting passed between them, only a smile of mutual understanding, content. Nothing had happened since they parted, she told herself passionately, else he had not looked so happy, so content.

"We'll drop the bag at the hotel, if you don't mind."

"Like we did the first time you came," Margaret answered. His hand lay near hers and he pressed it, keeping it in his.

"We might have tea there, on that iron table, as we did that day," he said.

"And hear the sea, watch the waves," she murmured in response.

"You like me better than you did that day."

"I know you better." She found it difficult to talk.

"Everything is better now," he said with a sigh of satisfaction. It was twenty minutes' drive from the station to the hotel. He was telling her of an old oak bureau he had seen, of the way the workmen were progressing, of a Spode dinner service George was going to give them. Once when they were between green hedges in a green solitude, he raised the hand he held to his lips and said:

"Only three days more."

She was in a dream from which she had no wish to wake.

"You don't usually wear a veil, do you?" he asked. "There is something different about you today...."

"It is my new trousseau," she answered, not without inward agitation, but lightly withal. "The latest fashion. Don't you like it?" Now they had left the sheltering hedges and were within sight of the white painted hostelry.

"The hat and dress and everything are lovely. But your own loveliness is obscured by the veil. It makes you look ethereal; I cannot see you so clearly through it. Beloved, you are quite well, are you not?" There was a note of sudden anxiety in his voice. "It is the veil, isn't it? You are not pale?" She shook her head.

"No, it is the veil." They pulled up at the door of the hotel. There was another fly there, but empty, the horse with a nose-bag, feeding, the coachman not on the box.

"The carriage is to wait. You can take the bag up to my room," he said to the porter. Then turned to help Margaret.

"Send out tea for two as quickly as you can. The table is not occupied, is it?"

"There is a lady walking about," the man said. "I don't know as she 'as ordered tea. She's been here some time, seems to be waiting for some one."

"Oh! we don't want any one but ourselves," Margaret exclaimed, still with that breathless strange agitation.

"I'll see to that, milady." He touched his cap.

When they walked down the path to where, on the terrace overlooking the sea, the iron table and two chairs awaited them, Margaret said reminiscently:

"I sat and waited for you here whilst you saw your room, washed your hands...."

"And today I cannot leave you even to wash my hands."

The deep tenderness in his voice penetrated, shook her heart. He remembered what they had for tea last time, and ordered it again when the waiter came to them: Strawberry jam in a little glass dish, clotted cream, brown and white bread and butter. "The sea is calmer than it was on that day," he said when the waiter went to execute the order.

"The sky is not less blue," Margaret answered, and it seemed as if they were talking in symbols.

"How wonderful it all is!" That was his exclamation, not hers. She was unusually silent, but was glad of the tea when it came, ministering to him and spreading the jam on the bread and butter.

"Let me do it."

"No," she answered. When she drew her veil up a little way to drink her tea one could see that her lips were a little tremulous, not as pink as usual. Gabriel, however, was too supremely happy and content to notice anything. He poured out all his news, all that had happened since she left, little things, chiefly details of paper and paint and the protection of their property from her father and stepmother's destructive generosity.

"It will be all right. I had a chat with Travers." Travers was the foreman of the painters. "He will do nothing but with direct orders from us. The concrete in the basement won't affect the general appearance, we can put back the old boards over it. But I think that might be a mistake although the boards are very interesting, about four times as thick as the modern ones, worm or rat eaten through. They will make the pipes for the bath as little obtrusive as possible. The electric wire casings will go behind the ceiling mouldings. They are not really mouldings, but carved wood, fallen to pieces in many places. But I am having them replaced. Margaret, are you listening?"

She had been. But some one had come out of the hotel. Far off as they were she heard that turkey gobble and impedimented speech.

"You can tell Dr. Kennedy that I would not wait any longer. Tell him I have gone straight up to Carbies. I shall see Mrs. Capel."

"The lady from Carbies is here, ma'am; having tea on the terrace, that's her carriage."

Gabriel had not heard, he was so intent on Margaret and his news. The sea was breaking on the shingle, and to that sound, so agreeable to him, he was also listening idly, in the intervals of his talk. The strange voice in the distance escaped him. The familiar impediment was not familiar to him. Margaret was cold in the innermost centre of her unevenly beating heart.

"Are you listening?" he asked her, and the face she turned on him was white through the obscuring veil.

"I am listening, Gabriel."

"I will go down and speak to her," Mrs. Roope was saying to the waiter. "No, you need not go in advance."

Margaret's heart stood still, the space of a second, and then thundered on, irregularly. She had no plan ready, her quick brain was numbed.

"Mrs. Capel!"

Gabriel looked up and saw a tall woman conspicuously dressed as nun or nursing sister, in blue flowing cloak and bonnet. A woman with irregular features, large nose and coarse complexion. When she had said "Mrs. Capel" Margaret cringed, a shiver went through her, she seemed to shrink into the corner of the chair. "You know me. I wrote to Dr. Kennedy Wednesday and the letter required an immediate answer. Now I've come for it."

"He went up to London to see you," she got out.

"I shall have to be sure you are telling me the truth."

"You can ask at the station."

Gabriel looked from one to the other perplexedly. But his perplexity was of short duration, the turkey gobble and St. Vitus twist it was impossible to mistake. He intervened sharply:

"You are Mrs. Roope, my sister's so-called 'healer.' When Mrs. Capel assures you of anything you have not to doubt it." He spoke haughtily. "Why are you here?"

"You know that well enough, Gabriel Stanton."

"This is the woman who blackmailed you?" The "yes" seemed wrung from her unwillingly. His voice was low and tender when he questioned Margaret, quite a different voice to the one in which he spoke again to the Christian Scientist.

"How dare you present yourself again? You ought to have been given in charge the first time. Are you aware that blackmailing is a criminal offence?"

"I am aware of everything I wish. If you care for publicity my motive can stand the light of day."

"You ought to be in gaol."

"It would not harm me. There is no sensation in matter."

"You would be able to test your faith."

"Are you sure of yours?"

Margaret caught hold of his sleeve:

"Don't bandy words with her, Gabriel. She says things without meaning. Let her go. I will send her away." She got up and spoke quickly. "Dr. Kennedy has gone up to town to see you. To … take you what you asked. When he does not find you in London he will come straight back here. They will have told him, I suppose, where you have gone? He has the money with him."

"What are you saying, Margaret?" Gabriel rose too, stood beside her.

"Wait a minute. Leave me alone, I have to make her understand."

Margaret was in an agony of anxiety that the woman should know her claims had been met, that she should say nothing more before Gabriel. She did not realise what she was admitting, did not see the change in his face, the petrifaction.

"Why don't you go up to his house, wait for him there?" Then she said to Gabriel quickly and unconvincingly:

"This is Dr. Kennedy's affair. It was Dr. Kennedy for whom you were asking, wasn't it?" Mrs. Roope's cunning was equal to the occasion.

"It is Dr. Kennedy I have got to see," she said slowly.

"If he misses you in London he will get back as quickly as possible." Margaret's strained anxiety was easy to read. Afterwards Gabriel followed her, as she moved quickly toward the hotel.

"What has she got to do with Dr. Kennedy or he with her?" he asked then. Margaret spoke hastily:

"She sent back the post-dated cheque. It is all settled only they missed each other. Peter went up to town to find her and she misunderstood and came after him. He has the other cheque with him."

She was purposely incoherent, meaning him to misunderstand, hoping against hope that he would show no curiosity. Mrs. Roope came after them, planted herself heavily in their path.

"I'll give him until the last train."

"Telephone to your own house and you will find he has been there," Margaret said desperately. "Let me pass."

"You may go."

"Insolence!" But Margaret hurried on and he could not let her go alone.

"I will go into the drawing-room. Get the carriage up. We mustn't stay here...." She spoke breathlessly.

"You are not frightened of her?" He hardly knew what to think, that Margaret was concealing anything from him was unbelievable, unbearable.

"Frightened? No. But I want to be away from her presence, vicinity. She makes me feel ill...."

Margaret thought the danger was averted, or would be if she could get away without any more explanation. She had obscured the issue. Peter Kennedy would come back and pay all that was asked. Gabriel would never know that it was the second and not the first attempt at blackmailing from which they were suffering. But she underrated his intelligence, he was not at all so easily put off. He got the carriage round and put her in it, enwrapping her with the same care as always. He was very silent, however, as they drove homeward and his expression was inscrutable. She questioned his face but without result, put out her hand and he held it.

"We are not still thinking of Mrs. Roope, Gabriel?"

"Have you seen her since I was here last?" he asked.

"Not until she came up to us this afternoon." She was glad to be able to answer that truthfully, breathed more freely.

"Nor heard from her?"

"Nor heard from her."

"How did you know Dr. Kennedy had gone up to town to see her?"

"He told me so this morning. I ... I advised him to go."

"Was this morning the first time you saw him?"

"No, I saw him yesterday. Am I under cross-examination?" She tried to smile, speak lightly, but Gabriel sat up by her side without response. His face was set in harsh lines. She loved him greatly but feared him a little too, and put forth her powers, talking lightly and of light things. He came back to the subject and persisted:

"Why did she send back the post-dated cheque? Had she another given her?"

"I ... I suppose so."

"Why?"

"I don't like the way you are talking to me." She pouted, and he relapsed into silence.

When they got back to Carbies she said she must go up and change her dress. She was very shaken by his attitude: she thought his self-control hid incredulity or anger, found herself unable to face either.

He detained her a moment, pleaded with her.

"Margaret, if there is anything behind this ... anything you want to tell me...." She escaped from his detaining arm.

"I don't like my word doubted."

"You have not given me your word. This is not a second attempt, is it? Why did she force herself upon you? I shall see Kennedy myself tomorrow, find out what is going on."

"Why should there be anything going on? You are conjuring up ghosts...." Then she weakened, changed. "Gabriel, don't be so hard, so unlike yourself. I don't know what has come over you."

He put his arms about her and spoke hoarsely:

"My darling, my more than treasure. I can't doubt you, and yet I am riven with doubt. Forgive me, but how can you forgive me if I am wrong? Tell me again, tell me once and for always that nothing has been going on of which I have been kept in ignorance, that you would not, could not have broken your word to me. You look ill, scared.... I know now that from the moment I came you have not been yourself, your beautiful candid self. Margaret, crown of my life, sweetheart; darling, speak, tell me. Is there anything I ought to know?" He spoke with ineffable tenderness.

He was bending over her, holding her, her heart beat against his heart; she would have answered had she been able. But when her words came they were no answer to his.

"Darling, how strange you are! There is certainly nothing you ought to know. Let me go and get my things off. How strange that you should doubt me, that you should rather believe that dreadful woman. I have never seen her since you were down here last, nor heard from her...."

Her cheeks flamed and were hidden against his coat, she hated her own disingenuousness. It had been difficult to tell him, now it was impossible. "Let me go."

He released her and she went over to the looking-glass, adjusted her veil. She had burnt her boats, now there was nothing for it but denial and more denial. Thoughts went in and out of her aching head like forked lightning. *He would never know. Peter would arrange, Peter would manage.* It was a dreadful thing she had done, dreadful. But she had been driven to it. If the time would come over again ... but time never does come over again. She must play her part and play it boldly. She was trembling inside, but outwardly he saw her preening herself before the glass as she talked to him.

"I think we have had enough of Mrs. Roope. You haven't half admired my frock. I have a great mind not to wear my new teagown tonight. I should resent it being ignored. We ought to go out again until dinner, the afternoon is lovely. I can't sit on the beach in this, but I need only slip on an old skirt. Shall I put on another skirt? Do you feel in the humour for the beach? I've a thousand questions to ask you. I seem to have been down here by myself for an age. I have actually started a book! What do you say to that? I want to tell you about it. What has been decided about the door-plates? What did the parents say when they heard I'd fled?"

"I didn't see them until the next day."

"Had they recovered?"

"They were resigned. I promised to bring you back with me on Monday."

"And now you don't want to?"

"How can you say that?"

"Did I say it? My mood is frivolous, you mustn't take me too seriously. The beach ... you haven't answered about the beach. Perhaps you'd rather walk. I don't mind adventuring this skirt if we walk."

"You are not too tired?"

"How conventional!"

Something had come between them, some summer cloud or thunderstorm. Try as they would during the remainder of the day they could not break through or see each other as clearly as before. Margaret talked frivolously, or seriously, rallied, jested with him. He struggled to keep up with her, to take his tone from hers, to be natural. But both of them were acutely aware of failure, of artificiality. The walk, the dinner, the short evening failed to better the situation. When they bade each other good-night he made one more effort.

"You find it impossible to forgive me?"

"There is nothing I would not forgive you. That's the essential difference between us," she answered lightly.

"There is no essential difference; don't say it."

"The day has been something of a failure, don't you think? But then so was the day when you cut yourself shaving." She maintained the flippant tone. "That came right. Perhaps tomorrow when we meet we shall find each other wholly adorable again." She would not be serious, was light, frivolous to the last. "Good-night. Don't paint devils, don't see ghosts. Tomorrow everything may be as before. Kiss me good-night. Sleep well!" He kissed her, hesitated, kept her in the shelter of his arms:

"Margaret...." She freed herself:

"No. I know that tone. It means more questions. You ought to have lived in the time of the Spanish Inquisition. Don't you wish you could put me on the rack? There *is* a touch of the inquisitor about you. I never noticed it before.... Good-night!"

CHAPTER XV

Margaret slept ill that night. Round and round in her unhappy mind swirled the irrefutable fact that she had lied to her lover, and that he knew she had lied. Broken her promise, her oath; and he knew that she was forsworn. She passionately desired his respect; in all things he had been on his knees before her. If he were no longer there she would find the change of attitude difficult to endure. Yet in the watches of the night she clung to the hope that he could know nothing definitely. He might suspect or divine, but he could not know. She counted on Peter Kennedy, trusted that when the five hundred pounds were paid the woman would be satisfied, would go quietly away, that nothing more would ever be heard of her.

Wednesday next they were to be married. She told herself that if she had lost anything she would regain it then. Perhaps she would tell him, but not until after she had re-won him. She knew her power. If, too, she distrusted it, sensing something in him incorruptible and granite-hard, she took faint and feverish consolation by reminding herself that it was night-time, when all troubles look their worst. She resolutely refused to consider the permanent loss of that which she now knew she valued more than life itself. The possibility intruded, but she would not look.

In short snatches of troubled sleep she lived again through the scenes of the afternoon, saw him doubt, heard him question, gave flippant answers. In oases of wakefulness she felt his arms about her, and the restrained kisses that were like vows; conjured up thrilled moments when she knew how well he loved her. She began to dread those nightmare sleeps, and to force herself to keep awake. At four o'clock she consoled herself that it would soon be daylight. At five o'clock, after a desperate short nightmare of estrangement from which she awoke, quick-pulsed and pallid, she got up and put on a dressing-gown, drew up the blind, and opened wide the window. She watched the slow dawn and in the darkness heard the breakers on the stony beach. Nature calmed and quieted her. She began to think her fears had been foolish, to believe that she had not only played for safety but secured it, that the coming day would bring her the Gabriel she knew best, the humble and adoring lover. She pictured their coming together, his dear smile and restored confidence. He would have forgotten yesterday. The dawn she was watching illumined and lightened the sky. Soon the sun would rise grandly, already his place was roseate-hued. "Red sky in the morning is the shepherd's warning," runs the old proverb. But Margaret had never heard, or had forgotten it. To her the roseate dawn was all promise. The day before them should be exquisite as yesterday, and weld them with its warmth. She would withhold nothing from him, nothing of her love. Then peace would fall between them? and the renewal of love? At six o'clock she pulled down the blinds and went back to bed again, where for two hours she slept dreamlessly. Stevens woke her with the inevitable tea.

"It can't be morning yet? It is hardly light." She struggled with her drowsiness. "I don't hear rain, do I?"

"There's no saying what you hear, but it's raining sure enough, a miserable morning for May."

"May! But it is nearly June!"

"I'm not gainsaying the calendar."

"Pull up the blind."

A short time before she had gazed on a roseate dawn, now rain was driving pitilessly across the landscape, and all the sky was grey. No longer could she hear the breakers on the shore. All she heard was the rain. Stevens shut the window.

"You'd best not be getting up early. There's nothing to get up for on a morning like this. It's not as if you was in the habit of going to church." Margaret was conscious of depression. Stevens's grumbling kept it at bay, and she detained her on one excuse or another; tried to extract humour from her habitual dissatisfaction.

"It will be like this all day, you see if it isn't. The rain is coming down straight, too, and the smoke's blowing all ways." She changed the subject abruptly, as maids will, intent on her duties. "I'll have to be getting out your clothes. What do you think you'll wear?"

"I meant to try my new whipcord."

"With the wheat-ear hat! What's the good of that if you won't have a chance of going out?"

"One of my new tea-gowns, then?"

"I never did hold with tea-gowns in the morning," Stevens answered lugubriously. "I suppose Mr. Stanton will be coming over. Not but what he'll get wet through."

"I shouldn't be surprised if he came all the same." Margaret smiled, and the omniscient maid reflected the smile, if a little sourly.

"There's never no saying. There's that telephone going. Another mistake, I suppose. I wish I'd the drilling of them girls. Oh! I'm coming, I'm coming!" she cried out to the insensitive instrument. "Don't you attempt to get up till I come back. You're going to have a fire to dress by; calendar or no calendar, it's as cold as winter."

Margaret watched the rain driving in wind gusts against the window until Stevens came back. Somehow the rain seemed to have altered everything, she felt the fatigue of her broken night, the irritability of her frayed nerves.

"It's that there Dr. Kennedy. He wants to know how soon he may come over. He says he's got something to tell you. 'All the fat's in the fire,' he said. 'Am I to tell her that?' I arst him. 'Tell her anything you like,' he answered, 'but find out how soon I can see her.' Very arbitrary he was and impatient, as if I'd nothing to do but give and take his messages."

"Tell him I'm just getting up. I can be ready in half an hour."

"I shall tell him nothing of the sort. Half an hour, indeed, with your bath and everything, and no breakfast, and the fire not yet lit. Nor one of the rooms done, I shouldn't think...."

"Tell him I'll see him in half an hour," Margaret persisted. "Now go away, that's a good woman, and do as you are told. Don't stand there arguing, or I'll answer the telephone myself." She put one foot out of bed as if to be as good as her word, and Stevens, grumbling and astonished, went to do her bidding.

Half an hour seemed too long for Margaret. What had Peter Kennedy to tell her? Had he met or seen Mrs. Roope? "All the fat was in the fire." What fat, what fire? The phrase foreshadowed comedy and not tragedy. But that was nothing for Peter Kennedy, who was in continual need of editing, who had not the gift of expression nor the capacity of appropriate words. She scrambled in and out of her bath, to Stevens's indignation, never waiting for the room to be warmed. She was impatient about her hair, would not sit still to have it properly brushed, but took the long strands in her own hands and "twisted them up anyhow." Stevens's description of the whole toilette would have been sorry reading in a dress magazine or ladies' paper.

"Give me anything," she says, "anything. What does it matter? He'll be here any minute now. The old dressing-gown, or a shirt and skirt. Whichever is quickest. What a slowcoach you're getting!"

"Slowcoach! She called me a slowcoach, and from first to last it hadn't been twenty minutes."

Margaret, sufficiently dressed, but without having breakfasted, very pale and impatient, was at the window of the music room when Peter came up the gravel path in his noisy motor, flung in the clutch with a grating sound, pulled the machine to a standstill. There was no ceremony about showing him up. He was in the room before she had collected herself. He, too, was pale, his chin unshaved, his eyes a little wild; looking as if he, also, had not slept.

"You've heard what happened?" he began, abruptly.... "No, of course you haven't, how could you? What a fool I am! There's been a hell of a hullabaloo. That's why I telephoned, rushed up. You know that she-cat came down here?" He had difficulty in explaining his errand.

"Yes. I saw her, she waited for you at the hotel. Go on, what next?"

"I didn't get back until after nine o'clock. And then I found her waiting for me. The servants did not know what to make of her; they told me they couldn't understand what she said, so I suppose she talked Christian Science. Fortunately I'd got the cheque with me. I had not been able to change it, the London banks were all closed. She took it like a bird. Not without some of the jargon and hope that I'd mend my ways, give up prescribing drugs. You know the sort of thing. I thought I'd got through, that it was all over. The cheque was dated Saturday, she would be able to cash it first thing Monday morning. It was as good as money directly the banks opened. I never dreamt of them meeting."

"Who?" asked Margaret, with pale lips. She knew well enough, although she asked and waited for an answer.

"She and Gabriel Stanton. It seems she was too late for the last train and had to put up at the hotel...."

"At the King's Arms?"

"Yes. He met her there, or rather she forced herself on him. God knows what she had in her mind. Pure mischief, I suspect, though of course it may have been propaganda. It seems he came in about ten o'clock and went on to the terrace to smoke or to look at the sea. She followed him there, tackled him about his sister or his soul."

"How do you know all this?"

"Let me tell the story my own way. He met her full-face so to speak, wanted to know exactly what she was doing in this part of the world. Perhaps she didn't know she was giving away the show. Perhaps she didn't know he wasn't exactly in our confidence. There is no use thinking the worst of her."

"She knew what she was doing, that she was coming between us." Margaret spoke in a low voice, a voice of desperate certainty and hopelessness.

"Well, that doesn't matter one way or another, what her intentions were, I mean. I don't know myself what had happened between you and him. Although of course I spotted quick enough he'd had some sort of shock...."

"Then you have seen him!"

"I was coming to that. After his interview with her he came straight to me."

"To you! But it was already night!"

"I'd gone to bed, but he rang the night bell, rang and rang again. I didn't know who it was when I shouted through the tube that I'd come down, that I shouldn't be half a minute. When I let him in I thought he was a ghost. I was quite staggered, he seemed all frozen up, stiff. Just for a moment it flashed across me that he'd come from you, that you were ill, needed me. But he did not give me time to say the wrong things. 'Mrs. Roope has just left me,' he began. 'The devil she has,' was all I could find to answer. I was quite taken aback. I needn't go over it all word by word, it wasn't very pleasant. He accused me of compromising you, seemed to think I'd done it on purpose, had some nefarious motive. I was in the dark about how much he knew, and that handicapped me. I swore you knew nothing about it, and he said haughtily that I was to leave your name out of the conversation. And now I'm coming to the point. Why I am here at all. It seems she tried to rush him for a bit more, and he, well practically told her to go to blazes, said he should stop the cheque, prosecute her. He seemed to think I was trying to save myself at your expense. ASS! He is going up this morning to see his lawyer, he wants an information laid at Scotland Yard. He says the Christian Science people are practically living on blackmail, getting hold of family secrets or skeletons. And he's not going to stand for it. I did all I knew to persuade him to let well alone. We nearly came to blows, only he was so damned dignified. I said I believed it would break you up if there was another scandal. 'I have no doubt that Mrs. Capel will see the matter in the same light that I do,' he said in the stiffest of all his stiff ways." Peter Kennedy paused. He had another word to say, but he said it awkwardly, with an immense effort, and after a pause.

"He'll come up here this morning and tackle you. You don't care a curse if I'm dead or alive, I know that. But if ... if he drives you too far ... well, you know I'd lay down my life for you. He says I've no principle, and as far as you're concerned that's true enough. I'd say black was white, I'd steal or starve to give you pleasure, save you pain. That's what I've come to say, to put myself at your service." She put up her hand, motioned him to silence. All this time he had been standing up, now he flung himself into a chair, brushed his hand across his forehead. "I hardly know what I'm saying, I haven't slept a wink."

"You were saying you would do anything for me."

"I meant that right enough."

Without any preparation, for until now she had listened apparently calmly, she broke into a sudden storm of tears. He got up again and went and stood beside her.

"I can't live without him," she said. "I can't live without him," she repeated weakly.

"Oh, I say, you know...." But he had nothing to say. The sniffing Stevens, disapproval strongly marked upon her countenance, here brought in a tray with coffee and rolls. Margaret, recovering herself with an effort, motioned her to set it down.

"You ought to make her take it," Stevens said to Dr. Kennedy indignantly, "disturbing her before she's breakfasted. She's had nothing inside her lips." He was glad of the interruption.

"You stay and back me up, then." Together they persuaded or forced her to the coffee, she could not eat, and was impatient that Stevens and the tray should go away. Her outburst was over, but she was pitiably shaken.

"He'll come round, all right," Peter said awkwardly, when they were alone again. She looked at him with fear in her eyes:

"Do you really think so?"

"Who wouldn't?"

"You don't think he would go up to London without seeing me?"

"Not likely."

She spoke again presently. In the interval Peter conjured up the image of Gabriel Stanton, speaking to her as he had to him, refusing compromise, harshly unapproachable, rigid.

"I could never go through what I went through before."

"You shan't."

"What could you do?"

"I'll find some way ... a medical certificate!"

"The shame of it!" She covered her face with her hands.

"It won't happen. She's had her money. He may have rubbed her up the wrong way, but after all she has nothing to gain by interfering."

"If only I had told him myself! If only I hadn't lied to him!"

Peter, desperately miserable, walked about the room, interjecting a word now and again, trying to inspirit her.

"You had better go," she said to him in the end. "It's nearly ten o'clock. If he is coming up at all he will be here soon."

"Of course he is coming up. How can I leave you like this?" he answered wildly. "Can't I do anything, say anything, see him for you?" Margaret showed the pale simulacrum of a smile.

"That was my idea, once before, wasn't it? No, you can't see him for me."

"I can't do anything?"

"I'm not sure."

She spoke slowly, hesitatingly. In truth she did not know how she was to bear what she saw before her. Not marriage, safety, happiness, was to be hers, only humiliation. Death was preferable, a thousand times preferable. She was impulsive and leaped to this conclusion.

"Can't I do anything?" he said again.

"Peter, Peter Kennedy, you say you would do anything, anything, for me. I wonder what you mean by it…. How much or how little?"

"Lay down my life."

"Or risk it? There must be a way, you must know a way of … of shortening things. I could not go through it all again … not now. If the worst came to the worst, if I can't make him listen to reason, if he won't forgive or understand. If I have to face the court again, my father and stepmother to know of my … my imprudence, all the horrors to be repeated. To have to stand up and deny … be cross-examined. About you as well as him…."

Again she hid her face. Then, after a pause in which she saw her life befouled, and Gabriel Stanton as her judge or executioner, she lifted a strained and desperate face. "You would find a way to end it?"

She waited for his answer.

"I don't know what you mean."

"Yes, you do. If it became unbearable. Life no longer a gift, but leprous…."

"It isn't as if you had done anything," he exclaimed.

"I've promised and broken my promise, lied, deceived him. It was only to secure his happiness, mine ... ours.... But if he takes it differently, and must have publicity...."

"I don't believe you could go through it," he said gloomily. "One of those heart attacks of yours might come on."

"You know the pain is intolerable."

"That amyl helps you."

"Not much."

"Morphia."

"Was a failure last time. Peter, *think*, won't you think? Couldn't you give me anything? Isn't there any drug? You are fond of drugs, learned in them. Isn't there any drug that would put me out of my misery?"

He listened and she pressed him.

"Think, *think*."

"Of course there are drugs."

"But *the* drug."

"There's hyoscine...."

"Tell me the effect of that?"

"It depends how it is given ... what it is given for."

"For forgetfulness?"

"A quarter of a grain injection."

"And, and...."

"Nothing, nothingness."

"If you love me, Peter.... You say you love me.... If the worst came to the worst, you will help me through...?"

"Don't."

"I must.... I want your promise."

"What is the good of promising? I couldn't do it."

"You said you could die for me."

"It isn't my death you are asking. Unless I should be hanged!"

"You can safeguard yourself."

"You will never ask me."

"But if I did?"

"Oh, God knows!"

"If I not only asked but implored? Give me this hope, this promise. *If* I come to the end of my tether, can bear no more; then ask you for release, the great release...?"

"My hand would drop off."

"Lose your hand."

"My heart would fail."

"Other men have done such things for the woman they love."

"It won't come to that."

"But if it did...?"

She pressed him, pressed him so hard that in the end he yielded, gave her the promise she asked. His night had been sleepless, he had been without breakfast. He scarcely knew what he was saying, only that he could not say "No" to her. And that when he said "Yes," she took his hand in hers a moment, his reluctant hand, and laid her cheek against it.

"Dear friend," she said tenderly, "you give me courage."

When he went away she looked happier, or at least quieter. He cursed himself for a fool when he got into the car. But still against his hand he felt the softness of her cheek and the fear of unmanly tears made him exceed the speed limit.

Margaret, left alone, calculated her resources and for all her whilom amazing vanity found them poor and wanting. What would Gabriel say to her this morning, how could she answer him? If he truly loved her and she pointed out to him, proved to him that their marriage, their happiness, need not be postponed, would he listen? She saw herself persuading him, but remembered that her father in many an argument had failed in making him admit that there was more than one standard of ethics, of right conduct. If he truly loved her! In this black moment she could doubt it. For unlike Peter Kennedy he would put honour before her love.

Gabriel, her lover, came late, on slow reluctant feet. He loved her no less, although he knew she had deceived him, kept things back from him, complicated, perhaps, both their lives by her action. He knew her motives also, that it was because she loved him. He had no harsh judgment, only an overwhelming pang of tenderness. He, too, had faced the immediate future. He knew there must be no marriage whilst this thing hung over and menaced them. Yet to take her into his own keeping, guard and cherish her, was a desire sharp as a sword is sharp, and too poignant for words. He thought she would understand him. But more definitely perhaps he feared her opposition. The fear had slowed his feet. She did not know her lover when she dreaded his reproaches. When he came into the music room this grey, wet morning, he saw that she looked ill, but hardly guessed that she was apprehensive, and of him. He bent over her hands, kissed her hands, held them against his lips.

"My dear, my dear." Her mercurial spirits rose at a bound.

"I thought you would reproach me."

"My poor darling!"

"I wish I had told you."

"Never mind that now."

"But that was the worst of everything. You don't know how I have reproached myself."

"You must not."

"You have not left off caring for me, then?"

"I never cared for you so much."

"Why do you look so grave, so serious?"

Her heart was shaking as she questioned him. In his tenderness there was something different, something inflexible.

"My darling," he said again.

"That means…?"

"I am going to ask you to let me stop that cheque."

"No."

"Fortunately it is Sunday. We have the day before us. I am going up by the two-o'clock. I've sent my bag down to the station. I've already been on to my lawyer by telephone and he will see me at his private house this afternoon. In my opinion we have nothing at all to fear. The King's Proctor will not move on such evidence as she has to offer, she has overreached herself. We ought to have her in gaol by tomorrow night."

"In gaol!"

"That is where she should be. She frightened you … she shall go to gaol for it. Margaret, will you write to your bankers … let me write…."

"No!" she said again.

"Sweetheart!" and he caressed her.

"No. Gabriel, listen to me. I am overwhelmed because I broke my promise to you, was not candid. But though I am overwhelmed and unhappy...."

"I will not let you be unhappy...."

She brushed that aside and went on:

"I am not sorry for what I have done. There is not a word of truth in what she says. As you say, I have admitted guilt, being innocent. Gabriel, I was innocent before, but racked, tortured to prove it. Here I have only paid five hundred pounds. Oh, Heaven! give me words, the power to show you. I am pleading with you for my life. For my life, Gabriel ... ours. Let the cheque go through, give her another if necessary, and yet another. I don't mind buying my happiness." She pleaded wildly.

"Hush! Hush!" He hushed her on his breast, held her to him.

"Dear love...." She wept, and the tortures of which she spoke were his. "If only I might yield to you."

"What is it stops you? Obstinacy, self-righteousness...."

"If it were either would I not yield now, now, with your dear head upon my breast?" She was sobbing there. "Dear love, you unman me." His breathing was irregular. "Listen, you unman me, you weaken me. We were both looking forward, and must still be able to look forward. And backward, too. Not stain our name, more than our name, our own personal honour. Margaret, we are clean, there must be no one who can say, 'Had they been innocent, would they have paid to hide it?' And this fresh charge, this fresh and hideous accusation! And you would accept all, admit all! My dear, my dear, it must not be, we have not only ourselves to consider."

"Not only ourselves!" He held her closer, whispered in her ear.

She had heard him discuss commercial morality with her father, had seen into both their souls; learnt her lover's creed. One must not best a fellowman, fool though he might be, nor take advantage of his need nor ignorance. She had learnt that there were such things as undue percentage of profit, although no man might know what that profit was. "Child's talk," her father had called it, and told him Wall Street would collapse in a day if his tenets were to hold good. Margaret had been proud of him then, although secretly her reason had failed to support him, for it is hard to upset the teaching of a lifetime. To her, it seemed there were conventions, but common sense or convenience might override them. In this particular instance why should she not submit to blackmail, paying for the freedom she needed? But he could not be brought to see eye to eye with her in this. She used all the power that was in her to prove to him that there is no sharp line of demarcation between right and wrong, that one can steer a middle course.

The short morning went by whilst she argued. She put forth all her powers, and in the end, quite suddenly, became conscious that she had not moved him in the least, that as he thought when he came into the room, so he thought now. He used the same words, the same hopeless unarguable words. "Being innocent we cannot put in this plea of guilty." She would neither listen nor talk any more, but lay as a wrestler, who, after battling again and again until the whistle blew and the respite came, feels both shoulders touching the ground, and suddenly, without appeal, admits defeat.

When Gabriel wrote the letter to the bank stopping the cheque that was to be paid to Mrs. Roope on the morrow, she signed it silently. When he asked her to authorise him to see her father if necessary, to allow either or both of them to act for her, she acquiesced in the same way. She was quite spent and exhausted.

"I will let you know everything we do, every step we take."

"I don't want to hear." She accepted his caresses without returning them, she had no capacity left for any emotion.

Then, after he had gone, for there was no time to spare and he must not miss his train, she remained immobile for a time, the panorama of the future unfolding before her exhausted brain. What a panorama it was! She was familiar with every sickening scene that passed before her. Lawyer's office, documents going to and fro, delay and yet more delay. Appeal to Judge in Chambers, and from Judge in Chambers, interrogatories and yet more interrogatories, demands for further particulars, the further particulars questioned; Counsel's opinion, the case set down for hearing, adjournments and yet further adjournments.

At last the Court. Speeches. And then, standing behind the rail in the witness-box, the cynosure of all eyes, she saw herself as in the stocks, for all to pelt with mud ... herself, her wretched, cowering self! Gabriel said they were clean people; she and he were clean. So far they were, but they would be pelted with mud nevertheless; perhaps all the more because their cleanliness would make so tempting a target. The judge would find the mud-flinging entertaining, would interpolate facetious remarks. The Christian Science element would give him opportunity. The court would be crowded to suffocation. She felt the closeness and the musty air, and felt her heart contract ... but not expand. That slight cramp woke her from her dreadful dream, but woke her to terror. Such a warning she had had before. She was able, however, to ring for help. Stevens came running and began to administer all the domestic remedies, rating her at the same time for having "brought it on herself," grumbling and reminding her of all her imprudences.

"No breakfast, and lunch not up yet; I never did see such goin's-on."

She had the sense, however, in the midst of her grumbling to send for the doctor, and before the pain was at its height he was in the room. The bittersweet smell of the amyl told him what had been already done. What little more he could do brought her no relief. He took out the case he always carried, hesitated, and chose a small bottle.

"Get me some hot water," he said, to Stevens.

"Morphia?" she gasped.

"Yes."

"Put it away."

"Because it failed once is no reason it should fail again."

"I'm in … I'm in … agony."

"I know."

"And there's no hope."

"Oh, yes, you'll get through this."

"I don't want to … only not to suffer. Remember, you promised." He pretended not to hear, busying himself about her.

"He has gone. I've stopped the cheque. Peter…." The pain rose, her voice with it, then collapsed; it was dreadful to see her.

"Help me … give me the hyoscine," she said faintly. His hand shook, his face was ashen. "I can't bear this … you promised." The agony broke over her again. He poured down brandy, but it might have been water. His heart was wrung, and drops of perspiration formed upon his forehead. She pleaded to him in that faint voice, then was past pleading, and could only suffer, then began again:

"Pity me. Do something … let me go; help me…."

One has to recollect that he loved her, that he knew her heart was diseased, that there would be other such attacks. Also that Gabriel Stanton, as he feared, had proved inflexible. There would be no wedding and inevitable publicity. Then she cried to him again. And Stevens took up the burden of her cry.

"For the Lord's sake give her something, give her what she's asking for. Human nature can't bear no more ... look at her." Stevens was moved, as any woman would be, or man, either, by such suffering.

"Your promise!" were words that were wrung through her dry lips. Her tortured eyes raked and racked him.

"I ... I can't," was all the answer.

"If you care, if you ever cared. Your miserable weakness. Oh, if I only had a man about me!" She turned away from him for ease and he could hardly hear her. In the next paroxysm he lifted her gently on to the floor, placed a pillow under her head. He whispered to her, but she repelled him, entreated her, but she would not listen. All the time the pain went on. "You promised," were not words,—but a moan.

Desperately he took the cachet from the wrong bottle, melted it, filled his needle. When he bade Stevens roll up her sleeve, she smiled on him, actually smiled.

"Dear Peter! How right I was to trust you!..." Her voice trailed. The change in her face was almost miraculous, the writhing body relaxed. She sighed. Almost it seemed as if the colour came back to her lips, to her tortured face. "Dear, good Peter," were her last words, a message he stooped to hear.

"Thank the Lord," said Stevens piously, "she's getting easier." She was still lying on the floor, a pillow under her head, and they watched her silently.

"Shall I lift her back?"

"No, leave her a few minutes." He had the sense to add, "The morphia doesn't usually act so quickly." Stevens had seen him give her morphia before in the same way, with the same preliminaries. He had saved her, he must save himself. He was conscious now of nothing but gladness. He had feared his strength, but his strength had been equal to her need. She was out of pain. Nothing else mattered. She was out of pain, he had promised her and been equal to his promise. He was no Gabriel Stanton to argue and deny, deny and argue. He wiped his needle carefully, put it away. Then a cry from Stevens roused him, brought him quickly to her side.

"She's gone. Oh, dear! Oh, dear! She's gone!" He lifted her up, laid her on the sofa, the smile was still on her face, she looked asleep. But Stevens was there and he had to dissimulate.

"She is unconscious. Get on to the telephone. Ask Dr. Lansdowne to come over."

Then he made a feint of trying remedies. Strychnine, more amyl, more brandy, artificial respiration. He was glad, glad, glad, exulting as the moments went on. He thanked God that she was at rest. "*He giveth His beloved sleep.*" He called her beloved, whispered it in her ear when Stevens was summoning that useless help. He had sealed her to him, she was his woman now, and for ever. No self-righteous iceberg could hold and deny her.

"Sleep well, beloved," he whispered. "Sleep well. Smile on me, smile your thanks."

He recovered himself with an immense, an incredible effort. He wanted to laugh, to exult, to call on the world to see his work, what he had done for her, how peaceful she was, and happy. He was as near madness as a sane man could be, but by the time his partner came he composed his face and spoke with professional gravity:

"I am afraid you are too late."

Dr. Lansdowne, hurrying in, wore his habitual grin.

"I always knew it would end like this. Didn't I tell you so? An aneurism. I diagnosed it a long time ago." He had even forgotten his diagnosis. "I suppose you've tried ... so and so?" He recapitulated the remedies. Stevens, stunned by the calamity, but not so far as to make her forget to pull down the blinds, listened and realised Dr. Kennedy had left nothing undone.

"I suppose there will have to be an inquest?"

"An inquest! My dear fellow. *An inquest!* What for? I have seen her and diagnosed, prognosed. You have attended her for weeks under my direction. Unless her family wish it, it is quite unnecessary. I shall be most pleased to give a death certificate. You have informed the relatives, of course?"

"Not yet."

Stevens emitted one dry sob which represented her entire emotional capacity, and hastened to ring up Queen Anne's Gate. Dr. Lansdowne began to talk directly she left them alone. He told his silent colleague of an eructation that troubled him after meals, and of a faint tendency to gout. Then cast a perfunctory glance at the sofa.

"Pretty woman!" he said. "All that money, too!"

Peter, suddenly, inexplicably unable to stand, sank on his knees by the sofa, hid his face in her dress. Dr. Lansdowne said. "God bless my soul!" Peter broke into tears like a girl.

"Come, come, this will never do. Pull yourself together, or I shall think.... I shan't know what to think...."

Peter recovered himself as quickly as he had collapsed, rose to his feet.

"It was so sudden," he said apologetically. "I was unprepared...."

"I could have told you exactly what would happen. The case could hardly have ended any other way."

He said a few kind words about himself and his skill as a diagnostician. Peter listened meekly, and was rewarded by the offer of a lift home. "You can come up again later, when the family has arrived, they will be sure to want to know about her last moments.... Or I might come myself, tell them I foresaw it...."

CHAPTER XVI

I woke up suddenly. A minute ago I had seen Peter Kennedy kneeling by the sofa, his head against Margaret's dress. He had looked young, little more than a boy. Now he was by my side, bending over me. There was grey in his hair, lines about his face.

"You've grown grey," was the first thing I said, feebly enough I've no doubt, and he did not seem to hear me. "My arm aches. How could you do it?"

"Do what?"

"She was so young, so impetuous, everything might have come right...."

"She is wandering," he said. I hardly knew to whom he spoke, but felt the necessity of protest.

"I'm not wandering. Is Ella there?"

"Of course I am. Is there anything you want?" She came over to me.

"I needn't write any more, need I? I'm so tired." Ella looked at him as if for instructions, or guidance, and he answered soothingly, as one speaks to a child or an invalid:

"No, no, certainly not. You need not write until you feel inclined. She has been dreaming," he explained.

It did not seem worth while to contradict him again. I was not wide-awake yet, but swayed on the borderland between dreams and reality. Three people were in the dusk of the well-known room. They disentangled themselves gradually; Nurse Benham, Dr. Kennedy, Ella in the easy-chair, Margaret's easy-chair. It was evening and I heard Dr. Kennedy say that I was better, stronger, that he did not think it necessary to give me a morphia injection.

"Or hyoscine."

I am sure I said that, although no one answered me, and it was as if the words had dissolved in the twilight of the room. Incidentally I may say I never had an injection of morphia since that evening. I knew how easy it was to make a mistake with drugs. So many vials look alike in that small valise doctors carry. I was either cunning or clever that night in rejecting it. Afterwards it was only necessary to be courageous.

I found it difficult in those first few twilight days of recovering consciousness to separate this Dr. Kennedy who came in and out of my bedroom from that other Dr. Kennedy, little more than a boy, who had wept by the woman he released, the authoress whose story I had just written. And my feelings towards him fluctuated considerably. My convalescence was very slow and difficult, and I often thought of the solution Margaret Capel had found, sometimes enviously, at others with a shuddering fear. At these times I could not bear that Dr. Kennedy should touch me, his hand on my pulse gave me an inward shiver. At others I looked upon him with the deepest interest, wondering if he would do as much for me as he had done for her, if his kindness had this meaning. For he was kind to me, very kind, and at the beck and call of my household by night and day. Ella sent for him if my temperature registered half a point higher or lower than she anticipated, any symptom or change of symptom was sufficient to send him a peremptory message, that he never disregarded. Ella, I could tell, still suspected us of being in love with each other, and she dressed me up for his visits. Lacy underwear, soft chiffony tea-gowns, silken hose and satin or velvet shoes diverted my weakness into happier channel and kept her in her right *milieu*.

Then, not all at once, but gradually and almost incredibly the whole circumstances changed. Dr. Kennedy came one day full of excitement to tell us that a new treatment had been found for my illness. Five hundred cases had been treated, of which over four hundred had been cured, the rest ameliorated. Of course we were sceptical. Other consultants were called in and, not having suggested the treatment, damned it wholeheartedly. One or two grudgingly admitted a certain therapeutic value in selected cases, but were sure that mine was not one of them! The medical world is as difficult to persuade to adventure as an old maid in a provincial town. My own tame general practitioner, whom I had previously credited with some slight intelligence, was moved to write to Dr. Kennedy urging him vehemently to forbear. He was fortunate enough to give his reasons, and for me at least they proved conclusive!

On the 27th of May I took my first dose of thirty grains of iodide of potassium and spent the rest of the day washing it down with glasses of chlorine water masked with lemon. I was still the complete invalid, going rapidly downhill; on a water bed, spoon-fed, and reluctantly docile in Benham's hard, yet capable hands. On the 27th of June I was walking about the house. By the 27th of July I had put on seventeen pounds in weight and had no longer any doubt of the result. I had found the dosage at first both nauseous and nauseating. Now I drank it off as if it had been champagne. Hope effervesced in every glass. The desire to work came back, but without the old irritability. Ella, before she left, said I was more like myself than I had been for years. Dr. Kennedy had unearthed this new treatment and she extolled him, notwithstanding her old prejudices, admitted it was to him we owed my restoration, yet never ceased to rally me and comment on the power of love. I agreed with her in that, knowing hers had saved me even before the drug began to act. It was for her hand I had groped in the darkest hour of all. Even now I remember her passionate avowal that she would not let me die, my more weakly passionate response that I could not leave her lonely in the world. Now we said rude things to each other, as sisters will, with an intense sense of happiness and absence of emotion. I criticised Tommy's handwriting, and she retorted that at least she saw it regularly. Whilst as for Dennis....

But there was no agony there now to be assuaged. My boy was on his way home and the words he had written, the cable that he had sent when he heard of my illness, lay near my heart, too sacred to show her. I let her think I had not heard from him. Closer even than a sister lies the tie between son and mother. Not perhaps between her and her rough Tommy, her fair Violet, but between me and my Dennis, my wild erratic genius, who could nevertheless pen me those words ... who could send me the sweetest love letter that has ever been written.

But this has nothing to do with me and Dr. Peter Kennedy, and the curious position between us. For a long time after I began to get well it seemed we were like two wary wrestlers, watching for a hold. Only that sometimes he seemed to drop all reserves, to make an extraordinary *rapprochement*. I might flush, call myself a fool, remember my age, but at these times it would really appear as if Ella had some reason in her madness, as if he had some personal interest in me. At these times I found him nervous, excitable, utterly unlike his professional self. As for me I had to preserve my equanimity, ignore or rebuff without disturbing my equilibrium. I was fully employed in nursing my new-found strength, swallowing perpetually milk and eggs, lying for hours on an invalid carriage amid the fading gorse, reconstructing, rebuilding, making vows. I had been granted a respite, if not a reprieve, and had to prove my worthiness. The desire for work grew irresistible. When I asked for leave he combated me, combated me strenuously.

"You are not strong enough, not nearly strong enough. You have built up no reserve. You must put on another stone at least before you can consider yourself out of the wood."

"I won't begin anything new, but that story, the story I wrote in water...." I watched him when I said this. I saw his colour rise and his lips tremble.

"Oh, yes. I had forgotten about that." But I saw he had not forgotten. "You never saw your midnight visitor again?"—he asked me with an attempt at carelessness—"Margaret Capel. Do you remember, in the early days of your illness how often you spoke of her, how she haunted you?" He spoke lightly, but there was anxiety in his voice, and Fear … was it Fear I saw in his eyes, or indecision? "Since you have begun to get better you have never mentioned her name. You were going to write her life …" he went on.

"And death," I answered to see what he would say. We were feinting now, getting closer.

"You know she died of heart disease," he asked quickly. "There was an inquest...."

"I saw her die," I answered, not very coolly or conclusively. His face was very strange and haggard, and I felt sorry for him.

"How strange and vivid dreams can be. Morphia dreams especially," he replied, rather questioningly than assertively.

"I thought you agreed mine were not dreams?"

"Did I? When was that?"

"When you brought me their letters, told me I was foredoomed to write her story. Hers and his. I can't think why you did."

"Did I say that?"

"More than once. I suppose you thought I was not going to get better." He did not answer that except with his rising colour and confusion, and I saw now I had hit upon the truth. "I wonder you gave me the iodide," I said thoughtfully.

"I suppose now you think me capable of every crime in the calendar?"

That brought us to close quarters, and I took up the challenge.

"No, I don't. Your hand was forced." Then I added, I admit more cruelly: "Have you ever done it again?"

He had been sitting by my couch in the garden; a basket-work chair stood there always for him. Now he got up abruptly, walked away a few steps. I watched him, then thought of my question, a dozen others rising in my mind. It was eleven years since Margaret Capel died and a jury of twelve good men and true had found that heart disease had been the cause of death. There had been a rumour of suicide, and, in society, some talk of cause. Absurd enough, but, as Ella had reminded me, very prevalent and widespread. The rising young authoress was supposed to have been in love with an eminent politician. His wife died shortly before she started the long-delayed divorce proceedings against James Capel, and this gave colour to the rumour. It was hazarded that he had made it clear to her that remarriage was not in his mind. Few people knew of the real state of affairs. Gabriel Stanton shut that close mouth of his and told no one. I wondered about Gabriel Stanton, but more about Peter Kennedy, who had walked away from me when I spoke. What had happened to him in these eleven years? Into what manner of man had he grown? He came back presently, sat down again by my couch, spoke abruptly as if there had been no pause.

"You want to know whether I have ever done for anybody what I did for Margaret Capel?"

"Yes, that is what I asked you."

"Will you believe me when I tell you?"

"Perhaps. Why did you first encourage me to write Margaret Capel's life and then try and prevent my doing it?"

"You won't believe me when I tell you."

"Probably not."

"I wanted to know whether she had forgiven me, whether she was still glad. When you told me you saw and spoke to her...."

"It was almost before that, if I remember rightly."

"It may have been. Do you remember I said you were a reincarnation? The first time I came in and saw you sitting there, at her writing-table, in her writing-chair, I thought of you as a reincarnation."

The light in his eyes was rather fitful, strange.

"I was right, wasn't I, Margaret?" He put a hand on my knee. I remembered how she had flung it off under similar circumstances. I let it lie there. Why not?

"My name is Jane." It came back to me that I had said this to him once before.

"You don't care for me at all?"

"I am glad you thought of the intensive iodide treatment. It has its advantages over hyoscine."

"You have not changed?"

"I would rather like you to remember this is the twentieth century."

He sighed and took his hand off my knee, drew it across his forehead.

"You don't know what the last few months have meant to me, coming up here again, every day or twice a day, taking care of you, giving you back those letters, knowing you knew...."

"You had not the temptation to rid yourself of me again?"

"You have grown so cold. I suppose you would not look at the idea of marrying me?"

"You suppose quite correctly," I answered, thinking of Ella, and what a score this would be to her.

"It would make everything so right. I have been thinking of this ever since you began to get better, before, too. You will always be delicate, need a certain amount of care. No one could give it to you as well as I. Why not? I have almost the best practice in Pineland, and I deserve it, too. I've worked hard in these eleven years. I've given an honest scientific trial to every new treatment. I've saved scores of lives...."

"Your own in jeopardy all the time."

"She asked me to do it, begged me to do it...." He spoke wildly. "Gabriel Stanton was inflexible, the marriage was to be postponed whilst Mrs. Roope was prosecuted, or the case fought out in the Law Courts. And every little anxiety or excitement set her poor heart beating ... put her in pain ... jeopardised her life. I'd do it again tomorrow. I don't care who knows. You'll have to tell if you want to. If you married me you couldn't give evidence against me...."

His smile startled me; it was strange, cunning. It seemed to say, "See how clever I am,—I have thought of everything."

"There, I have had that in my mind ever since you began to be better."

"It was not because you have fallen in love with me, then?" I scoffed.

"When you are Margaret, I love you ... I adore you." The whole secret flashed on me then, flashed through his strange perfervid eyes. We were in full view of a curious housemaid at a window, but he kneeled down by my couch, as he had kneeled by Margaret's.

"You are Margaret. Tell me the truth. There is no other fellow now. You always said if it were not for Gabriel Stanton...."

I quieted him with difficulty. I saw what was the matter. Of course I ought to have seen it before, but vanity and Ella obscured the truth. The poor fellow's mind was unhinged. For years he had brooded and brooded, yet worked magnificently at his profession, worked at making amends. The place and I had brought out the latent mischief. Now he implored me to marry him, to show him I was glad he had carried out my wishes.

"Your heart is now quite well ... I have sounded it over and over again. You will never have a return of those pains. *Margaret*...."

I got rid of him that day as quickly as possible, not answering yes or no definitely, marking time, soothing him disingenuously. Before the next day was at its meridian I had hurriedly left Carbies. Left Pineland, all the strange absorbing story, and this poor obsessed doctor. I left a letter for him, the most difficult piece of prose I have ever written. I was writing to a madman to persuade him he was sane! I gave urgent reasons for being in London, added a few lines, that I hoped he would understand, about having abandoned my intention of turning my morphia dreams into "copy"; tried to convey to him that he had nothing to fear from me....

I never had an answer to my letter. I parried Ella's raillery, resumed my old life. But I could not forget my country practitioner nor what I owed him. A peculiar tenderness lingered. However I might try to disguise names and places he would read through the lines. It was difficult to say what would be the effect on his mind and I would not take the risk. I held over my story as long as I was able, even wrote another meantime. But three months ago I became a free woman. I read in the obituary column of my morning paper that Peter Kennedy, M.D., F.R.C.S., of Pineland, Isle of Wight, had died from the effects of a motor accident.

The obituary notices were very handsome and raised him from the obscurity of a mere country practitioner. It mentioned the distinguished persons he had had under his care. The late Margaret Capel, for instance. But not myself! I suspected Dr. Lansdowne of having sent the notices to the press, *his* name occurred in all of them, the partnership was bugled.

Peter Kennedy died well. He was driving his car quickly on an urgent night call. Some strange cur frisked into the road and to avoid it he swerved suddenly. Death must have been instantaneous. I was glad that he died without pain. I had rather he was alive today, although my story had remained for ever unwritten. So few people have ever cared for me. Had I chosen I do believe his reincarnation theory would have held. And I should have had at least one lover to oppose to Ella's many!

Lightning Source UK Ltd.
Milton Keynes UK
UKHW011946260722
406426UK00002B/40